PRAISE FOR *FORTUNE*

"The unique premise of a DNA lottery had me hooked from the very first pages! Ellen Won Steil's *Fortune* is an emotionally written tale demonstrating what happens when the power of a woman with the wealth and drive to find out the truth is pitted against three friends from high school with secrets to hide. The suspense culminates with the inevitable countdown to the DNA lottery."
—Georgina Cross, author of *Nanny Needed*, *One Night*, and *The Stepdaughter*

"With an irresistible premise that gets more unsettling by the page, *Fortune* is so much more than a random game of chance. Every ticket is a potential clue; every character has a fiercely guarded secret. You won't be able to look away until the final name is drawn."
—Jessica Strawser, author of *A Million Reasons Why*

"This emotional and tense debut held me locked in its grip through each roller-coaster twist! Steil's confident prose immerses the reader in a small town's past—and the lives of four formidable women—using the modern premise of blood for money in a way I did not see coming. Clear your weekend; then prepare to be sucked into the heart-stopping secrets of *Fortune*."
—Elle Marr, Amazon Charts bestselling author of *The Family Bones*

BECOMING
MARLOW
FIN

ALSO BY ELLEN WON STEIL

Fortune

BECOMING
MARLOW
FIN

A Novel

ELLEN
WON STEIL

LAKE UNION
PUBLISHING

Published by Lake Union Publishing, Seattle

www.apub.com

Amazon, the Amazon logo, and Lake Union Publishing are trademarks of Amazon.com, Inc., or its affiliates.

ISBN-13: 9781662512124 (paperback)
ISBN-13: 9781662512131 (digital)

Cover design by Kathleen Lynch/Black Kat Design
Cover images: © Cunfek / Getty; © Windhi Hermanto / 500px / Getty; © Hayden Verry / Arcangel

Printed in the United States of America

For my parents, Jung and Kyung Won

CHAPTER 1

ISLA

1995

The night we found Marlow, I saw her face when I looked in the mirror.

I climbed out of the old copper tub, its metal starting to show patches of cyan. The shock of cold made me tingle, warm bathwater still slippery around my legs as I stepped on the footstool. The fog in the mirror gave way to my methodical hand swipes.

But instead of my own reflection, there she was again. Staring at me with those eyes, like she did through the window that morning.

She's not letting you go.

The doorknob rattled. My shoulder met my chin as if cradling me.

"Isla. Your mother would like to take a bath sometime tonight." Dad had this habit of never knocking. He was a doorknob shaker.

She's here. She came back for me.

I turned back to the mirror. She had vanished once more, leaving me with an image of my own face, melting into something almost unrecognizable.

"Stella, our eight-year-old daughter seems to think our cabin is her own personal spa," I heard Dad say through the dark cedar door, his words coming in waves of baritone and brass.

Mom pushed the door open. I clutched my towel against my chest, a purely involuntary reflex. Her straw hair was still damp from the lake, and her skin had a slimy sheen. She blinked her glassy lapis eyes at me and then focused them on the puddles I had created all over the black vinyl floor.

"Sweetie, I hope you saved some hot water for me," she said, a hint of bemusement in her voice.

I remained still.

"Isla?" she asked with a head tilt.

"Are we having dinner soon? Is Moni cooking?" I stammered.

"Yes and yes." She patted my head tenderly and then scooted me out.

Dad stood behind her. I could see them looking at each other in the mirror, the stark contrast in their colorings. The angles in their facial bones, the shapes of their eyes, all distinctive landscapes. Dad's deep, dark hair seemed to fluff Mom's into a near-champagne cloud. He caressed her neck and I kept walking.

"Moni!" I called out. My hand traced the metal banister as a few drops of rain started to splatter over the main room's wall-size windows.

We were at the tail end of our annual cabin getaway, which usually meant some sort of delectable hot dish Moni would create with whatever leftovers still lingered like stray kittens waiting to be finally taken in.

As a baby, I had failed to properly pronounce the Korean word for grandmother, *Halmoni*. "Moni—Moni!" I'd babbled.

The nickname had stuck and she was forever my Moni.

I found her in the kitchen, her petite form hovering over the rice cooker plugged in next to the unused gas range. A bright-red broth bubbled up, and she gave it a stir with her oversize silver spoon.

"Vacation food always tastes better out of a rice cooker," she said in Korean.

She cracked a square of ramen and handed me half. I slid my half in, and she stirred the noodles, their stiffness giving way to the hot liquid, their squiggly foam strands making my mouth water. A handful of chopped green onions, a few bits of red meat, and some oval-shaped rice cakes were tossed in as she tasted the liquid with her spoon, then offered me a sample. I sipped it, the broth nearly burning my tongue. The top of her salt-and-pepper head bent down over the pot to inspect further.

I wanted to tell her then. About the face I saw in the window that morning. The first time she showed herself to me.

———

One look was all it took to haunt me.

A round, bundled mass of chestnut flesh, two luminous coals gaping at me, magnetically in focus upon whatever fell in their sight.

My chest filled with fright and wonder. The rest of me static, locked in on her stare. I blinked and shifted my eyes. The early morning had started to extend glints of light across Lake Superior. The vibrant waves lapped curiously hard against our dock, each crash saying *See her, see her*.

I looked again. The glass of the window grew thick and foreboding. The face seemed to float and then dissipate in and out of the speckled mix of light and shadows.

Isla.

I heard someone calling for me. Was it Moni? Dad?

I tried to draw myself away from the gaze, our connection pulling like taffy as I broke free, the snap of it practically shaking my core.

Isla. Isla.

When I looked back a third time, Dad touched my shoulder, and whatever amazement had taken over my body dissolved like a white seltzer tablet.

"Isla. Let's go, sweetie."

I turned to see his perplexed expression.

"Are you still up for that hike?"

I nodded.

He drove the green-and-brown Jeep to Birch Trading Post, my face pressed against the window, looking for her the entire time. Would she have followed us? Was she running along the lines of emerald pines soldiering the shoreline of the water, a blur whipping between each tree trunk already emblazoned, buried like a mealworm inside me?

Dad took my hand and led me inside the trading post. At the time it was the biggest store in Grand Marais, a hodgepodge of necessities and camping supplies. I passed an abandoned can of Spam perched in a basket of shiny Lake Superior pins set next to a turning rack of generic birthday cards and campy postcards.

"Last trip for the season, Mr. Baek?" the store clerk asked, scanning two cans of Diet Coke and a bottle of red wine.

"Last one," Dad replied, thumbing a few bills from his wallet.

"Better add some batteries, Patrick. Storm is supposed to be bad."

Sheriff Vandenberg slapped a pack of AAs on the counter. He had a bald head and a smooth face. Even his eyebrows looked sparse. He smiled at me as he sidestepped toward the register.

"That bad, huh?"

"Rolling in tonight. Predicting it to be one for the ages. Make sure you hunker down with the fam." He closed both hands into fists as if to flex his arms.

"Taking Isla for one last hike to Covet Falls," said Dad, pulling the brown grocery bag up to his chest.

"Better make it a quick one, Patrick. Wouldn't want you two getting stuck there in the storm."

We ate our packed lunches of tuna on marble rye and peeled grapefruit near the top of the falls. I kicked my legs out and let the mist drop on my face as I ran my tongue against a pink sac of fruit stuck in my teeth. Our cabin was the closest one to Covet Falls, a mere half-hour hike from our yard.

"Did you know, if I dropped this fruit peel into the stream, it would go down that fall and disappear forever?" Dad asked.

"Maybe. Or maybe it would show up someday."

"Mmmm," he murmured, throwing the last of his sandwich into his mouth.

"I don't know if I like that word."

"What word?"

"Forever."

We had ventured to that very spot many times before, Dad and me. He would always tell me about the mysteries of Covet Falls while I watched its white churning jets stampede over the rocks, over and over again, relentless. Stories of kayaks getting lost. A boy nearly drowning. A man who never came back once he went over that cliff.

Dad never told me if they were actually true.

On the way home we spotted Mom swimming in the lake, her arms straight, hair spread out like floating seaweed. I called to her, but she didn't hear me. I helped Dad put some of our hiking gear back in the storage shed. He stuffed a tattered yellow tent and its poles into the garbage bin.

"Why are you throwing that tent out?" I questioned with raised brows.

"It's old. We'll need to get a new one." The metal poles popped back up like pesky squirrels.

"Maybe a red tent? When we get the new one?"

"Sure, Isla."

I jumped in the lake to join Mom. The shock of cold washed away the heat that clung to my skin like a membrane. For a moment, I forgot what I saw that morning. I floated on my back, tucked my chin into my chest, and could see the long, shimmery dock, a millipede leading to our cabin. The endless plush forest behind it, a blanket of vegetation covering with thick and opaque arms.

We sat down on the floor of the main room for dinner, our knees bumping the bottom of the coffee table. The windows were already getting pummeled with rain. Dad popped open the bottle of red wine he'd bought earlier and poured three glasses. He toasted our time spent this summer at the cabin. His cheeks grew rosy, and Mom pinched one of them playfully. Moni kept spooning more noodles into my bowl. I gladly slurped them, the warmth of each slippery mouthful soothing me as my cold, wet hair still dried.

The meal created a buzz among the four of us as we ate, chirping about the last week, the wonderful swims we had, how the kayak had held up for one more summer, how great this last meal was, if the rain would let up soon. When the last bite was taken, the buzzing ceased, a silence that was met with the increasing roar of the storm. The stronger the booming and clapping of the sky, the tighter my chest felt.

Dad turned on the television. "Severe thunderstorm. Tornado watch until ten thirty. Stella, do you know where I put those extra flashlights?" He scratched the side of his face roughly, as if chiding himself for not preparing.

Moni rose to clear the bowls; the clanking of them made me twitch to alertness.

I thought about her then, the girl from the window. What would she do in this storm? She was out there. At least I thought someone was out there.

I must have conjuring powers, because as soon as I had thought it, I saw her face again in the window, a pleading flash.

I stood up and flung the back door open, drenched within seconds. My mouth gaped open as I sputtered from the water.

I followed her. She looked back and kept running.

I followed her calls. Until I realized they were pleas behind me, calling my name. Begging me to stop.

CHAPTER 2

THE INTERVIEW

2021

The following is a transcript of the televised and streamed interview of model and actress Marlow Fin that aired July 3, 2021, on NBC. More than 36.1 million people worldwide have watched the interview. Veteran journalist Jodi Lee was specifically chosen by Ms. Fin for the interview.

When asked about the interview, Ms. Lee would later say, "I still wake up and think about it. I do . . . I really do. I can't get any of it out of my mind. And that makes me think I can't be the only one who feels this way."

[Introduction from set]

JODI LEE: Good evening. Thank you for joining me on this Fourth of July weekend. In one of the most anticipated interviews in the last decade, maybe even going further back, I had the privilege of speaking with Marlow Fin. Under Ms. Fin's strict direction, I was chosen as the interviewer. Under the terms of our agreement, the interview was prerecorded. NDAs were signed on a very small, closed set. No one, and I mean no one other than a select few, has seen or heard the contents of this interview.

I begin with Marlow Fin. Who is she? That may seem a strange question, as the world knows her well. One of the most prominent models and actresses of our time. But now we all want to know another side of her. Could it be possible? Was she involved in the tragic incident that occurred on September 7, 2020?

[Roll package]

JODI LEE: You've seen her on every magazine cover. Her ads are everywhere you look. "That Face," as people have deemed her. Many say it's an unforgettable one. You can't look at "that face" without staring. Modeling since she was a teen, Marlow almost instantly became the staple for every major fashion house, eventually foraying into acting. Growing up in Henley, Minnesota, a small suburb of the Twin Cities, Marlow's childhood did not start out like any other. That's because Marlow doesn't remember much before the age of six.

[Studio]

JODI LEE: You say you don't have any memory before the age of six. Does that still hold true?

MARLOW FIN: For the most part.

JODI LEE: Hello, by the way. I don't think we ever actually said hello to each other.

[Extends hand out, they shake]

MARLOW FIN: *[Laughs]* Hello, Jodi Lee. Do you know why I chose you?

JODI LEE: Chose me?

MARLOW FIN: I would not do this interview unless it was you.

JODI LEE: I guess I have wondered that. Why me, then?

MARLOW FIN: What happened to you was an injustice. I always thought that—that you should have stayed as cohost. It could have

8

and should have been the start of something that meant so much to so many. The way you were ousted was wrong.

JODI LEE: [*Shifts in seat*] I think . . . I've managed okay since.

MARLOW FIN: Of course. But doesn't it bother you? *He* got you kicked off the show. And now *he* remains untouched. I suppose he will have to be left to karma. So I'm handing you the biggest interview of your life.

JODI LEE: Well . . . I don't know how to respond to that. But this isn't just a big interview. This is the only interview you have ever given. Up until right now, this moment, you have never given an interview.

MARLOW FIN: Correct. I never liked the idea of talking to someone where every phrase, word, syllable of their question was simply a leech in the air, to eventually land on me and take all it could.

JODI LEE: And this interview is different from that?

MARLOW FIN: You're not a leech. And I am here to speak a truth.

JODI LEE: How do we know you are telling the truth?

MARLOW FIN: I have nothing to gain from lying.

JODI LEE: That's something I want to believe, Marlow. That the viewers want to believe, in fact. But here we are sitting across from each other. We are here because people want to know something. They want to know how a beautiful, successful, famous person such as yourself could possibly be involved with what happened on September 7, 2020.

MARLOW FIN: Of course they do. People are fascinated with anything that deflects from themselves. Why do you think they're fascinated with questioning someone before a potential downfall? We are a culture that puts our hands on the back of anyone standing on the edge of a cliff.

JODI LEE: I don't think many people would disagree with that.

MARLOW FIN: People love to put other people in glass jars. America loves a good, tasty interview, Jodi.

JODI LEE: Aren't you deflecting now?

MARLOW FIN: Not at all.

JODI LEE: Before we get to that Labor Day weekend nearly a year ago, I think it's time people knew more about you. Before you were famous. Before all the cameras and glamorous photo shoots. Let's go back to how your childhood was a little . . . different, shall we say? Would you say you had a good childhood?

MARLOW FIN: I had a decent childhood. For the most part anyways. I really did. I feel lucky I was given that because I don't think I would be here today if I hadn't been. I don't think anyone can say their upbringing was completely normal. Sure, there are skeletons. Did it start out normal? No. There is nothing normal about what happened.

JODI LEE: Can you take us back to that day? To what you do remember? Twenty-six years ago. That's a long time, I know. But what can you recall?

MARLOW FIN: I was found in the woods near Grand Marais, Minnesota, along Lake Superior. I was six years old when she found me.

JODI LEE: Who found you?

MARLOW FIN: Isla.

JODI LEE: What's your first memory?

MARLOW FIN: Waking up to rain. Cold, wet rain. It fell in little spurts on my face. I was so tired . . . the achy kind of tired. I wanted to go back to sleep, but whenever the rain would fall on my face I would wake right back up. When I finally sat up, I didn't know where I was or how I got there. There were leaves in my hair, inside my mouth. I remember spitting a bunch out. The rain had stopped, and I got up like someone gets out of bed. It felt like being born, like that was my birth moment. The beginning of it all and I didn't know any other way.

When I did finally stand, I toppled over. Whap! Like a tree being cut down. For some reason my legs were weak. I tried again and clung to a tree trunk for God knows how long, trying to stand without trembling. When I regained steadiness, I started walking. I walked because I didn't know what else to do. Or where to go, for that matter.

JODI LEE: Those are remarkable details. How is it you think you can remember that, but so little from before?

MARLOW FIN: I wish I had the answer. But there are some moments that are so crystal clear they're like little clips I can play in my head on command.

JODI LEE: You were a six-year-old girl. Alone, without any idea who you were. Weren't you scared?

MARLOW FIN: No. I was too new to the world to feel anything. I didn't know what to be scared of. I only knew I had to start moving. As I walked, I remember bits of rock and sharp twigs on the ground poking the bottoms of my bare feet. They kept digging deeper and deeper the more I started walking. Eventually, a piece of wood punctured my skin and blood started spilling out. I bent down and looked at the cut. I took my finger like that [*gestures*] and swiped at it. I see that bright red still.

And then I followed it. I followed where I could see the light. The sun was starting to shine through the tops of the trees. I kept walking to where it would show itself. I remember the woods were patterned with this light, little spots shining here and there. I don't remember how I got to the cabin or even approaching it. Only that when I did see it, it appeared out of nowhere. At least that's how I remember it. In my memory the cabin is much bigger than it actually is. It looked like it could swallow me whole.

JODI LEE: What did you do when you found the cabin?

MARLOW FIN: I walked up to the cabin. I was drawn to it, as if I already knew the cabin and it knew me. I found myself standing up against a massive window. There were windows everywhere.

She was standing there, staring back at me. She looked . . . scared. She was the scared one.

JODI LEE: Isla?

MARLOW FIN: Yes.

JODI LEE: Did she come out to help you? Did she go get someone?

MARLOW FIN: No.

JODI LEE: Did that bother you?

MARLOW FIN: She was a little girl. Just like I was. What's there to be bothered about? I'm not sure she knew what she saw. I don't really remember what happened after she saw me. That's where it gets a little fuzzy. But I tell you what, Jodi. You know what should be bothersome?

JODI LEE: What?

MARLOW FIN: A six-year-old girl gets discovered wandering in the woods, and it makes the local news. That's it.

JODI LEE: You think it should have been covered more widely?

MARLOW FIN: I think if I had been a little white girl instead of a little Black girl, you would have been interviewing me when I was six.

[Pause]

JODI LEE: Do you remember when you were finally rescued?

MARLOW FIN: I'll never forget being rescued.

CHAPTER 3

ISLA

1995

I still remember Dad's face when he found me pointing, my little hand stretched out as if I were showing him something I had created, like an art project or crayon drawing. *Look, look what I did!* The lines on his face were severe from the stinging downpour, his eyes wide in disbelief, his mouth an open shock wave. I kept pointing as though putting my finger down would make it difficult for any of them to see what I had led them to.

I had ignored their calls for me to come back. Their desperate shouts pressed me to run faster. This was our first game of tag, she and I. I wasn't going to let her down. The sky had an unnatural hue, a faded chartreuse that lit the silhouette of her head as it bobbed up and down until it disappeared, dropping with such rapidity it looked as though she had fallen down a rabbit hole.

I didn't lose her.

The ripping gusts shrieked, creating a white noise that strangely calmed me. Moni came up behind me and tugged my arm, wrapping me inside her torso, pulling me away as I fought her.

"Moni! She is there. Do you see her?"

"Isla—"

"She's right there!"

"No more. Stop it! Dangerous!" But she couldn't help herself either. She kept her grip on my arm as she looked over her shoulder. She too had to see her, as if there were no chance of it being real otherwise.

The girl was curled up, like a stone sitting under the large pine. Lightning hissed in the sky, illuminating the outline of the tree's height and her dark head. She twitched and curled herself up even tighter.

Mom suddenly appeared, flashlight in hand, her eyes squinting from wetness. She lurched back when she saw what was under the pine, as if a pest had encroached upon her feet. With her arms crossed, she stood silent, examining what lay so still.

Tornado sirens blared. Even as the atmosphere blackened, I could see the alarmist, motherly hairs rising up all over her.

"Patrick—the storm. This isn't safe!" she shouted as he approached us.

Dad took a step away from the pine, his body following her command.

"We can't leave her!" I cried with my hand still out.

The three of them looked at me, as if I made no sense at all. But it was the only sense that mattered.

Dad bent down to touch the girl on the head, gingerly, as though she really was something wild that could turn on him. She didn't move.

Mom looked around like she was searching for someone else to jump out at us—a trap for having touched her. She grabbed Moni's arm and jerked us both farther away from Dad.

"Patrick . . ."

He didn't say anything as he scooped the girl up in his arms. It looked so easy, like a pillow being lifted off the bed.

She kept her head burrowed, hands clenched into little fists, a titan of a fetus propped on Dad's arms. He placed a finger under her nose.

"Is she breathing?" asked Mom.

"Yes," he answered. Quickly, gruffly.

She didn't wait another second. She took my hand and ran, my little legs stumbling every other step, her pace far too quick. I looked back to see Moni following as best she could. She appeared even smaller than usual with her head ducked down to shield herself, arms up in surrender. The storm was strengthening, daring us as we tried to escape her, the intensity of each downdraft practically lifting us off the ground. We ran through sheet after sheet of water, disorienting and exquisite.

I looked up for one second to see the glow from our cabin for the first time, the gleaming dot making me ache a little. Was it only a moment ago that we were all sitting around the coffee table, bellies full and heads humming with untroubled thoughts? When it was just the four of us, our rhythms with each other having been fine-tuned over the years, a painstaking balance not to be disrupted? What would happen when we crossed that doorway? What had we done?

The sirens grew noisier the brighter the light from our cabin windows became.

Mom threw a wool blanket from the couch over me as soon as we fell through the doorway, as if I were on fire and it needed to be snuffed out.

"Are you okay?" she kept asking me, as though I were the one who had been found in the woods.

Moni sat quietly in the tan saddle-style armchair, a little puddle of water at her feet. I pushed away from Mom and sat on Moni's lap, wrapping us in the blanket, little pieces of woolly fuzz already caught on my damp lips.

Dad surged through the door, the girl still in his arms. He looked at us expectantly, as if we should have already formed a concise plan for what to do next.

"Towels first. Then blankets," he ordered—mostly to Mom, who had withdrawn into a motionless state, arms slack at her sides.

The girl lay on the wood floor, her head and upper body on the maroon-and-cream-speckled rug. She looked straight up at the ceiling, like a patient would in a dentist's chair, with eyes that took up half her face. Her feet were bare and marred by scratches, blood dried in some areas and fresh in others. Her body was covered in dirt, its grimy linear patterns like some sort of crude tattoo. Even with all the mud that coated her, the pink shirt and shorts she wore were visible. Tiny straw-berries lined the edging of her sleeves, a big one over her belly. Her hair was split into pigtails, held by pink bobble elastics, each section soaked and limp. Who had dressed her in those clothes? Who had done her hair like that and placed each elastic so carefully around each pigtail?

Who had left her?

She began to open her mouth and then close it, like a fish searching for water. Yet her breathing remained steady, her chest rising up and going down in a rhythmic fashion. A soft moan crawled from the back caverns of her throat and whistled out.

"Stella, keep her warm. I'm calling for help," Dad said. He lifted the cordless phone out of its cradle and dragged its antenna up with his teeth.

Mom dried her off, rubbing vigorously with a blue towel. Instantly it became caked in mud. I wondered if it was the same towel I had used getting out of the bathtub.

"I need an ambulance. We found a girl in the woods by our cabin . . . I'd say six or seven . . . Yes, she's breathing. Yes, she's con-scious . . . You don't understand. We found her out in this storm. She needs medical attention . . . You can't what?"

Mom grabbed another towel and continued to rub harshly. The girl's head vibrated.

"What? What do you mean you can't get anyone out here?" Dad's voice rose with each syllable, the agitation ringing in a way I had never heard from him before.

I leaned forward out of Moni's lap, my feet hitting the floor softly as I placed the wool blanket over the girl so only her head was exposed. She had gone still. Mom rocked back on her heels and put her head in her hands. I wasn't sure if it was from exhaustion or dread. Maybe it was both.

"Please. First thing in the morning. Sheriff Vandenberg, he knows me. Tell him I said it's an emergency. Patrick Baek. B, A, E, K."

"She need bath. She need hot." Moni finally spoke.

Mom's head jolted up. She met Moni's eyes and nodded. "I'll go run it," she said quietly. She patted my head, telling me to stay where I was.

Dad held the phone low at his side, the metal antenna tapping his leg. "No one can get here tonight," he finally said.

"What?"

"The roads are flooded and blocked by downed trees. They said since she doesn't seem injured, we should keep her warm and hydrated."

"Until when?" Mom demanded, her voice near shrill, her hand clutching the banister as she took a step back down.

He shrugged and narrowed his eyes. "I don't know, Stella. Until they can get here."

The tenderness they had shared earlier in front of the mirror seemed like decades ago. The night had swept that moment away.

Mom studied the creature who had abruptly disturbed her last evening on vacation. Like a classmate chiding the one who had ruined a field trip for the rest of the class. I was not used to such apathy from her, the woman who swam in the lake with me, her carefree strokes and tossing of the head. Her gentle caress with a towel when we got out together.

"Well, let's get her warm," she said.

The girl screamed when placed in the copper tub upstairs. Dad shouted at Mom, accusing her of making the water too hot, that she should have tested it. She denied it, making him test it himself. The water became clouded from the mud. The girl calmed down after some coaxing from Moni while I sat on the toilet, knees tucked in, covering my ears from her screams. Her eyes, those fawn-like eyes, shone when they came upon Moni, as if she drew comfort from simply looking at her.

She became calm enough to be dressed in a pair of my pajamas. The leggings were too long; the tips of her fingers barely made it out of the sleeves.

"Hold her for a second, Stella. I want to take her temperature," Dad urged.

Mom pulled the girl into her lap, sighing as though she were surrendering to all the nonsense. When the girl looked up at her, Mom unstiffened ever so slightly, like a cold stick of butter that had just been set out.

The girl made a noise, a burble and then a cough.

She vomited all over Mom, dark muddy water spreading like poison across her lap.

CHAPTER 4

ISLA

Labor Day: September 7, 2020

I stared out over the lake as it shone, a spotlight with a pitch-black audience. The tops of the trees shook and encroached, watching over what was happening below.

I could not scream that night at the lake.

The light from the porch flickered weakly, afraid to show me. The long dock of the cabin an illusion that never ended. Plank after plank, row after row, elastic and unfathomable—a gleaming wet runway pointing to a figure.

There was someone at the end of the dock.

My feet were implanted in each wood grain, tied down tight so I couldn't escape. I could smell remnants of fish . . . guts and frothy blood. Its belly torn open earlier, the knife placed on the dock as if left for me. A gleam from the blade flashed over as I passed it.

I paused mid-step, the arch of my foot bent and disturbed. I heard it right then.

The faint laps of water at first. They grew stronger. Thicker. Pulsating. The water churned, loud and roaring. I ran closer to the edge, straining to see and hear as the surface broke so viciously.

The brief moments of complete silence in between each violent splash sickened me. I was a useless tower of fear, stuck on those planks.

A circle of matted hair sank into the water before a hand burst out and then disappeared. I reached out as if I could touch it, my arm extending so far that it hurt.

There was a force that drew me into the dark waters. Sucking me in, the top of the water a gaping mouth, starved for me to enter. I was submerged in all that was cold and calm. I floated, then sank farther.

A gurgle. A choke.

Then all silence.

CHAPTER 5

ISLA

1995

As the girl turned and looked at me from the hospital bed, the pillow beneath her head was so stiff it crunched. I didn't say anything to alert anyone else in the room. Mom's arms were crossed and Dad was hunched over as they quietly talked with the doctor in the corner under the mounted box television set.

I opened my mouth to say hi. Nothing came out, but she tilted her head as if to let me know she understood anyway. She placed two fingers on the IV catheter, tapping it at first and then trying to rip it out. I shook my head at her and gently held her wrist still. She stared back at me, like a baby would, before going right back to yanking at the catheter. I wrapped my hand around it, trying to keep it in.

A plump, red-haired nurse walked in and rushed over.

"No. No," she said, each time in the same level tone. It seemed directed more at me as she lightly pushed me away from the bed, glancing over at the doctor. She decided not to interrupt and turned her attention back to the IV catheter. The girl's free hand shot out and then retracted back as fast as a party horn.

"Oh . . ." the nurse gasped under her breath.

She touched the thick part of her forearm, where the girl had pinched her.

The girl looked up from under the sheets with a blank expression, then slowly turned back to stare at me.

The nurse's hands remained motionless above the bed, curled in. A few seconds later, she lowered them. "You've been through a lot," she whispered, justifying her decision to be idle on the whole matter, nodding at me as if I was in agreement. She checked the saline bag, tucked the sheet up farther, and left the room.

The girl still hadn't said a word.

The previous night, we had stayed up as long as we could. Sleeping would've somehow made us even more vulnerable to what had happened—what exactly we were still grasping. I woke up in the middle of the night next to Moni, who had fallen asleep in my bed due to my pleading. I had become suddenly panicked as the storm raged on while Mom and Dad took turns watching over the girl in their bed. The trauma of the evening had finally become too much for me.

By then the rains and winds had ceased. It was like being in a different cabin, this one so still and nearly soundless. I left my bedroom as Moni snored softly. I crept into the bedroom across the hall, the cedar floorboards under my feet cold and creaky. I did not find the room in silence. Instead, a low and muted dialogue—hushed in some waves but then sharp and stabbing in others, quickly reciprocated with an even coarser tone, only to die back down to an abrupt whisper.

It was Mom and Dad speaking livid words that I could not decipher, but I could sense the hostility coming from both of them. I stiffened by the door and slid down, willing myself not to make another move, as if their arguing were my fault. I dared not cause even more disturbance.

I woke up in the hallway, my head resting on my stretched-out arms. I looked back into the room. Both of them were passed out, Dad face down into his pillow, Mom on her side, her knees tucked in.

The girl lay between them, wide awake. It was strange seeing another girl where I had so often been—a replacement that did not stir up jealousy, but curiosity. If she noticed me, she gave no sign of it.

An ambulance arrived right at dawn. Sheriff Vandenberg pulled his brown prowler behind it, its lights ceremoniously swirling. A blue-and-red show flashed on our cabin exterior.

Dad carried the girl out. She seemed bigger, as if she had grown overnight. A young female paramedic opened a stretcher and guided her down onto it.

"Sorry, Patrick. Roads were blocked. Trees knocked over everywhere. Never seen anything like it," Sheriff Vandenberg said as he pulled his hat off.

"I'm just glad you're here now. She seems okay. But she hasn't said a word."

"Is that so?" Sheriff Vandenberg muttered.

"Did a tornado actually touch down?" Dad asked. He looked over his shoulder to check on the girl as the paramedic monitored her vitals. Mom stayed in the doorway with me, her hand resting on my head.

"I don't think so. But it sure felt like it, didn't it?"

"Should we follow the ambulance to the hospital?"

"If you want. I could question all of you down there if you don't mind. Girl doesn't have anyone else right now, does she?"

Dad looked up at Mom. She stepped forward, her hand still on my head.

"No. She doesn't . . . Have there been any car accidents nearby? Maybe she survived and ran into the woods?"

"None in the last week or so. There was a white Oldsmobile that skidded into one of the guardrails on 61. But the driver was a local teenage girl, and that was two weeks ago at least. Been a quiet last month of summer, believe it or not. Well—until now."

Dad anxiously tapped his foot. "What about missing persons reports? Children missing in the area?"

Sheriff Vandenberg shook his head. "Not in Grand Marais and nothing immediate on the wire that would match this. I can check the state database with her description. I'll let you know what I find."

"Please do, thank you," Dad said. He placed his fingers over his mouth, then dragged his hand away. "What does this mean for us? I hate to ask, but are we required to take care of her?"

Mom drew me in, her hands folded over my chest.

"This means nothing right now. But when child services gets involved, the state will take over. She will be questioned. Once she talks, that is."

Dad rubbed his arms as if a sudden draft had blown on him. "We don't mind coming down to the hospital. Part of me feels responsible for her in some strange way. North Shore Memorial?"

On the ride to the hospital, Mom kept looking over at Dad, who never once returned her glances. Instead, his hands steadily adhered to the steering wheel as if they had become a part of it.

"Patrick, that girl will get help. It just may not be from us," Mom said coolly.

"She doesn't have anyone."

"You heard the sheriff. The state will take her in."

"And do what with her?" Dad asked, still refusing to look at her.

Moni patted my hand and pressed her lips together, breathing in hard, then stared out the window.

"Find her a home," Mom answered.

"Stella, do you have any idea what foster homes can be like?"

"There are plenty of wonderful foster homes."

"We have a chance to do the right thing. To give her a home that has more certainty. She came to us, Stella. She came to our house."

Mom groaned. "The right thing? This isn't a lost puppy, Patrick. This is a child."

"Please don't talk to me like that," he said sternly, then abruptly glanced up in the rearview mirror. His dark eyes focused on me as if he noticed for the first time that I had joined them in the Jeep.

Mom looked at him and then back at me. She gave one of those smiles parents give when they try to slap a bandage on whatever their child shouldn't have been privy to.

"Isla, should we see what they have at the hospital cafeteria? You're probably starving. Would you like that?"

I shrugged.

And then she said what all mothers say.

"You need to eat something."

Later, after I had been cajoled into eating jiggly cafeteria eggs and drinking a small orange juice, Moni took me to walk around the hospital while Mom and Dad were questioned by Sheriff Vandenberg.

"Are Mom and Dad in trouble?" I asked.

"Trouble? Why trouble?" She folded up an extra napkin I hadn't used and prudently tucked it into her pocket.

"Because they have to talk to the police."

"They . . . cooperate. Police cooperate."

"Will I get in trouble?"

"Why?" she asked, her eyes crinkling with concern.

"For following her. I was the one that ran out into the woods."

She shook her head and then spoke in Korean. "You should not have gone out like that, tearing outside like a crazy person. You nearly gave Halmoni a heart attack. We're lucky everyone is okay. But are you in trouble? No, my child, you are not. You were good to lead us to her."

"You really think that?"

"Yes. For how else would we have been able to save her?"

I stopped walking. "So you want her to live with us too?"

She sighed and flattened her lips together. "I want what is best for our family."

The girl was discharged from the hospital at the end of the week. Dad and Mom agreed to take her in as emergency guardians. I stayed at the cabin with Mom and Moni to clean and pack while Dad went to go pick up the girl.

I stood at the end of the dirt path leading to the cabin. The same dark, stained cedar framed the abundant windows, giving it the appearance of a fish tank. Black metal roofing topped the first and second levels; gray and white stones lined the stairs leading up to the front door. I could see Moni in the kitchen, wiping down the inside of the oven. Mom was on the second floor, taking off the bedding in my room for the wash.

But it wasn't the same cabin anymore.

Her presence had morphed the very bones of its structure. Bending and twisting it into something that we all recognized but knew was incongruent with what we had lived in before.

It was immeasurable. But we felt it unmistakably.

Two local papers printed stories about the girl. The *Cook County News Herald* made it their front-page story, quoting Sheriff Vandenberg and even Dad. He read the story once at breakfast, folded it, and put it to the side. Mom later tossed it in the trash.

The *Duluth News Tribune* printed a picture of our cabin with a smaller article on the third page. She was still known as "girl found in woods." No name.

Eventually, she would have one.

And everyone would know it.

CHAPTER 6

WREN

Minneapolis, 1980s

She couldn't ignore them any longer. The tight, pressurized pains that invaded her midsection. It was like a vacuum had been inserted under her skin, suctioning and stretching all her muscles until the off button was finally pressed and she was able to breathe again.

It was nothing close to what the books had mentioned. These were sporadic. She couldn't time them even if she tried.

"Liars," she muttered and then clenched her teeth as another wave hit her.

A week after she found out she was pregnant, she had sat on the floor of a bookstore as she sucked on saltines to help with the nausea. There was no one else in the back corner. Just a half row of pregnancy and parenting books and the crinkle of the transparent packaging she dipped her hand into after every few pages.

Was this what she was already? A "back-corner mother"?

She had wanted to take one of the books with her. Instead, she placed a few on hold. Pretending to be able to buy something was better than not buying it at all.

"Your name?" the bookstore employee had asked politely, his pen poised over the white scrap of paper.

She had looked down at her belly that was still flat, then up at him. "Wren."

The name had slid with rawness off her tongue.

She had left the store before he could even finish writing it.

The pain was now making it hard to remain in a sitting position. She opened and closed her hands until her belly loosened. She had promised to call when this happened. But she wanted a little more time. She wanted to keep her safe inside for a little bit longer.

Her.

When the tech announced it was a girl, she had smiled. She had rubbed her belly, sang to her tenderly, and done all the things she was sure she would never do. Maternal, loving things. Things she never had growing up.

She slid her hands onto the base of the roundness that overtook her petite frame and lifted, as if that would alleviate the pressure. For the first time, she moaned out loud. Sweat dampened dark strands against the sides of her face and down her neck.

The nearest phone was at the Somali deli a block away. She would have to make it down there before it got worse.

Not yet. Not just yet please. Hang in there with me a little longer, baby girl.

She never imagined it would be this hard.

She never imagined she would be all alone.

She wanted more time. A sliver of time. That was all she was asking for.

A sigh of relief breezed out of her as the contractions suddenly ceased. She tilted her head back and tucked her knees in.

Something tore inside her. There was no pain. A gush of warm liquid seeped down her legs. The trickling taunted her, a faint chime that time was up.

That phone call couldn't wait any longer.

CHAPTER 7

THE INTERVIEW

2021

[Roll package]

JODI LEE: She was only six when her life began. At least that's what Marlow Fin says, as we learn more about her harrowing start to some more hopeful early years. Patrick and Stella Baek legally adopted Marlow, becoming the only parents she has ever known. But what were those beginning years like?

[Studio]

JODI LEE: Why do you think the Baek family took you in?

MARLOW FIN: You know, I've never really asked myself that. I think it's because I don't want to know the real answer.

JODI LEE: Is that because you don't like the possibilities?

MARLOW FIN: I think it's because I will never fully know. But what I can guess? They felt obligated. That doesn't scream love, I know. But I always felt my father pushed for it. As a man who always thought he was doing the right thing. My mother was never quite all there for me. Did she fulfill all her duties as a mother? Yes. But I could sense that she wouldn't miss me. That if I were to suddenly disappear, she wouldn't be sad—not really, anyways.

JODI LEE: That's a tough, tough thing to think as a child. That your mother wouldn't miss you?

MARLOW FIN: She did her best. I won't fault her for that.

JODI LEE: Most people would be less forgiving. Maybe even unforgiving.

MARLOW FIN: I never said I was forgiving.

JODI LEE: You call them your mother and father. Yet you don't share their last name?

MARLOW FIN: I legally changed it.

JODI LEE: Why? A family that takes you in. Legally adopts you. Raises you. Why get rid of their very name?

MARLOW FIN: It wasn't out of spite, if that's what you're getting at.

JODI LEE: A lot of people find that hard to believe.

MARLOW FIN: [*Smiles*] I'm sorry. I smile anytime I get emotional. It's like a reflex. It makes me look like a psychotic clown, I know . . . but yeah. I can see why people think that.

JODI LEE: Fin. That's the name you chose instead, right?

MARLOW FIN: Yes. My agent suggested—well, told me—to change it when I was eighteen. I told her no way. But then I kind of liked the idea. It was stupid—I mean, who knows what I was thinking? I sure as hell don't, I was a kid. It sounded cool, rebellious, you know? So I changed it to Fin. I was booking some of my first shows in Paris when I got the idea for that. I know [*rolls eyes*], exceptionally cliché—a model visiting Paris for the first time decides to go with something French. I think we all have regrets from our youth. Though I can't say I fully regret this one.

JODI LEE: Why Fin?

MARLOW FIN: It means "end" in French.

JODI LEE: As in . . .

MARLOW FIN: The end.

JODI LEE: I'm going to jump back a little here. You're six years old. You aren't speaking. You don't have any memory. A family takes you in. Do you remember those first moments? Days? Weeks . . . being with your new family?

MARLOW FIN: A lot of what happened the night I was found— and those moments leading up to the hospital—is a blur. I can recall bits and pieces. I know someone put a blanket on me. I remember my sister's face in the hospital. How she kept looking at me. I don't remember any of the doctors or nurses. But I remember Isla.

JODI LEE: What do you remember about Isla from the hospital?

MARLOW FIN: She was always at my side.

JODI LEE: Anything else?

MARLOW FIN: No. Just that. But the first night out of the hospital is pretty clear, though. Yeah . . . that's a good memory.

JODI LEE: Yeah?

MARLOW FIN: We drove in this old Jeep. I don't think it's around anymore. But we drove it all the way back to the Twin Cities. My father pulled up into the driveway. It was dark enough where I didn't see the house. But he held me and carried me inside.

When he opened the front door, there was suddenly so much light . . . so much brightness. I don't know if that's actually what I saw or if I'm only remembering it this way. It was such a light after being in the dark so long. Being in that house was its own blanket for me. That's the only way I can describe it.

There was very little talking. Everyone was quiet, like they were afraid if they talked too much it would startle me or become too much for me. Instead, I got fed something warm and wonderful by Moni. That's my grandmother . . .

JODI LEE: Are you okay?

MARLOW FIN: Yes. I'm fine . . .

JODI LEE: You sure?

MARLOW FIN: My Moni. A white bowl full of thick beef broth and rice. I devoured it. She was the one who put me in bed. I think I slept for days. I really did. When I woke up, she was still sitting there, making sure I was okay. Isla would pop her head under her arm.

31

JODI LEE: Why does mentioning your grandmother, Moni, bring up such emotion?

MARLOW FIN: She was the best of all of us. I haven't really talked about her much.

JODI LEE: And your mother, Stella Baek? Where was she?

MARLOW FIN: She checked in on me too. I heard her talk on the phone quite a bit. Asking questions—I can only assume it was the doctor. She took my temperature. Brought me meals. Everything she was supposed to do.

JODI LEE: Supposed to do.

MARLOW FIN: Yes.

JODI LEE: Marlow, do you think your mother wanted you in the family?

MARLOW FIN: [*Silence*]

JODI LEE: Marlow . . .

MARLOW FIN: What good does it do answering that now?

JODI LEE: What was your father, Patrick Baek, doing during those first weeks?

MARLOW FIN: He was also on the phone a lot. Trying to see if there were any missing children who matched my description. At this point they weren't sure if I still had anyone out there. As far as they knew, I was temporary.

JODI LEE: You say that word, temporary, with such weight.

MARLOW FIN: [*Shrugs*]

JODI LEE: Now, this is 1995. I dislike saying this, but things were still a little different at that time. Did you ever feel people looked at your family in a strange way?

MARLOW FIN: Are you trying to ask if people cared that I was Black, my mom was white, my dad was Asian, and my sister was a mixed-race child? Yes. There were of course people who cared. Plenty of people care [*gestures*] about things that have no significance. Did it matter to me? No.

JODI LEE: What about to the rest of the family?

MARLOW FIN: You mean my family. I'm sure it crossed their minds before bringing me in that the particular makeup of our family was not going to be typical in our neighborhood. There were plenty of lingering eyes. The first time we went out as a family, I distinctly recall a white girl my age who wouldn't stop staring at me. As if I were the first Black person she had ever seen. Just as you said, 1995 . . . we were all still pretending then, right?

JODI LEE: Marlow, did you ever feel like an outcast in your family? And I ask this not because of race. But because of the manner you were brought in. Found in the woods and then adopted. A mother who did not seem particularly . . . close to you. Did you feel like the outcast?

MARLOW FIN: Of course. I feel like an outcast wherever I go. It's part of my makeup. And I don't mean that in the physical sense. I've never felt comfortable blending in anywhere.

JODI LEE: Did that anger you? Upset you?

MARLOW FIN: At times, yes.

JODI LEE: Were you prone to violence during this time?

MARLOW FIN: No. I'm not a violent person.

JODI LEE: I have a police report here from September 1995. [*Shuffles papers*]

MARLOW FIN: And?

JODI LEE: Can you tell me why the police were called to the house after the first month you were there?

MARLOW FIN: It was a misunderstanding.

JODI LEE: Tell us about it. Tell us what this misunderstanding was.

MARLOW FIN: I recall there being a lot of arguing. Moni took me and Isla into her room. But I got out and went back downstairs to see what the fuss was. The noise was coming from the kitchen.

I could see the kitchen light shining hard on my mother's blonde hair. It was so shiny in that moment it looked like a helmet. She was shaking her head, my father yelling something back. I wanted to make it stop. I think I ran at them. My mother fell somehow trying to avoid me. She ended up falling backward and clipping her cheek on the counter.

JODI LEE: The counter. That's what the police report also says. That it was the counter.

MARLOW FIN: My father never struck my mother.

JODI LEE: Then how did she get . . . the police report says a three-inch laceration on her cheek? That is a pretty bad cut. You're saying the counter did that?

MARLOW FIN: Yes. And it's really unfortunate that it happened. My mother still has a slight scar from it if you look really hard.

JODI LEE: Have there ever been any other incidents of violence that involved you?

MARLOW FIN: It depends.

JODI LEE: On?

MARLOW FIN: On what you consider violence.

CHAPTER 8

ISLA

1995

"Don't wake her up," Mom said as she flipped a pancake on the smooth stone griddle.

"But we're having pancakes," I said, as if that were a critical reason for anything.

"She needs rest," she replied without looking up, then reached for the glass measuring bowl full of yellowish batter. Her face was placid but her grip on everything was hard, her hand on the handle a little too tight, each flick of her wrist sharp and restrained.

Dad looked over his morning coffee and swallowed whatever comment he was about to send her way.

I sat perched on my stool at the counter. "Then why did you wake me up?" I asked, looking over at Dad as if to say *if you're not going to speak, I will.*

I slid an inch off my seat. "I'm going to go get her. It's Saturday and—"

"Isla. No," Mom cut me off fast, holding up her spatula warningly.

She was always doing this—holding on to any moment she could without the girl. A Saturday morning of pancakes, yes, wonderful. But not with *her.* Let's keep her away. Just for a little bit longer.

It had been a month since the girl had been living at our home.

Her silence remained. Every time she didn't answer a question or gave us a blank look, it was another reminder of that night. How her being here was not of the ordinary.

The first week she mainly stayed in the spare room upstairs, sleeping. Moni would tend to her as Mom and Dad were on the phone relentlessly—it was *always* ringing. A reporter wanting to ask questions for a follow-up story. Child services scheduling a visit. Mom talking to the doctor and repeatedly asking when she should bring "the girl" in next for an evaluation.

And of course, Dad's back-and-forth with Sheriff Vandenberg.

"Any leads? I'm sorry to be calling again but it's been nearly a week. Don't you think anyone who knew her would have reached out by now?"

He would hang up the phone in his office, throw a Tic Tac into his mouth, and chew it rapidly. When he noticed me standing at the french doors to his office, he would quickly smile and offer me one.

"We don't know where her mom and dad are yet?"

He would shake his head and pretend to turn back to his work.

By the time school started, the calls became less frequent, the conversations with Sheriff Vandenberg sparser.

In class, my third-grade teacher, Mrs. Elefson, would pull me aside and quietly ask me how I was doing.

"Fine," I would say each time.

"And—that little girl. Is she doing okay?"

Her face was sympathetic, but I could still see it, that sloppy, gossipy eagerness in her eyes, wanting the latest on "that girl found near Grand Marais."

Most of the time I'd just shrug.

When she was strong enough, she finally emerged and joined us for meals. Otherwise, she remained in what was now turning into "her room." The doctor and child psychologist had both agreed: "too much stimulation" would be ill advised right now.

"She needs consistency. Stability. That's what the doctors told us," Mom would say—her rationale for keeping the girl in her room.

"What's wrong with her?" I finally asked one morning, as Mom folded laundry into neat stacks on her and Dad's bed. A tower of white socks here, a column of folded shirts there.

She didn't even pause as she kept her focus on a towel she placed against her chest and brought the corners up. "She suffers from PTSD. That means something bad happened to her before we found her. It was enough to make her not talk."

"Something bad?"

"Yes. Something that . . . scared her."

I sat on the edge of the bed. "Do we know what was so scary?"

Her hands tightly held the folded towel.

"Will she ever talk again?"

She finally looked up at me. "I don't know, Isla."

Dad walked by the room. He looked at the two of us, but longer at Mom. She seemed to hold her breath around him. The same way she did that night at the cabin.

I saw them again from that night. Dad standing by Mom in the foggy bathroom mirror. The careful caress of her neck.

But it had not been simply a tender moment. That had been their truce. A ceasefire between them after the dust had settled from the days before.

Those days before were not as adoring. A livid whisper, quick and scorching, replaced by straight smiles when I entered the room. Moni, hastily taking me by the hand and outside, while the faint shouts of their fight echoed after us.

"What do you expect me to do now? Just ignore it again?"

"No. But you could lower your voice. She'll hear you."

"Maybe she should hear it? Maybe she should know."

"Quiet. I'm warning you . . . quiet."

But at dinner, they would be holding hands again, a brief intermission from whatever had fueled their fiery exchange this time. "Would you like more glazed carrots, Isla?" one of them would ask with a straight face. They were so good at it. So good at recovering from their battle wounds to make it home to me.

Earlier that week, I had woken up to find Dad absent from breakfast. Mom looked puffy, her eyes saggy. She played along and talked to me and Moni for a while, answered my questions, but said nothing if Dad was mentioned. She eventually excused herself.

She didn't notice me follow her, a shadow behind her as she went up to their room and planted her face into the bed, heavily breathing and motionless. I left, not wanting to see her face when she got up. Not wanting to see her reaction to finding out I had watched her. Instead, I waited outside the rest of the day.

Dad came back to the cabin later that evening. But *happy* was not the word I would use to describe Mom right then. *Relieved.* She seemed like a woman who had gotten off an amusement park ride she had been somehow talked into. It was over and she was pleased to never have to go on it again.

I wonder what she would have done had she been warned about what was to happen that week. That her family would never be the same. That a girl would enter their lives and there would be no going back.

I sometimes wished her away.

In the weeks that followed, I would lie in bed and wish her away. I would wish that she never existed. That I never saw her face and followed her into the woods. That she belonged to another family, and they would come and take her away.

When we returned home with her, I would hear them at night. Mom and Dad in the big bed that used to be full of such light and embraces, where I was tucked in, safe and treasured.

Where mornings were spent under those cream blankets. Dad's hair stuck up in the front and flat in the back. I was their little "squish" in between, tucked in as we hugged and lazily rolled around. My legs kicking up excitedly, not wanting it to ever end. Until there was the mention of bacon and french toast by Mom, a whisper, a promise in my ear and I would bolt up. We hardly stayed home on weekends. There was always some festival, restaurant, bookstore, or coffee shop to visit, the three of us in a constant burst of affection and laughter.

We had been inside our own snow globe, a molded and carved scene of brilliance.

Only then did I pause at this idea. The glass in the globe cracked.

Did I remember it the right way? Was the morning light in their room as bright as I envisioned? Was the french toast as sweet as it tasted in my memory? Or was it all a little duller in reality, embroidered by things I had seen on TV or read about?

And then I would be brought back to what it had become. The girl now inside with us. Their whispers at night.

"Do you think she knows? Do you think she'll ever remember?"

CHAPTER 9

ISLA

1995

I would slip into the girl's room whenever I could, bringing her some of my dolls and books. I didn't know if she even liked them or knew what to do with them. I would sometimes color on the floor with her, showing her how to clutch the fat red crayon in her small hand. When she grew bored of that, I would cut shapes out of construction paper. Her eyes would remain focused on the shears as they opened and closed, little colored pieces of paper falling to the floor like confetti.

Occasionally I thought she smiled at me, the corners of her mouth barely moving upward. Her thick matte eyelashes mimicked my dolls, blinking in a random pattern. I would pat her arm, whisper soothingly, copying what I saw Moni do with her.

For whatever reason, Moni was so natural with the girl. She would gently brush her hair, singing a Korean lullaby. The notes were so familiar to my ears as she had sung the very same ones to me. She would fold her ever so cautiously into bed, as though she were a paper doll that could be crushed easily. Her words were cooing in nature, a constant reassurance she would be okay.

"Goodness, goodness," she would say in Korean.

The barrier of words and language was nothing for Moni and the girl. Their connection went deeper than that, requiring nothing but compassion.

Most meals, Moni would be the one to feed her. Each spoonful, each bite, was so patiently inserted into her mouth. A small wipe there. A light caress of the cheek there. The girl seemed nearly in a trance with Moni, a willing subject that would do whatever she asked.

When Mom was home to feed her, it would be transactional. Like a slot machine she fed coins into, motorized and monotonous. She would barely look at her with each spoonful, as though she were afraid to make eye contact, or the very sight of her was too much.

One night Mom bathed her, since Moni had gone to a Korean church fundraiser. The splash each time Mom dipped the washcloth in the water and cleaned a part of the girl's body was oddly soothing. I took the yellow duck and placed it on the girl's chest as she lay back in the water. She touched it with one finger and pushed it, watching it float and then go idle toward Mom. Their eyes met when she suddenly reached out and touched Mom's arm.

Mom jerked upward, as if she had been electrocuted. She stared down at the little hand on her forearm. Quickly, she peeled it off and kept washing her, as if nothing had happened. Later, I would see her tracing the very spot the girl had touched her, rubbing it slightly as if it had imprinted and left a burn.

On weekends, when Dad wasn't giving a lecture or going back to campus for a meeting, he would give most of his attention to the girl. Bringing home cream-filled doughnuts or peanut butter cookies was his attempt at getting her to talk. He would take whatever treat he had bought and bring it to her room. The girl, sitting in a small blue wooden chair—part of a tea party set that used to be mine—would wait expectantly. Dad would sit in the pink one, his long legs awkwardly jutting out, giving him the appearance of a marionette. I would watch from the doorway as he slid the goods across the table. She would take

41

only a moment to examine it before bringing it toward her mouth with both hands.

"I'm Patrick. What's your name?"

The girl would take a bite and look back at him.

"Do you have a name?"

Chewing.

"Does your mommy have a name?"

More chewing and then licking her fingers.

"Do you know where your mommy is? Your daddy?"

I could always see the patience eventually fall off his face, the more questions he asked and empty voids he got in return. Frustration clung to him, and maybe even a shade of irritation.

"You're pushing her too much," I heard Mom say before dinner, the plates hitting the table a little too hard. Had they skin, it would have bruised.

"Well one of us has to try talking to her," Dad said in a brusque tone as he took his plate and retreated to the office.

Their arguing must have increased in velocity, as Moni took me and the girl to her room to sleep that night.

The next morning, Mom had a cut on her cheek, the skin around the slice like a puff pastry. She silently fixed a bowl of cereal for me, until Moni entered the kitchen with the girl. The girl stood with one hand in Moni's, the other touching her cheek. Mom's face flared with discomfort as she hurriedly went back upstairs.

I said nothing and went with Dad in the Jeep to school. He turned the volume up on the radio as if to drown out any questions I may have had in my mind.

By the end of the month, as the weather turned cooler, I would bring the girl with me to the neighborhood playground. Mom was hesitant at first.

"She could use some fresh air. Being around other kids," I argued.

Mom bit her lip, something she seemed to be doing more frequently. "Keep her close. And don't let her wander."

"Fine."

"Isla."

"I will. Don't worry so much."

I could see her face in the front door window as I held the girl's hand and led her down the sidewalk, leaves circling our feet from the warm afternoon gusts.

Most of the neighborhood kids thought nothing of this new creature who had landed in their world—one who had caused "grown-up" talk among their parents, low-voiced conversations at the dinner table.

So that girl they found, she's really staying with them?

Not often you see something like that happen . . . I mean, we would do the same, I'm sure.

Would we though?

But to the children she was just another body on the field. Another kid to wait behind before their turn on the slide. Harmless at best, and nothing to be fussed over.

Except for one. There is always one.

She lived two blocks away from us. I wish I could remember her name. Shaina, Shawna, one of those names that sounded like it had to be said with a twang. Her father worked for John Deere and would get transferred to another state the following spring. We never saw her again.

You would think I would remember her name after what happened.

At first Shaina, or whatever her name was, would give hard stares. These elevator eyes that never stopped traveling over the girl, one finger twisting her long, wavy, flaxen hair. I would give them right back to her, a learned skill from my already seasoned time on the playground.

"Can I help you?" I asked her, clutching the girl's hand. She looked up at me and then over to Shaina.

"She can't be your sister."

"Why is that?"

Her nose wrinkled as if she smelled something repulsive. "You look nothing like each other. Sisters are supposed to look alike."

"Who said we were sisters?"

"My mom did. She said it was going to raise a lot of questions for the both of you if they took her in."

Everything felt hot in my face.

"Like I said. You can't be sisters."

I felt the skin under my eyes tingle and cheeks go red. I wanted to tell her that her mom didn't know what she was talking about. That she was shaming me. That she made me feel less than her. I wanted to tell her to go to hell.

But another word and the tingling would turn into something even more embarrassing than saying nothing at all.

I sat on a bench with the girl still holding my hand. She looked at Shaina and then back at me, a peculiar look in her broad eyes.

We went home. Mom, of course, seeing that we survived the ordeal of the playground, sent us back the next day despite me dragging my heels over it.

Shaina was there again. She was too busy on the spinning carousel, pretending to be surfing with her arms out, laughing, to notice I was back with the girl.

The girl tugged at my arm. I pulled her in closer. She tugged again. I looked down at her to find the blankness replaced by an eagerness, an urgency to be freed.

I let her hand go.

I watched her for a while but soon grew tired of keeping tabs on her. It wasn't until I realized I couldn't see her anymore that I actively searched. There was no panic; somehow I knew she wouldn't run away from me.

I found her five minutes later in the crawl space under the green tube slide. Shaina was there, too, her mouth in a stunned O shape, one hand holding a fistful of her own hair, the other palm up in the air, as if she, too, wasn't sure how she ended up like this.

The entire left side of her hair had been cut off.

A pair of scissors lay in the pebble gravel. A pair I recognized.

Later, when they asked me about it, I pretended not to know how it happened. Maybe Shaina did it herself?

The girl looked at me and stood up.

The next day she started talking.

"Do you have Mickey waffles? My name is Marlow," she said the morning the dam broke, and her words began to flood out, as though there had been so much to say and it had been blocked from exiting her mouth. Her wavy hair was a wild nest, her nightgown twisted overnight like a Rubik's Cube, half of it tucked into her underwear.

A switch had gone off in her head.

Someone or something had figured out how to reprogram the girl's brain. She woke up a different girl. One who spoke like she had never stopped in the first place.

"More syrup, please," she said clear as day to Moni.

Moni smiled, unfazed—as if she knew the girl would eventually speak—and handed Marlow the plastic dispenser shaped like a maple leaf. She squeezed an excessive amount and messily patted the waffle with her blue plastic fork.

She barely finished her breakfast before she was taken to see the child psychologist. Mom and Dad rushed her over as if she had been physically injured and required medical attention. *Fix this, it seems to have broken.*

"She still has no memory of anything prior to being found by your daughter," the doctor said, closing the door with Marlow inside what looked like a playroom, little wooden tables and chairs with puzzles, dolls, and books in various colored bins. I could see her through the window, examining a rag doll with black yarn for hair and yellow button eyes.

"Why do you think she suddenly started talking?" asked Dad.

The doctor, a Hispanic woman with hair tied in a severe knot at the nape of her neck, nodded before Dad finished his sentence.

"It is quite remarkable how quickly she came back from whatever trauma she experienced."

"Quickly? Dr. Ciruelos, it was overnight," said Mom.

"Indeed. Children tend to heal faster than adults. They are truly amazing when it comes to recovering. We did some initial assessments. She will have to come back for continued therapy and evaluation, of course, but she is very much at the level of a six . . . I'd say seven-year-old child. You should be very proud."

Mom stepped back. "Well, she is not our child."

"Stella," Dad muttered under his breath.

Dr. Ciruelos dipped her head down and then up. "That does bring me to my next question. Have either of you thought about what your plans are after the emergency guardianship?"

"Our plans," repeated Mom flatly.

"Marlow doesn't remember anything before her life with you. Your family is the only one she has ever really known, as far as we know. We have yet to find out anything about her past. Whether she even has any surviving relatives. If you aren't planning to keep developing this—this relationship with her—then it is best to break things off now. Give her the chance to start with whoever will be there in the long run."

Her calmness did nothing to squelch the tightening I could see in Mom's face. Dad reached over and tapped Mom on the arm, as if to check her.

"We haven't talked about it in detail. But it's something we will have to discuss in private," Dad said, looking over at me, suddenly remembering I was there.

"I understand," said Dr. Ciruelos. "In the meantime, please keep me posted if you notice any significant changes in Marlow."

She moved toward the door to retrieve her.

"Do you think she may regain any of her memory?" Mom abruptly asked.

"Only time will tell. She may remember everything tomorrow. She may never remember it ever again."

Mom nodded slowly, looking at Marlow through the window. She smiled at her, holding the doll up.

A week later, Sheriff Vandenberg pulled up in our driveway. He had grown a beard. Dad seemed surprised to see him.

"Please, come in," he said, holding the front door open.

Moni offered him tea but he declined.

"Can't stay long. I'm in the Cities on a separate matter so I thought I would drop by. Heard we got ourselves a little miracle."

Marlow entered the kitchen. She was already a stunning sight. Sheriff Vandenberg paused to look at her.

"Marlow, is it?" he asked kindly.

"I'm six."

"You are? Well, that's great. Do you remember me?"

"No," she said bluntly and hid behind Moni, tugging on her shirt.

Mom placed her hands on my shoulders instead of Marlow's. "She's still a little skittish. She talks a lot when it's only us."

Sheriff Vandenberg nodded gently. "I spoke with Dr. Ciruelos. She advised it was too early to question the little lady."

"I would think that would be wise. One step at a time," said Dad.

"Right. But since I'm here, mind if I ask Isla a few questions?"

Dad's eyebrows lifted high. He studied me and then shrugged. "I don't see why not."

I followed Sheriff Vandenberg to the living room. Mom and Dad stayed in the kitchen, while Moni took Marlow up to her room to play.

"Where would you like to sit?"

I looked around and then down. "The floor."

"Ahh, sure. I'm going to warn you, my knees aren't what they used to be."

We sat on the cream carpet. I ran my hands over it, picking up little tufts instead of looking up at him.

"Isla, do you still remember the night you found your friend Marlow?"

"She's not my friend."

His eyes narrowed slightly. "She isn't?"

"Well not really."

"It was a pretty scary night."

"Yes." I looked up at him. His beard looked thick and oily, in stark contrast to his shiny, smooth head.

"Do you remember what you were doing right before you found Marlow?"

"Yes. We ate noodles. They were a little spicy."

"Was everyone in the cabin when you ate?"

"Yes. Moni. Mom. Dad."

He popped a white Chiclet into his mouth. It crackled as he paused.

"Isla, did you notice anything different about that night?"

"What do you mean by different?"

"Anything out of the ordinary. Something maybe Mom, Dad, or your grandmother did that they usually don't do."

I shook my head. "We ate our last dinner of cabin week. Moni always cooks it."

"Nothing else seemed a little weird or off?"

I could smell the mint and sweetness from his mouth.

"No."

"All right, then. Good girl."

He took a pink Chiclet from his pocket and handed it to me. I let it stay warm in my palm. It left a pink smudge. I opened and closed my fist, feeling its stickiness.

I looked up to see Marlow sitting cross-legged on the foyer floor. Copying my hand motions and staring back at me.

CHAPTER 10

ISLA

1996

"There's a moving truck across the street!"

I pressed my nose against my bedroom window. Knees tucked in, I perched on the white wooden reading nook, leaning in to get a better look.

Marlow climbed up next to me. She placed both hands on the glass and stared out.

"Who is that?" she asked, pointing to an elderly woman standing on the lawn.

She had dyed red hair as bright as a fire engine, her roots white so I could see them even from where I sat. Her hands were on her wide hips as she seemed to be saying something to one of the movers.

"Must be who's moving in."

We both looked to the left and then to the right, scanning for more evidence of who our new neighbors were.

"Isla! Marlow!"

Moni's calls floated up the stairs.

I took Marlow's hand and dragged her from the windowsill, her head craned to maintain her view.

My hand entwined with Marlow's.

This had become the ordinary over the last eight months or so. She had remained with us, the guardianship extended. "Through spring," Dad had said. The harsh winter solidified her presence more and more, like layer after layer of snow, packed in deep until it turned into an unmoving and glacial form.

Our daily domestic routine had slowly circled around her, bringing her in to become one of us. Moni constantly poked food into her mouth with chopsticks, to the point where Marlow would simply turn her head for the next bite. An elderly Korean woman was now attached to her as if a thread connected them.

Dad stayed busy at the university, grading papers in his office when he was home. But I would see his hand on Marlow's head at the end of the night, a soft pat—the lost puppy we had let stay with us for shelter. His eyes studied her as he asked Mom the same questions. "How were the girls? Were they good for you today? Did Halmoni get a break?"

I could see Mom ever so slightly bend to our new clan, the repetition and cycle of each day swaying her toward a reticent acceptance. Each morning she'd get us out of bed, help us each struggle with the toothbrush, do extra loads of laundry, and make an extra plate of food at dinner. This, too, was becoming part of her system, her makeup, her household habitat, whether she wanted it to or not.

It was hard going anywhere without comments from strangers. Strangers would look back at Marlow as she passed, her striking features an open invitation to marvel and ask questions, as if she were giving permission by her appearance alone. I would secretly feel defensive, wanting to shield her from these voyeurs.

"Your daughter is beautiful," a woman said to us at the grocery store, pointedly looking at Marlow. I sat crouched inside the cart, clutching a box of Fruit Loops in front of my chest, shielding myself from any confusion. Of course, she wasn't talking about me.

Mom opened her mouth to correct her. But this time . . . this time she said nothing. Her hands stayed poised on the green rubber handle of the cart. Her shoulders dropped and the lines around her mouth hardened. She averted her eyes from Marlow's upward gaze and pushed forward.

Only Mom was good at ignoring Marlow.

When Marlow asked a question or looked at you, there was no disregarding her. She overwhelmed with a heaviness that dripped like syrup, coating you inward. Her light, honey-colored eyes watched you with wonder and a possessiveness that made you feel wanted. That you mattered to her. That you mattered at all . . .

Moni called for us a second time.

I clutched Marlow's hand and pulled her out of my room.

"Moni wants us," I said, bending down to her ear.

"But the new neighbors—"

"They're not going anywhere."

We found Moni downstairs in the kitchen. She looked up from tying a bow out of stiff, plasticky pink ribbon.

"What you girls doing?" she asked, tying the bow tighter.

"Watching the new neighbors," I said.

She held up a round plastic container, the pink ribbon lopsided on top, and placed it in my hands. It felt warm and smelled of garlic.

"This is for new neighbor. Come on. We go say hello."

"What? They just got here." I flattened my hands out underneath the container.

"Yes. Welcome gift."

Marlow poked at the container. "What's a welcome gift?"

Moni rushed us all forward at the front door. For such a small woman, she had immense strength and forcefulness. "Don't you know what welcome means?"

"And why are you bringing them that?"

"In Korea you show respect to a new neighbor. You welcome them with a gift," she said in Korean, practically shushing Marlow as if she had said something bad.

With all the time she had spent with Moni, Marlow had quickly picked up on some of the language, furthering their bond, a taut and tightening rope.

We followed Moni, little ducklings in a line, as she walked hurriedly—there was never any time to waste.

The red-haired woman we saw earlier from upstairs poked her head out from behind the large yellow moving truck. Her brow furrowed as she stepped onto the lawn with a wide gait. She was sweating despite the chilly April weather.

"Hello. Can I help you?" she asked with solid, separated words.

Moni smiled pleasantly and bowed her head slightly as she pushed me closer. "Give to her," she whispered loudly.

I wiggled forward and held up the container. "Welcome to our neighborhood," I said ceremoniously. "We live there." I pointed to our blue house with dark shutters.

She squinted with one eye and looked up.

"Ahh. I see. And what's that you got?"

"I am the grandmother," Moni said, smiling and patting me. "I cook some food for you. Please enjoy. Welcome."

"Smells wonderful." She held the container up to her nose. "My name is Clara Ada Yates. But you can call me Ada."

"My name Young-Mi. But everyone call me Halmoni."

"Where does a name like that come from?" Ada asked. She had a gruff and brash voice that did not pause for anything.

"Korea."

"My younger brother fought over there. But he's no longer with us."

Moni lowered her eyes. "I'm so sorry."

"Ahh. I never liked him. He was an alcoholic. Beat his wife."

I could see the startled expression on Moni's face but she quickly hid it. "We need go now. Please, again welcome."

"Go? Nah. Stick around. Help us unload some of this crap. I'm telling you, most of this I could have dumped before we left."

The lack of boundaries this woman had was nothing new to my Moni. Since coming to this country, she had quickly learned some Americans never really had them. But I had watched her stealthily step around this before. She had practice over the years in how to handle these one-sided, clashing circumstances.

"Oh. I so old," she joked and took my hand and Marlow's.

"Old? You don't look it," Ada said with a deep-throated cackle.

"This is Isla and Marlow," Moni said, putting us in front of her like two small buffers.

Ada looked behind her and then around the back of the truck. "Did I mention I moved here with my grandson? He's likely about your age. Will be really nice to have some kiddos to play with in the neighborhood.

"Sawyer. Sawyer!" She looked around again. "Boy must be in the backyard somewhere. Go find him, will you? And thank you for this!" She patted the container like a drum.

Moni lifted one eyebrow. "You're welcome."

She left us to find the boy and scuttled her way back inside the house, looking over her shoulder a few times.

I took Marlow's hand and walked across the patchy brown-and-green yard around to the back. The house had pale-yellow siding and a gray shed on the edge of the property. A large lilac bush shook. I watched petals fall down, a shower of purple confetti.

A skinny boy emerged with limbs like a young deer, angled every which way. His sandy hair hung over his green eyes as he peered at us both.

"There's a wasp nest at the top of that shed," he said, pointing a long stick upward and tapping the roof.

Marlow looked up and then took a step behind me.

"Are you two sisters?"

"Huh?"

"Sisters. You both have the same look on your face."

I shook my head as if that would make sense of it. "Are you Sawyer?" I asked as I looked up to try to find the nest.

"Yup." He whacked the black shingled roof again with the stick. A single wasp buzzed out and disappeared into the sky. "My grandma and I drove here from Wyoming. You ever been there? We have moose that walk around. Ever see a moose?"

"Not in real life." I batted at another wasp. Marlow ducked. "Why did you move to Minnesota then?"

"I had to come here with Grandma Ada."

"Why?"

"My dad left."

Something in his voice made me stop asking questions. He hit the roof even harder; bits of bark flew everywhere.

"Don't do that," I ordered.

"I'm getting the nest."

"But you'll knock the nest. And then all the wasps will fly out, angry. We'll get stung."

"My Grandma Ada says you can suck the venom out. You'll be fine."

I scoffed. "I don't want to get stung. And I don't even know if *she's* allergic or not."

Marlow nodded emphatically. "Yeah. We don't want to get stung. So, stop it."

Sawyer pulled the stick down. "How'd you know my name?" He squinted one eye as his upper lip stretched across his oversize, crooked front teeth.

"Your grandma. She told us to find you."

He put one of his hands in his pocket and looked down for a moment as if considering his options.

"And you?"

"Me?"

"Your name."

"Isla."

"Her?" He pointed with his stick.

"Marlow."

"All right, Isla and Marlow. I won't try to knock that nest down." He bent to get rid of the stick. A small plastic figurine landed in the grass. I leaned in and looked down. It was in the shape of a knight, the head covered in a closed helmet and visor. It was shiny and blinked at me in the sunlight.

"Sawyer!"

"That's Grandma Ada. I better go help her. See you all around."

He waved his arm in a sort of salute and ran around the side of the shed, his hair flopping as he disappeared around the corner.

Later that night, after dinner, Dad came home with a cookie cake. He held the white box out for us to open.

"Marlow. This is really for you, sweetie."

She clapped her hands in delight as he revealed the large chocolate chip cookie decorated in white and black icing.

"Oh, so nice," Moni declared, immediately going to the pantry to retrieve paper plates.

Mom stood behind the counter, drying a pot from dinner with a dish towel. "When did you find time to get that, Patrick?" she asked with a tightened jaw.

"I shortened my office hours a little."

"Your students didn't mind?"

He stared back hard. "They didn't. And besides, this is a special occasion."

"What's so special?" I asked, pulling the box down to get a better look.

Marlow stuck her finger in the white icing and put it in her mouth.

Dad glanced at Mom. "Tomorrow we're all going down to the courthouse."

"What for?"

He took a deep breath. "Well . . . Marlow is going to officially be part of our family."

I found myself quickly looking at Mom, whose cheeks went flush.

Moni came back with a stack of paper plates lined with blue and pink flowers. "Very special day."

"We're adopting Marlow. She'll be your sister, Isla," said Dad, chest out, a wide smile plastered on his face.

"I thought she already was." I fingered the icing like Marlow did, dipping it in the black instead.

"Hey, hey. Let Moni cut you piece," she said, swatting me away.

"Marlow, do you know what this means?" Dad asked, bending down next to her.

She smiled. "I don't have to leave?"

"Oh. Sweetie. No, you don't. You're part of our family. I'm your Dad and Stella is your Mommy."

Mom put the pot away, closing the cabinet door forcefully.

"Mom. That means you're going to have two daughters," I said.

She said nothing to me and suddenly stood in front of the cookie cake. Her face went even redder before reaching out and hitting the cake hard with a serving spoon. Once, twice. Before dipping her head down toward the cracked confection. "Now. Who wants a piece?" she asked calmly, reaching for a plate.

In the middle of the night, I sat up in bed. I could hear murmurs and whispers, low at first and increasing to loud pitches that hit my ears like arrows. I couldn't make out any of the words. I tried not to. Too afraid to hear what was being said in those incensed tones.

I didn't know when I noticed her, but when I did, I wasn't startled. Only curious as to when and how she got there.

She sat in the corner surrounded by my bevy of stuffed animals and plush dolls. She rose slowly and then hurried over to me, covered my ears with her small hands, pressing hard until all I could hear was her breathing near my chest.

CHAPTER 11

THE INTERVIEW

2021

[Studio]

JODI LEE: So, you wouldn't consider yourself a violent person, then?

MARLOW FIN: I'm like any normal human being. If left alone, I'm not going to lay a finger on you. If provoked, of course I'm going to react. We are reactionary, as people. We're not sea coral.

JODI LEE: Some people might say you have been known to have a reputation.

MARLOW FIN: A reputation for what?

JODI LEE: You are known, by some, to have a . . . temper, shall we say? In particular, this temper has been channeled toward members of the press.

MARLOW FIN: Leeches aren't members of the press. They aren't journalists. You are a journalist, Jodi. They are not.

JODI LEE: These leeches you keep bringing up. Paparazzi?

MARLOW FIN: Worse.

JODI LEE: How so?

MARLOW FIN: Paparazzi take pictures. It sucks, yes. But leeches write lies. Do you know how to remove a leech, Jodi?

JODI LEE: I've never encountered one actually.

MARLOW FIN: Where I'm from, you have to find its mouth. That's the trick, get it where it talks.

JODI LEE: Can I give you some nicknames the "press"—and I say that for now to give it a label—have dubbed you with in the past?

MARLOW FIN: Sure. Why not?

JODI LEE: "Mad Marlow"? "Fiery Fin"? "Mental Mar"?

MARLOW FIN: Sweet, isn't it?

[Roll package, footage of Marlow and press]

JODI LEE: There is no question that Marlow has earned a reputation for shunning the press and even acting out. In 2006, she was involved in an altercation outside The Ivy in which she pushed a photographer into the street, breaking his arm. He filed a lawsuit the following spring, but it was settled out of court, and the details remain undisclosed. In 2010, Marlow was sued again, this time for pouring a bottle of water over a reporter's head in New York City.

[Studio]

MARLOW FIN: I never touched anyone. Not in a violent way. I stand by that. The photographer outside The Ivy pushed me. I was only trying to get out of there safely.

JODI LEE: By yelling and screaming? "Tantrums," as the press called it.

MARLOW FIN: [*Shrugs*] They can say what they want. Just because it's in print doesn't make it true. Scary world, isn't it?

JODI LEE: I'm going to go to a place now that may be hard to talk about. But can we try?

MARLOW FIN: You are so polite. I like that about you, Jodi.

JODI LEE: Does that mean I can go there?

MARLOW FIN: Go there.

JODI LEE: You've had some addiction problems. I will flat out say it. [*Motions hands outward*] Do you think you are fully recovered?

MARLOW FIN: I'll never be recovered. But I think I am in a better place for sure.

I've been in some really, really dark holes. I don't think that's what people understand. That someone on magazines, billboards—that's an image. Those are only images of me. But they are nothing close to anything resembling me.

JODI LEE: Can you tell me about some of those dark holes? I've interviewed a lot of people who have had and still have addictions. But the one thing they all have in common is that moment when they knew something had to give. What was it for you? The darkest moment when you knew something had to change?

MARLOW FIN: There are . . . [*Holds up two fingers*]

JODI LEE: Tell me about the first one.

MARLOW FIN: My first time modeling in Europe. You always hear about these models being crazy and partying. Snorting. Doing lines. But it wasn't like that. Not for me, or initially anyway. I really tried to keep to myself—focus on the jobs and staying levelheaded. I truly liked the work back then. But I swear, the more I tried to stay on this . . . this tightrope . . . the higher I got and the harder I was going to fall.

I took one hit. One hit of pot at a party in Barcelona. Seems innocent right? But I was all too curious. I was . . . maybe I wanted to go there. Maybe I wanted to fall. A week later I was drinking heavily. Empty bottles don't lie. A month later I was doing coke and ecstasy pretty much every night, then all day every day. I blurred my life out. I won't sit here and lie and say I regret using. Because I loved it. I loved the burn and numbing power it had. My head lifting away from my body . . . it was peace. But . . . [*pauses*]

JODI LEE: But?

MARLOW FIN: There were many times I woke up unsure of where I was. What I had done. What someone had done to me.

I remember it was a Sunday. I heard a lot of church bells that morning. I woke up in a hotel in Florence completely naked. Even the sheets were stripped off the bed. There was no one else. I couldn't tell you what had happened because the night before was a complete blackout. I put some clothes on—they weren't even my clothes—and took a walk outside. I was beyond hungover. I was at the point where hungover was better than the state I was in. The world had gone silent. Dead. And everybody who walked past me didn't seem to see me. It was as if I were a ghost.

That's when I knew.

JODI LEE: How old were you?

MARLOW FIN: Eighteen. A kid. But I felt fifty.

JODI LEE: You sought help.

MARLOW FIN: I did. [*Scratches forehead*] I did.

JODI LEE: Did it work?

MARLOW FIN: Well—I'm still here now, aren't I?

JODI LEE: What did your family think of all this?

MARLOW FIN: They didn't. At least at this time in my life they didn't. It was so easy to hide because when I went home, I would put on this spectacular show of being fresh and excited about all the travels I had done and my fantastic career. But really? I wanted to be alone.

JODI LEE: There is a rumor that I'm wondering if you could clarify for me.

MARLOW FIN: All right.

JODI LEE: Your sister, Isla, got married in 2012. You attended her wedding?

MARLOW FIN: Yes.

JODI LEE: Were you sober?

MARLOW FIN: No.

JODI LEE: Is it true that you were not welcome?

MARLOW FIN: That is not true. I was very much welcome. I was her maid of honor. She had us all wear mint dresses. [*Smiles*]

JODI LEE: Is it true that you got into an altercation with your mother, Stella Baek?

MARLOW FIN: There is so much more to this than a really simple answer to that question.

JODI LEE: So there was no altercation?

MARLOW FIN: I didn't say that. There was, yes, an altercation between myself and my mother at the wedding.

JODI LEE: Okay. Here goes: Is it true, Marlow, that you tried to strangle your mother?

CHAPTER 12

ISLA

1996

Sawyer slid the worm onto the hook, a fleshy accordion bunched up over the wet metal. He handed the pole to me, letting the bait dangle. The line shimmered in the sunlight.

"That's not how my dad does it," I said. The worm smelled metallic, the pond water still and hot.

"I've caught six sunnies this morning already. Toss her in."

Marlow sat on a large, speckled rock near the water's edge and scooted her purple jelly sandals out until her toes dipped. She leaned forward and skimmed the top of the water with her hands.

"Look, tadpoles." She pointed.

Sawyer knelt behind her and pulled her back by her white sleeveless cotton top. "You're going to fall in like that."

"The water is pretty shallow," I said, throwing the line in, the satisfying plop disturbing the pond water.

He led her closer to where he was and handed her his tackle box.

"Here. Pick a lure."

She slid it on her lap and opened it like a book, fingering a few of the brightly feathered ones and picking up a heavy silver drop as if it were an earring.

"Sawyer, can I have this one?"

He nodded, not really looking as his line bobbed down once and then hard.

"Got another one!"

The fish shook back and forth as he dragged it onto the grass and held it up. The green scales glistened; the orange underbelly heaved in and out.

Marlow jumped up next to him, the tackle box falling to the side.

"Don't step on it," he said.

She picked the sunnie up without even hesitating, squeezing a little and holding its mouth up to her own.

"Kiss it," she said to him.

"Marlow, hand it back," he said patiently.

She brushed it against her lips and giggled. "I did it!" she squealed, her eyes closed tightly.

"Gross," I groaned, reeling my line back in and then casting it out again.

Sawyer laughed at her and then looked at me with his mouth still wide, the freckles across his nose darkened from sunshine.

The summer had taken us all up to a height of familiarity, sweeping us away together with warm dusks cupping fireflies, sore tongues from too many popsicles, dirt-lined feet that never seemed to get all the way clean, a perpetual sweat at the base of our necks, hair clinging hot and fixed, our knees high-stepping in the tall grass, dancing until it got too dark as we were called back inside to settle in our beds, heads spinning from the dizziness of the pleasing day.

We were home.

This was where I remained. When I close my eyes, I can still feel this time, when there were no blue thoughts from morning to twilight, no unsettled visions about what the next moment would bring. A summer that drew a line, pure and untainted and never faltering, as it carried us and fulfilled its promise.

Each morning, we met in the field by the woods. A clearing full of big bluestems; they swayed to greet us on breezy days. The three of us, a peculiar meeting to determine the day's scheming. A collection of quarters to buy a pizza from the gas station a half mile away, a flag for our growing fort made of branches in the woods, a jar of tiny frogs we would release into the stream, a prized broken watch we found abandoned at the edge of the tree line.

This was our field. This was where the mystique of each summer day began.

We didn't go to the cabin that summer. Dad and Mom said nothing about it, as if the cabin didn't exist. Anything before Marlow didn't seem to exist. I didn't ask about it. This was the first summer Dad had decided to teach a few courses, while Mom returned to working full time as a copywriter for an ad agency. She was gone most days, with Moni usually watching Marlow and me.

Moni had taken to Sawyer as easily as she had to Marlow. She would hug each of us, the soft skin sagging at the underarms of her summer house dress, clucking us in for lunch.

"Eat more, Sawyer. You are growing boy," she would say.

His thin stature seemed to alarm her, instincts sweeping in to feed, feed, and then feed again, although she wasn't aware of the pantry of junk food Ada kept at their house. Ada would let us have a free-for-all as she kicked her legs up in the recliner and watched *All My Children*.

The inside of her kitchen was covered in dream catchers, their colorful feathers floating above our heads. Ada claimed she was one-sixteenth Lakota on her mother's side as she dusted her "healing crystals" and rocks that were strewn about the house. I would pick one up and ask what it was for.

"Sapphire. That one, little girlie, is for prosperity."

"And this?" I held up a light-green one.

"Fuchsite. Relaxation." She cackled so hard I could see her fillings. "But I got other tools for relaxation in that cabinet over there." She cackled again as I looked at the glass liquor bottles.

The initial meeting between Moni and Ada had created a wary neutrality. Yet they were always cordial to each other, a wave or a nod from across the street as we would scamper from one house to the other.

It was one of those off-and-on rainy days. A nearby cul-de-sac was having a neighborhood garage sale. There were more cars than usual zooming up and down our street. Moni was planting some purple verbenas around our mailbox while the rain had stopped. A man with square glasses in a Honda Civic pulled up near her. Marlow, who had been circling around on her bike in the driveway, stopped, while Sawyer and I paused with chalk in our hands.

"Do you know where Hammersmith Drive is?"

She paused from digging with her garden spade and wiped her brow. "Oh . . . I not so sure."

"Sorry?" the man asked loudly, his elbow hanging out of his window.

"I'm not sure," Moni said, matching his volume.

"Well don't you live here?"

The muffler on his car was shot, the engine sputtered.

"Yes."

"Then where is Hammersmith Drive? I'm late picking something up, can you help me?"

"Sorry. I . . ." she stammered.

"You people . . . learn English or get out of here."

I tightened my grip around the yellow piece of chalk. Each of his words seared in my ears, words that I hated. Not only because of what he said but because of the way they had such an effect on me. The clout this repulsive stranger had over me was too much to bear.

"No reason to talk like that."

Ada stood at the end of her driveway, arms crossed, making them look even bulkier.

The man turned forward, both hands on his steering wheel, and ignored her.

"That's right. Get the hell out of here. *You* get out of here," Ada nearly shouted.

He drove off, the pain he left behind floating all around us in the exhaust fumes.

Moni looked down our street, making sure the man was gone. She stood up.

"You don't need help me," she said indignantly.

"What's that?" Ada uncrossed her arms.

Moni said nothing and went inside the house, the verbenas left unplanted in their nursery containers.

A few weeks later, when Ada sprained her ankle going down the stairs, Moni cooked a whole grocery bag full of frozen food for her and Sawyer, containers of rice, bulgogi, and pajeon vegetable pancakes stacked inside. She left them on the doorstep as I watched from our front porch.

Moni sent me to retrieve the containers early one evening—good Tupperware was gold to her. I knocked but no one answered. The door was open; I could hear the television through the screen door.

I found Sawyer, sitting at the kitchen table, drawing on a Mead spiral notepad with a blue ballpoint pen. He put his fingers to his lips and then looked over to the recliner where Ada lay sleeping. Her mouth was a crooked gape, emitting a few light fluttered snores.

Sawyer pushed his chair back and carefully made his way over to her. I followed. We stood on each side of her, looking down at Ada's mostly still form. Her cheeks had a few lines of wetness, tributaries of tears trickling in the dry folds of her skin. Her hand rested on a small silver frame, glass plate side down, chest heaving up and inward.

He slid the frame out of her hand and placed it on the side table next to her. I leaned forward and looked at the woman in the frame. The photo looked older, but she was young. I saw shiny hair and a light-green blouse.

Her eyes matched Sawyer's, crinkled at the corners as she smiled. She had the same broad lip that stretched over the top half of her teeth.

She looked upward in the picture, and I wondered who she was looking at. Who was she smiling for?

I didn't ask Sawyer about the woman. Partly because his eyes went sad, an expression I wasn't used to seeing from him. And partly because I didn't get a chance to, as Moni called me home from outside.

Mom and Dad were heading out for a dinner date. I had heard them eagerly chatting about it in the days before. Some new restaurant opening in downtown Saint Paul that meant a new red dress. Mom hung it up, showing it off in a clear dry-cleaning bag on their bedroom door. I passed it each morning, admiring the fiery, silken fabric. The sheen made me want to smooth it over with my hands.

I returned home with Moni to be immediately assaulted with questions.

"Isla, have you seen my dress?" Mom demanded as she attempted to get the back of her earring on. Her blonde hair in perfect, hot-ironed curls arranged in rows over her shoulders.

"No," I answered quickly.

"Are you sure?" she asked again, this time with more urgency. I watched her mouth move, the red lipstick just outside the lines.

"Yes. I thought it was on your door?"

She shook her head. "Not there anymore."

Dad appeared shaking the car keys in his right hand as he slipped his wallet in his jacket. "Stella, please. We're already late."

She brought her arms up exasperated. "I don't understand. It's been there for days, Patrick. I bought it specifically for tonight."

He shrugged sympathetically. "I know but . . ." He waved toward the garage. "I doubt they will hold our table for much longer. Maybe wear a different dress?"

Mom breathily returned a few minutes later. Her curls were now scattered and out of place and she wore a plain, black sleeveless dress. She gave me a cursory kiss good night, trailing Dad who was already out the door when she halted, her eyes darting up the stairs.

I followed her gaze. There she was. Perched at the very top, staring down at us like a bird of prey. Half her face guarded by the shadows, her hands folded in her lap.

Three weeks later, I was playing near the creek with Sawyer when I found it. Drenched and covered in streaks of mud. Barely recognizable, the skirt end fraying. I poked it with a stick, letting it roll in the water like a crocodile barreling with agitation.

The red bled through, deep and questioning.

CHAPTER 13

ISLA

1996

There are days for the lambs. And there are days for the wolves.

Moni used to say that to me.

Days I would scrape my knee raw, the weather gave me the blues, the kid in class mercilessly teased me. Days the ice cream truck circled back, the new green dress got a flurry of compliments, the sun dried my skin until it tingled at the pool.

"Days for the wolves," she would plainly say, if I came into the kitchen sullen and worn.

A bowl of filling for *mandu* would be on the counter, a mosaic of minced pork, onion, cabbage, zucchini, and mushrooms. My nose would fill with brine and garlic; my eyes would take in her fingers so delicately pinching the dough, each drop of filling softly cocooned in a shell of white plushness. Each dumpling she would delicately drop in boiling water, then pull out onto a plate for me. It steamed in freshness as a drop of soy sauce and vinegar was added before my teeth sank in.

She would lean in, almost drinking in my satisfaction from her food. It never bothered me, her leaning in like that. Her round, forgiving face—beyond anything merely pleasant. Hers was a face of luminosity.

"Now. Time to let those wolves go. Let in room for the lambs."

She arrived in the US when she was twenty-four.

Young-Mi Baek was one of only a few women out of the select number of students allowed to come over under the pretense of studying. It was 1957 and she was secretly pregnant with a son. She never spoke of the father. Not even to Dad. She named him Patrick, after the pastor who helped her learn English at the Methodist church a block from her boardinghouse.

Moni never liked to tell me stories of those early years. Possibly because she didn't want me to pity her. Or maybe it was simply too much to repeat out loud, to live all over again. Dad once told me it was because she missed her family. She never saw them again after the war. There were too many stories like hers . . . I never pried.

But she loved telling me about Dad.

How he was the most beautiful little boy and all the other Korean mothers at church envied his button eyes and full lips. He loved hot dogs like all the other "American" boys but loved her *ge jjigae*, spicy crab stew, the most.

But he was teased the most.

"No one else look like your Daddy," she would say as she pruned bean sprouts over a metal bowl. "Oh, he handsome now. Everybody say that. But your Daddy . . . he had to be brave."

The kind of teasing that sticks like a barb in the chest, prickly, burrowing in further and further.

Her eyes would look a little bothered, as if she were worrying all over again about her precious son. He was the *only one*. The only one who ate kimchi. The only one who knew another language. The only one who wasn't white. I wondered how much of this story was still left inside him, a reluctant pioneer.

"He have to be perfect. Perfect in everything. Best grades, best student. Even now. You know that, Isla?"

She didn't have to use words for me to see how she ached over it. How she ached over him not having a father in his life. Maybe it was her drive that had pushed him to such rigorousness. She wore her mother's guilt like a badge, tattered and useless, as it would do nothing to right any wrongs she may have committed.

It was impossible for me to picture her as anyone but the lenient and soft Halmoni she had always been in my eyes. A pleasant, agreeable woman who wore the same floral pink apron when she cooked for her family. Who always gave the best parts of a dish to everyone else, keeping the lesser scraps for herself.

The sacrifice.

That was the only way she knew how to live. The only way she felt whole. As if her skin existed to protect us all, stretching far and wide, so thin and transparent it would inevitably snap. A tear at first, fissuring, then ripping all the way.

The first summer after Ada and Sawyer moved in, our kitchen had grown extra warm with the air conditioner being on the fritz. The heat swelled an already rising strain in the house.

Dad decided to scoop out ice cream for us all.

We ate around the kitchen table that was mostly quiet, a clink here and there against the bowls.

Mom ate slowly and methodically, as if forcing herself to ingest each bite. She sat directly across from Marlow. I never found out what Marlow did or didn't do. What her expression was or what she could have mouthed.

But whatever it was did not agree with Mom.

Her spoon dropped loudly, clanging like a cowbell in her dish. She dusted her hands and drew her chair back.

"Is there something wrong?" Dad asked without looking up, as if he didn't want to give her irritation any more life.

She looked over at him, eyes narrowing before retreating into weariness. "I'm not sure, Patrick. What could possibly be wrong?" Her hand took part of the light-green plastic bowl and held tight.

Moni's jaw clenched as she sucked in her breath.

Dad remained silent, his head bowed down before he dipped his spoon in again.

"That's right. We're all fine. Everything is fine," Mom said. She shook her head tightly, quick with irritation, before leaving us all in the kitchen.

I heard Moni exhale slowly and heavily. Her relief also washed over me.

Later that summer, Dad would take me to his office occasionally. The shelves on the wall were packed with books, the spines shiny and smooth under my finger. There would be students who popped in and left, a brief chat or question that had to be addressed. I didn't take that much notice for the most part.

But there was a woman with long, curly auburn hair. I remember her because I thought her to be especially pretty. She looked like Ariel incarnate. (I was fixated on *The Little Mermaid* right then.) I wanted to ask her if she knew her, but it seemed a silly question, so I kept my mouth shut. She never told me her name, yet she acted as if she knew me because she handed me a sticker book. It was brand new and there was a unicorn bookmark with a pink tassel tucked inside.

Dad told me to wait outside.

He closed the door, and I sat in one of the hard wooden chairs in the hallway. Some of the stickers were scratch and sniff. I put my nose deep into the one with a dancing grape. There were other times like that, with other stickers. Other trinkets and cheap toys to preoccupy me.

It's funny how you can remember such details. And then other things get washed away into an unintended indifference.

I can remember Moni's face whenever she made oxtail soup. Her eyes in a dull concentration as she skimmed fat off the boiling broth, tedious in getting every drop. But I can't remember what it looked like the last time I saw her. Was she smiling? Did she have on her glasses? Or did she leave them off, sitting on a stack of magazines in her bedroom?

There are the memories that stick to your bones, that feed you when there is nothing left to cling to. And there are the ones that fade in and out, a tattered cloth that ripples in the wind and then flaps away with one final gust.

CHAPTER 14

WREN

1980s

Wren looked around the basement apartment with blank eyes.

The cement walls, low ceiling, and single egress window would have deterred most from saying yes. She was new to the Twin Cities but she wasn't new to living in places like this. She nodded as the landlord stated the monthly rent and handed her a set of worn keys.

"I don't take late payments," the middle-aged woman said, a slight Eastern European accent curling at the end of her tongue. "You pay or you're out."

"I understand," Wren replied, taking note of the cobwebs in the corners and rusted pipework overhead.

The landlord suddenly eyed her. "How old? You even twenty-one?"

"Yes."

"You Chinese?" she asked.

"No. But I am part Asian."

The woman turned with a grunt; the door jammed a few times before it shut. Wren locked it instinctively, despite the woman's seeming to be harmless. She reached up to touch the dusty lightbulb, twisting it to stop its flickering. She suddenly felt so tired. The single mattress in a metal frame was her only piece of furniture. Her eyes fluttered into sleep quickly as she lay on it.

She spent the next few weeks looking for a job. Work. Anything to make a few dollars. Whenever her pen came to a certain part in an application, she would pause and then leave. There was nothing to put in those blanks. There was nothing to share.

She was a ghost that no one would hire.

Meals were often instant noodles or bags of chips. Anything that was cheap and could fill her up with calories. She turned to one of her previous habits of lingering near restaurant patrons dining outdoors. She didn't look the part of desperate; maybe that was why she could get away with it. There was an innocence to the shape of her face, a collegiate look. To most, she was a student sitting down for a meal. No one knew that the girl sitting at the café table was eating a stranger's leftovers.

At one of her haunts, a Mediterranean bistro, a server she had seen a few times seemed to catch on. He was a tall young man, hard to miss. She was in the middle of putting rolls into her purse when he strode toward her with his hands behind his back. She shot up, head ducked down, but his hand reached her shoulder first.

"Here," he said softly, as his smile stretched across his shiny dark cheeks.

She looked down to a white paper takeout bag. Her hand clutched the top of it, shaking with embarrassment.

"Thank you," she said as she began to exit.

"Julien." He placed his hand on his chest.

"Wren," her voice came out hushed.

When she reached the security of the basement apartment, she hurriedly opened the bag to find a container of creamy chicken pasta tossed with sundried tomatoes and herbs. Her eyes closed as she ate slowly, savoring each bite.

She was shy at first to return, but the thought of a decent meal over-rode any further inhibitions. Julien always spoke so gently to her, trying to probe more out of her. But she would only smile politely and eat as he did most of the talking. He told her about some work she could do for the restaurant owner—cash-under-the-table kind of work. A few early mornings a week, she brought in the day's crates of provisions and helped wash and peel all the produce the kitchen staff needed.

It was enough to survive. That was all she needed right then. Survival.

But as her stomach began to get nourished, other parts of her began to wake up. On her days off she would wander the streets of Minneapolis. Her eyes filled with images of how *other people* lived. Normal people. Couples. People who could rely on each other, hold hands, go to lunch, browse a clothing store, all with such ease. Such carefree airs that floated toward her, as if to invite her in.

She didn't envy them. It was more than that. She wanted to immerse herself in what they had. She wanted to somehow transform.

It was on one of her walks in late summer when she saw them. Sitting across from each other on the patio of an Italian restaurant in Uptown. Her breath caught and she placed a few fingers near her throat. She was disconcerted with her reaction to these two people. What was it that made her stop like that?

They glowed. A halo that only she could see lassoed around them. The woman had fair hair, the features of a beauty as if plucked out of a Scandinavian fairy tale. Her ice-pick eyes glinted as she sipped from her glass and listened intently to her companion. With a half-serene smile, she didn't take her eyes from him once.

Him.

It was *him* that really halted her. She watched him smooth back his jet-black hair; a lock kept straggling and she wanted to go put it back in place for him. The outline of his lips looked almost drawn—a light burgundy hue that perhaps was stained even further by the red wine he shared with his wife. She could see the bands on their fingers. He whispered something and she laughed. Their affection seemed genuine. They weren't putting on airs, were they? At least that was what she wanted to believe. They were beautiful to watch.

Beautiful.

"Are you ready to go, honey?" the woman asked, pulling her violet shawl over her gracefully sloped shoulders.

"Yes, yes, we should get going . . . I've got a big day tomorrow. My first faculty meeting."

He began to get up but she stopped him. She reached across the table and squeezed his hand.

"I'm so proud of you, Patrick."

CHAPTER 15

ISLA

1996

Mom smeared the orange paint across my cheeks. She paused to dab more on her brush and stepped back to look at her work.

"Do I look like a tiger yet?"

She shook her head and smiled. "But we're getting there, Isla."

Halloween always meant my birthday. Dad made a point to tell me the same story every year. How Mom's water broke right as they were about to leave for a party. She didn't even have time to take off her Marie Antoinette costume, I came out so quickly. Dad was dressed as Frankenstein and it was quite a scene to see him hold me, crying so loudly. He would shake his head when he said this part, then tousle my hair.

It always seemed like such a crazy story. And he remembered every detail like it was yesterday. I would ask to see a picture of them in costume, but they could never find it.

This year the story wasn't mentioned. Dad was too busy putting Marlow's ladybug costume on. He struggled with the black tights as she wriggled and played with the antennae headband, the two velvet balls at the ends bobbling sideways.

"Can you please stay still, sweetie?"

She tossed her head back and forth and then smacked her mouth a few times.

"Marlow . . ."

She giggled and leaned forward, patting his cheeks. "Okay, Daddy."

Mom stopped mid brushstroke. It was the first time Marlow had called him that.

Dad froze and then pretended that name was nothing new. That she had always called him that and there was no need to give it attention.

"There," said Mom as she put her hands on my shoulders and turned me to the bathroom mirror.

I looked up to see the black and orange streaks she had carefully created across my cheeks, my forehead white, my nose dotted with a tiny black heart.

"Do you like it?"

"Yes." I turned my head side to side to admire her work.

"Happy tenth birthday, my Isla," she said in my ear, her breath warm.

Marlow squirmed her head under Mom's elbow, clinging to her. "Happy birthday!"

I felt Mom go rigid. She awkwardly moved away from Marlow's head. I could see her staring at the three of us in the mirror. Our faces, each a different piece to a puzzle that didn't quite fit together.

She scooted us downstairs to the kitchen, where she made us a quick dinner of leftover porkchops. The microwave whirred as she took out the steaming breaded meat with some green beans on the side. The smell of her food circled around and danced with the lunch Moni had made earlier—one of my favorites, pan-fried mackerel with rice and kimchi. The synthesis of their distinct aromas wisped about the kitchen, entwining and creating a mixture that was nurturing to me—an essence of home.

A few of the neighborhood kids were invited over for cake and ice cream before we went trick-or-treating.

Sawyer arrived first. "Cool face paint!" he exclaimed, his voice muf-fled behind his red Power Ranger mask.

He was followed by the Bollinger twins, Topher and Greta, and then Oliver, who lived at the far end of the cul-de-sac.

They each handed wrapped gifts over to Mom, as if it were their entrance ticket to the house, and she judiciously stacked them on the kitchen table. Dad brought out the cake, Funfetti with white icing as I'd requested. Marlow sang the loudest in my ear, but I didn't mind. I blew out the ten candles but forgot to make a wish.

I opened the gift from the twins first, a K'Nex building set. From Oliver, a heart-shaped purple Polly Pocket. The last was Sawyer's. I held up the small dream catcher and smiled, knowing it had to be from Ada.

"She said you would like that one," he said as he shoveled a bite of cake in.

Moni handed out little plastic cups of red punch, the dye staining all our upper lips as we grabbed our buckets to go trick-or-treating.

"You sure one of us shouldn't go with them?" Mom asked, opening the front door and rubbing her arms.

"Nah. They aren't going to go too far. Right, kids?" Dad said—a statement, not a question for us.

"Mr. Baek, can I use your bathroom?" Oliver whined, clenching his legs together. He was nearly a year older than me but smaller. I always thought his skin, paler than the moon, looked like tissue paper.

"You bet, buddy. Over to your left there. And call me Patrick."

"Patrick!" Oliver called as he raced away.

"Anyone else?"

We set out together, a determined clan as the dusk settled on the neighborhood. We weren't more than four houses in when Marlow cried that she had lost her "ladybug ears."

"Antennas. Ladybugs don't have ears," I corrected her.

She frowned as Topher and Greta laughed behind their green gloved hands. Each dressed as a dinosaur, their fabric tails swished behind them.

"Help me find them!" she whined, stomping her feet and crossing her arms.

"Really, Marlow?" I said with annoyance.

Sawyer tilted his mask up on top of his head as he knelt. "We can look on the way back, Marlow."

"No. I need to find them now. I'm not a ladybug without it."

Her eyes went limpid; I could see her gathering up the tears.

I sighed. "Let's go look. You guys go ahead. We'll catch up."

Topher and Greta waddled away but Oliver and Sawyer stayed put.

"I'll help find them," Oliver squeaked, his voice high and almost alarming.

We backtracked to the first house. Unsuccessful in our search, Marlow began to whine again.

"Marlow, we'll have to go without them," I said, frustrated with the mere four pieces of candy shuffling around in my plastic pumpkin pail.

"I will *not* go on without them," she pouted.

"Fine. Then you can stay here." I turned around. My face suddenly felt itchy from the paint. I scratched my cheek, only to find orange paint under my nails.

"Sorry, Marlow," Sawyer said quietly, following me. "C'mon. This way you can get more candy."

"I'll find them myself!"

She shot through the tall arborvitaes that ran along the yard of the nearest house, her red plush back disappearing.

"Marlow!" I called.

We ran after her, darting between the trees. The windows of each passing house glowed more as the street was getting darker. I began to imagine, for the briefest of moments, that I had lost her. That my finding her in the woods was all for want, and she had disappeared—returned to wherever she'd come from.

Where did you go, Marlow?

Another group of trick-or-treaters bustled past us. A few shrieks made me jump as they ran up to the next house.

"Where is she?" I asked out loud with panic.

"There! Under that streetlamp," Oliver cried out.

I looked to where his small hand was pointing. A block down, her tiny figure was crouched down by the gutter.

"Marlow! Stay right there. We're coming to get you!"

I was breathless when we caught up to her. But she didn't move, a huddled mound in the street.

"Don't run off like that!"

"Are you okay?" Sawyer asked.

She rose slowly and turned around. Her head still bent, she held her hands out. It was hard to make out at first. Shiny and dark, a beak glinted in the moonlight.

A dead crow.

Her hand cupped its black head, lopsided and lifeless.

"Do you think we can make it better?" she pleaded, bringing it higher in the air.

"Put—put that down," I said immediately, pointing to the gutter.

"What is that?" Oliver leaned in and then jerked back.

She was calm as she stroked the feathers. "It was still alive."

"Marlow . . . what happened?" I asked in a low voice.

"I rescued it, though. See?"

Sawyer stepped closer. "Are you sure it was still alive?"

She remained quiet.

I placed my hand on her shoulder. "We can't take that with us, Marlow. Do you understand?"

She shook her head.

"Marlow. Put it back where you found it," I ordered.

Her hands seemed to squeeze the bird, as if that would make it better. As if that was how it would become hers.

The others turned away as she knelt and returned it to the ground. But I watched. I watched as she gripped its body tighter, her hands shaking with force.

Shaking with perhaps grief or rage, either way becoming hers to own.

CHAPTER 16

ISLA

1996

I would often watch Marlow in the morning. Her face always looked so clean. Maybe that was because she was covered in dirt when she was found. Her skin perpetually appeared as though it had been scrubbed, a sheen that never went away. Sometimes I would find myself wanting to reach out and poke her cheek, creating another dimple next to the two she already had. I would let my finger sink into it like a wooden dowel into fresh dough.

She would catch my gaze across the kitchen table at breakfast. Face still marvelous, still full of a secret I could never quite catch. A few slurps of her cereal and then a sip of orange juice before she would look away.

When Mom and Dad's backs were turned, her hands became flashes. Quick to move and create a secret commotion, then retreat back.

A bite of Dad's toast.

A fork would go missing, its new spot under a napkin where no one would find it.

Mom's pancake drenched with syrup.

The butter knife flashed while she stared at me, the glint of it a lighthouse signal. A pretend slice across her forearm before it was hidden in an instant.

My mouth would remain closed. I would say nothing. I was witness to nothing.

When Dad got home in the evenings, his dress shirt rumpled and the skin around his eyes just a little bit weary, he would pull her into his lap. Like a doll that he had misplaced, he would hold her in and then turn to me, asking me how school was. Whether I did well on that math test he helped me study for.

I answered his questions dutifully. All while watching her lean in, her head tucked perfectly near his shoulder. She would watch me as if she had asked the questions, too, and was waiting on my answers.

Where had my spot near his arm gone?

I tried to remember if I ever did that. Crawled into his lap like that. I must have.

I watched her on the playground when our recess periods overlapped. The sidewalk from the school went down a slight hill, and as I marched in our line I would spot her almost immediately, the curls bouncing, her smile dazzling even from a distance. She was the darling. The Shirley Temple of her class.

You would think I was envious. The jealous older sister of the cheery younger one. The one who drew everyone in around her, a storm cloud that sneaked in and wrapped around anything in its path. But that wasn't the case. I admired her.

I admired from afar.

She would make her way to my room some nights. I would fall asleep, only to wake up to find her tucked in next to me as if she had always been there. Sometimes she would talk out loud, her eyes still closed.

"We're sisters, right?"

I would nod and then say, "We are now."

This would make her press in closer to me. The top of her head felt damp from her bath; the baby shampoo smelled strong. I would look up at the glow-in-the-dark stars dotted all over the ceiling, and count them. Rearrange them in my head until I fell asleep again.

Sawyer began coming over to our house before and after school. Ada had started taking late and early shifts at a poultry processing plant outside the Twin Cities.

"Extra cheddar for me and the boy," she would say, laughing.

She said most things while laughing. A woman who liked to lessen the vinegar of life with her own sugary insertions.

Sawyer would shift a little when she said this. As if it were his fault his grandmother was working again. I never asked about his dad. But his unwillingness to talk about him said enough.

His presence was starting to grow roots, trickling in and settling down. Moni always had breakfast waiting for him, an extra plate automatically slid out like another card being dealt. He would politely eat before we hurried out to the bus stop.

On mornings he was not there, I felt a slight disappointment in my stomach. As if I had missed breakfast because he had.

After school, we would throw our backpacks in the kitchen chairs and slide onto our bellies in front of the television like seals.

"No TV. Snack and homework first," Moni would scold us.

But she would put bowls of mixed nuts and a few of those shrimp chips from the Asian market in front of us, muttering in Korean that we watched too much television in America.

"What Power Ranger do you think I would be?" Sawyer asked one afternoon, as he popped a shrimp chip into his mouth.

"Red. And I would be Pink, obviously."

"Nah. You'd be Green."

"What?"

"Green and Red are buddies!"

I rolled my eyes. "Pink."

"And me?" Marlow asked as she lay flat on the couch.

"You're too young."

Her nose scrunched in protest. "I'm not that much younger. I'll be eight in a few months!"

As she did not have an official birth record, Mom and Dad had decided to give her a birthday. Rather than give her an arbitrary date, they decided on January 1st. It was all she could talk about, her birthday, despite it still being two months away.

"You don't even like Power Rangers," I pointed out.

"Maybe I do. Maybe that's what I want for my birthday."

I chewed on some peanuts and pointed to the television screen. Green and Red Ranger had teamed up against Rita Repulsa.

"See? Buddies!" Sawyer said and then rolled onto his back.

The next afternoon, Mom took Marlow and me to the mall. Mall of America had opened to big fanfare a few years back, but she avoided it whenever she could.

"It's honestly too big. I can never get anything done," she often complained.

Despite our pleading, she took us to the more manageable Rosedale Mall.

"Marlow needs new sneakers," she stated right before we went inside, a mission for us to understand. The smells of hot pretzels, sweat, and rubber all assaulted us as we entered.

"Oooh, can we get an Orange Julius?" I asked, my eyes lasering in on the brightly lit Dairy Queen sign.

"Shoes," said Mom, holding my hand tighter.

I looked up at her. Her golden hair that used to shine and cascade in loose waves down to her shoulders looked ashen. She hadn't taken the time to get it cut in a while, and the ends splayed limply by her breasts.

"Mary Janes? Or red slippers?" Marlow inquired hopefully.

"You need comfortable ones, Marlow. The sneakers you have are too small."

"I don't need sneakers. You can't twirl in sneakers."

"I think you could if you tried."

She let go of Mom's hand as soon as we approached the children's shoe store and ran straight for glittery purple Mary Janes.

"Now these . . . these are shoes worth wearing." She held the pair up in the light.

"No, Marlow." Mom shook her head with slight frustration. "Go look in that corner. See how comfortable those look."

"I will. But *these* first."

Mom sighed. "Marlow. What did I just say?"

She continued to ignore her. She slipped the Mary Janes on easily and stood in the full-length mirror, admiring them. Her hands went behind her neck and pushed her hair up onto the crown of her head.

"Look. Look, Mom!" She turned to her expectantly, pointing one foot outward like a ballet dancer.

Mom turned her head. Her eyes widened briefly, and then the rest of her face tumbled. It was like watching a curtain rise and fall—all within a second.

"Mom."

She didn't respond, transfixed by Marlow's reflection in the mirror.

"Mommy?"

She pressed her lips tightly once and then placed her hands on the nearest shoes. Plain white leather tennies. Her hand trembled as she looked down at them, as if they were the most important pair in the store.

"Let's . . . keep looking," she said quietly.

I helped Marlow put the glittery shoes back, then took her hand. Mom stayed at the display in the front of the store, picking up pair after pair, glancing at them for a few seconds and then putting them down. She didn't seem to even take them in. She was on autopilot.

"Isla, I liked those," Marlow whispered loudly.

"Just—listen to Mom right now. Look for some comfy ones, okay?" I looked back over at her.

We browsed for a while longer before Mom walked back to me. "Where's Marlow?"

"Huh?" I looked around. She had just been there, next to me, pretending to twirl. She couldn't disappear again.

Or could she?

Mom's voice started to rise. "Where is she?"

"She was looking for comfy shoes . . . I told her to." I motioned to the corner but there was a boy and his father there instead.

"Well, she's not there."

Mom heaved her shoulders up and then down. I could see the panic swell up inside her and then snap into a calmness.

"Isla. Did you still want that Orange Julius?"

I peered up toward her. "Yeah . . . but don't we need to find—"

"Let's go, then. Before there's a line," she said briskly, snatching my hand and leading me out of the store.

I turned around for one last glance. One last look for Marlow. I didn't question Mom. Why should I?

Ten minutes later, I sat on a light-colored wooden bench next to Mom. I slurped the drink a few times and kicked my legs. The emptier my cup got, the stranger the feeling in my stomach became.

"Do you think we should go . . . look for her now?"

Mom had her hands in her lap. She hadn't moved much since we sat down.

"I could go check a different store. Maybe the toy store?" I suggested meekly.

She shook her head and stood up.

"It's getting late. Your father and Moni are probably wondering where we are."

"But . . ."

"Let's go, Isla," she ordered.

The orange liquid no longer tasted sweet. It had gone chemical in my mouth. I wanted to throw it away right then.

"I can't."

"What?"

"Without her."

I thought I saw Mom's eyes go wet. But she blinked twice with a harshness and then her mouth opened slightly.

Skipping toward us was Marlow, hand in hand with a mall police officer. He wore a jacket with navy fur on the collar that made him appear as if he had no neck.

"Mommy!" Marlow ran to us and hugged Mom, her hands looped around her waist.

Mom didn't move.

"Ma'am, is this your daughter?"

The officer looked at Marlow and then Mom, desperately trying not to show what was likely in his head.

This woman? This woman who looks like the poster child for Scandinavia is mother to these little ones?

"Yes," she answered.

"Were you looking for her?" He looked down at me, the drink in my hand and then back at Mom.

"We thought she was at the shoe store," answered Mom slowly.

The officer cleared his throat. "Is that right, little lady? Did you tell your mom you were going to the shoe store?"

Marlow stared at Mom. She let the wait for her answer linger a little too long and then blurted, "Sure did." She hugged Mom, tighter this time.

"Please don't let minors go to stores alone. Got that, ma'am?"

Mom nodded.

"Are *you* okay?" he asked.

"Yes. Yes," she sputtered.

He studied her for a bit and then slowly nodded. "All right. You ladies have a safe night, then."

She didn't wait for him to walk away. She grabbed our hands and took us to the Jeep, buckled us in, and peeled out of the parking lot.

No one said anything on the ride home.

CHAPTER 17

ISLA

1996

I kicked my legs behind me and sucked on another chocolate-covered cherry. The green cellophane crinkled as I dipped my fingers in the half-wrapped box for another. *The Sound of Music* was playing on television, and I tilted my head back and forth to Julie Andrews's singing. The thrill of Christmas morning—wrapping paper flying everywhere and chaos over who was going to open what present first—had died down throughout the day. I still believed in Santa . . . sort of. It was the kind of feigned enthusiastic belief that helped me stay a kid in the eyes of my parents.

The early-winter darkness seemed to have swept away the magic of the day. We were all let down after so much hype and preparation.

Marlow scooped in next to me and took a chocolate. She bit into the hard shell and slurped out the cherry juice.

"Who got these for us?" she asked.

"Ada and Sawyer. They dropped them off last night."

"Want to play with my American Girl doll?"

"Who, the Samantha one?"

"Yes. She came with a tea set and little petit fours just like in the book!"

I stared back at the screen. Maria had changed into a blue silk dress and was dancing with Captain von Trapp.

"I want to finish the movie."

Mom and Dad sat nestled in the couch. She had her head in his lap and he stroked her hair while he went between watching the movie and reading the new autobiography she got him. This one was about Nelson Mandela.

Moni peeled apples and oranges, legs crossed with the plate balanced on her lap. I loved watching the peel fall off in a perfect spiral, her hands effortlessly working the paring knife. She was always cutting fruit post-dinner.

"Fruit settles the stomach after a heavy meal," she would say in Korean.

The citrus of the orange woke me up a little from my zoning in on the movie. I took a piece and slid it into my mouth as I went to the front window. I could see Sawyer's light on across the street, his bedroom window on the second floor to the right. I wondered if he had gotten as many presents as I had. If he and Ada were also watching the same movie in front of the television. If he missed his mom or dad.

The next morning, a fresh powder of snow covered the existing six inches we got right before Christmas.

"The sparkly kind," Marlow exclaimed with glee as she dusted it with her red mittens.

The garage door opened across the street. Ada waved and started shoveling the driveway. Sawyer came out behind her.

"Jesus, child! Look before you cross!"

Ada adjusted her knit cap and went back to her shovel.

His breath created little clouds when he reached us. "It's not like there are any cars."

"Should we go to our field?" I asked.

He bit his lip as he grinned.

Our field was a white sheet. Untouched and perfect. Ready for us to mark its page with our trampling and laughter. Marlow threw herself on the ground and did snow angels. Snow caught in her lashes like lace. I scooped up a few balls and chucked them at her and then at Sawyer.

"Hey!" she said when one landed in her mouth. Her laughing only caused more to melt inside it.

"Thirsty?" I called out.

"Aren't you?"

She shot up and charged at me, throwing snow that sprayed everywhere.

Thunk!

A snowball hit my left ear. Sawyer sailed another one; this time he missed.

"Ha!"

He chased me and I tripped trying to run away. My chin tingled from the snow.

"Let's bury someone," Marlow declared. She stood up with her hands on her hips. A tiny dictator demanding the next event.

"Okay. Who?" asked Sawyer. He sat in the snow with one knee propped up, his arm resting against it.

"Isla!" she said determinedly.

"Oh shoot—" Sawyer began.

"What?" I asked, clapping excess snow off my mittens.

He brought one arm up in the direction of our houses. "I forgot to salt the sidewalk. Grandma Ada said she'd pay me ten bucks if I did it. I have to run. I'll come straight back!"

"Bring the orange sled when you do," I told him as he jogged away in the nearly knee-high snow.

Marlow hopped over and started to push me down.

"What are you doing?" I rang with annoyance.

"Burying you," she announced as if it were obvious.

"We're still doing that?"

"Yes. Pretend it's the beach and I'm putting sand on you."

I lay down and sank halfway in from my weight. She immediately began to pack my arms and legs with snow.

"*Lie still.*"

I obeyed her instruction. It didn't even feel that cold—the snow encasing me, a tomb blocking the wind. I stared up at the sky. I could hardly hear anything, my thick wool hat, coat, hood, and the snow blocking my ears.

"Isla," I thought I heard her say a few times, muffled and low.

The snow continued to pile on. My legs, torso, then my face. I closed my eyes and let the white powder fall on and cover me. I let her do it. I let her keep pressing the snow on top of me. It was starting to get hard to breathe, but I held my breath in. There was something gratifying about being able to hold my breath that long. I was swimming under the snow, and she was there to guide me.

I couldn't feel my chest.

It was so quiet. I don't know if I had ever heard such silence.

Marlow . . . can you hear me?

I began to hum.

It was a song I had heard only once in my life. One that had never left my ears, each note burned in the canal, the soot and singes blown into my mind so I could remember how it sounded. The trembling of my vocal cords reached the back of my throat.

The song that told me Marlow's secret.

She had been kept in her room for two weeks by then. The doctors wanted as little stimulation as possible. *Sensory overload.* I had overheard our mother say that on the phone.

Yet I would peep in. I would find her sitting up in bed, staring out the window. If she sensed my presence, she made no indication at first. A zombie of a little girl. I wanted to draw fake blood on her face, streams of red coming from her eyes and mouth. I wanted to trace each red river with my finger and then wipe it on my lips, a rosebud for a mouth.

She began to hold her hand out when no one else was in the room. I would take it and she would clutch it, looking out the window again. I never pulled away; I let her take it as long as she needed it. Her hand was sticky and warm, while mine was clammy. Sometimes my palm would have imprints from her fingernails, so long and sharp because no one had taken the time to cut them yet. She would see these marks and then stroke them a few times, looking at me as she did this as if to apologize for any harm she had caused.

Had she? Had she caused me harm?

She had not said a word. Not to Moni. Not to the doctors. Not to me. It was her spell she had cast, her power she wielded. We hung on to her every movement, waiting for the dam to break. The silence had more weight than any words she could scream. She was the girl who uttered not a peep. This was how she was to remain with us. Those were the rules.

But she broke them once for me.

I heard the humming. A gentle buzz and fluttering that hit me before I saw her. I came around the corner of the doorway, her back to me as she sat on the bed. She hummed a sweet line that turned into minor notes ringing dim, and they hit me like pellets. Her head slowly turned as she hummed, her lips a straight line until they suddenly split open, and words came out—the words to a song that only she and I would ever know.

She sang and stared at me, only her mouth moving with each word. Her hands were both on the bed, legs slack, head angled up like a ventriloquist's doll. She stopped and then tilted her head to the side.

"My mommy sings me that song. Do you know where she is?"

I shook my head.

She continued singing, kicking her legs, and then when it was over, she turned back to the window. She returned to her mute state.

I never told anyone what I had heard.

The snow seemed to harden then as I blinked once, my body growing numb. I felt like I was sinking. Deeper into ice and loss.

Where was she taking me?

A hand grabbed my arm tightly and pulled me up. The cold air was startling. Sawyer jerked me up to a sitting position.

"What in the heck are you girls doing?"

His eyes were round, his mouth twisted and disconcerted.

Marlow sat next to me. She said nothing for a while as the three of us breathed in and out. She finally turned to me, her eyebrows in an earnest, questioning furrow.

"What was it like? What does it feel like when you're drowning?"

CHAPTER 18

THE INTERVIEW

2021

[Studio]

MARLOW FIN: I've never strangled anyone in my life.

JODI LEE: There are rumors that you had an altercation at the wedding with your mother, Stella. There are eyewitnesses stating you lunged at her. And that your hands were around her throat.

MARLOW FIN: Lies. [*Shakes head*]

JODI LEE: So, you did not touch her at all?

MARLOW FIN: She had it out for me. Let's just say that. She had it out for me for the longest time and she finally got her way.

JODI LEE: There was an altercation with your mother? You are acknowledging that?

MARLOW FIN: Yes. And that is as far as I will go. But I did not strangle her.

[Roll package, photos of wedding]

JODI LEE: On September 15, 2012, photographers captured Marlow lunging at her mother. Tabloids called it "Mad Marlow and Mom." Her reps would later deny anything other than a "family argument that got too heated." Stella Baek never publicly commented on the incident. But what caused such a heated interaction between the two?

JODI LEE: Are you on good terms with your mother today?

MARLOW FIN: No. That would be a solid no. Especially after what happened.

JODI LEE: After what happened . . . you mean what you have been accused of? Or the wedding?

MARLOW FIN: Everything.

JODI LEE: Has she spoken to you? Reached out to you?

MARLOW FIN: [*Laughs*] If Stella Baek tells you she wants to talk to me, you can tell her she can come straight to me. That would be the day too.

No, she hasn't reached out. We don't speak.

JODI LEE: That's a sad thing. A mother and daughter who don't speak. I have a daughter myself and I can't imagine. Do you miss her? Are there days when you wish you were on good terms?

MARLOW FIN: I am happy for you and your daughter. And for any mother and daughter out there who have a great relationship. But that was never in the cards for me and Stella.

JODI LEE: You refer to her as Stella a lot.

MARLOW FIN: I do.

JODI LEE: I sense some agitation, so I'll move on, Marlow. [*Smiles*] There's a story that has been floating around the industry for a while now. This story is about how your big break in modeling was in large part due to your sister, Isla.

MARLOW FIN: Are you talking about the art project?

JODI LEE: The photo was taken in 2004. You were sixteen years old. And the person who took that photo was your sister, Isla.

MARLOW FIN: It was her final for an art class. That's one of my favorite photos to this day.

JODI LEE: Do you know what happened to that photo?

MARLOW FIN: No. But I would love to.

JODI LEE: Apparently, that photo taken of you in this composition is worth a lot. Sotheby's recently valued it at $1.6 million.

MARLOW FIN: [*Shakes head*] I've been around the world and met a lot of eccentric people. But it still surprises me how much people will pay for something. I hope I always remain surprised by that.

[Roll package, early modeling shots]

JODI LEE: Surprising as it was to her, the photo auctioned a week after our interview for over $2 million. Just why is this photo so famous?

Taken by her sister Isla in 2004 with a Nikon F-401, little did either of them know that it would launch the career of one of the most successful models in history. Isla presented the photo alongside a local news clipping about Marlow's rescue in 1995 as her senior art project. The black-and-white photo depicted Marlow staring straight into the camera, with her hand spread across her face.

Now here is the part that some may call fate . . . fortune.

The photo caught the attention of a prominent model scout who happened to be in Minneapolis at the regional art exhibition for his niece. He was so struck by the photo that he inquired for a month as to the identity of the girl in the picture. When he finally located Marlow, she was flown to New York City to Elite Model Management. She signed and the rest is, as they say, history. A year later, she was the youngest American model ever to land the cover of *Vogue*.

[Studio]

MARLOW FIN: Oh . . . my goodness. Is that it? [*Reaches for photo*]
JODI LEE: This is the photo. The one that launched your career.
MARLOW FIN: How did you get it?
JODI LEE: Sotheby's let us borrow it. After all, you are the subject matter, right?
MARLOW FIN: Unbelievable. [*Studies photo, camera zooms in*]

[Voice-over]

JODI LEE: I then quickly flipped the switch and turned to what everyone wanted to know. What the world had been buzzing over for nearly a year. Did Marlow really do it? Was she really capable of killing someone?

[Studio]

MARLOW FIN: This is truly wonderful. Thank you for sharing this. [*Hands photo back*]

JODI LEE: When you look at that photo, Marlow . . . what do you see?

MARLOW FIN: I see . . . I see a girl who should stay right where she is.

JODI LEE: And why is that?

MARLOW FIN: Because she's happy.

JODI LEE: I am going to turn to another police report now, Marlow. This one from September 8, 2020. It was created by the Cook County Sheriff's Department the day after the incident. Can I read you some of it?

MARLOW FIN: You may.

JODI LEE: "On the premises of the property is a shed, large enough to be a barn. Upon inspecting the inside of that structure, blood was found in the corner. Officer Bittner slipped in the area in which the blood was found. Samples were taken by a forensics team for a DNA analysis. Marlow Fin, the last person to see the victim, was questioned this afternoon at police headquarters."

I can see your reaction right now. You have no reaction.

MARLOW FIN: I have read the report before. Many times.

JODI LEE: "Slipped in the area in which the blood was found."

MARLOW FIN: Yes.

JODI LEE: Marlow . . . what happened that night?

CHAPTER 19

ISLA

1997

None of us wanted to go home.

We lay in our field surrounded by bent bluegrass, a soft bed for our heads. Only tiny feathery whiteflies bothered us, fluttering around in the glow of summer sundown. The sky was an orange creamsicle I wanted to pluck out and taste. A quiet evening symphony of creature sounds, croaking and strumming for us.

I took a blade of bluegrass and stroked my kneecaps with it in small circles. Sawyer chewed on the end of one while Marlow lay on her belly, drumming her fingers.

"Are you coming over for dinner?" I asked.

Sawyer took the grass out of his mouth, examined it, and placed it back in.

"Grandma Ada doesn't have to work the night shift. So I'll probably eat with her."

"Moni's making her chicken noodle soup you like so much."

"I know . . . but I think Grandma Ada wants me home. Sometimes she gets lonely. Especially after . . ."

His voice trailed off.

Especially after. I had learned what this meant a week earlier. Mom and Dad, post-dinner, talking in low voices, assuming I was upstairs playing with Marlow in her room. I had come back down to ask if we could have graham crackers.

"That poor boy. I had no idea."

I paused at the bottom of the stairs.

"I think that's why they moved here. Maybe let him start over," said Dad. I heard him set his wineglass down on the counter.

"But she works all the time."

"Yes. She has her grandson to support. I don't think social security is enough."

"Let's not get all political—" Mom paused to take a sip.

"It's not political. Anyhow, the father is out of the picture. Not much of a father, if you ask me."

"Well, that's hard to argue against. Abandon your son like that? After the mother dies from cancer?"

"From what I heard from Oliver's dad, he's always been quite the drinker."

Part of me had thought of Sawyer right then, apprehensive as to how I would act around him. Would he know that I knew? The other part enjoyed listening to them having a harmonious conversation. It eases children to hear their parents banter so smoothly. I would eventually revere these moments.

There was my own *especially after.*

Especially after what was to come later that week.

I looked at Sawyer as he sat up, staring out into the entrance of the woods. His hair was lighter from the pool's chlorine. A tan line showed at the nape of his neck. Did he ever hate his father? How could he be the Sawyer that he was? How could he go on as he did, after what had happened back in Wyoming? How had he not once brandished his pain or anger in front of anyone else, not even one ounce of it?

How could he not say one word to me about it?

I closed my eyes. I let the last of the sun's gleams probe my skin. When I opened them, Sawyer and Marlow had stood up.

"We should go," he said, taking Marlow by the hand. She was eight but he still treated her like a baby sister, a protectiveness that never faltered.

"Sawyer, will you eat with us for breakfast, though?" she asked, looking up at him.

"Maybe. Grandma Ada usually sleeps in."

I followed them, watching our three shadows in the field as we got closer to the trail leading back to our neighborhood. A sharp, ringing pain hit my finger. I looked down to see a wasp fly away, whizzing past my left ear. I didn't cry out. Instead, I froze and held my index finger up. The spot right under my nailbed throbbed.

"What's wrong?" Sawyer looked back to me.

"I think I got stung."

"Stung?"

"A wasp."

Marlow put her hand over her mouth. "Oh, Isla!"

He dropped her hand and, within a few strides, picked up my own and held up the finger. Without hesitating, he stuck it in his mouth.

"What are you doing?" I jerked my hand back.

"Sucking out the venom. Remember?" He half grinned and then spit on the ground. "Better?"

"No. It still hurts. A lot."

I wrung my hand a few times and then scrunched my hand in a fist.

"You're tough. I remember a boy back in Wyoming got stung and he wailed for an hour."

"I could use a wail."

"No. You're tough."

Our street was getting dark as we approached it. A red truck was parked in Ada's driveway. She came out as soon as she saw us, the screen door slamming behind her.

Sawyer halted.

"I know that truck," he muttered.

"Whose is it?" I asked.

But I already knew the answer.

The driver's side door swung out, followed by a long skinny leg. A man with shaggy hair and a beard climbed out. He stood with his hands in his pockets.

"Hey, son," he said. A cigarette glowed in his hand. He took a drag and then flicked it.

"I'm sure you're going to pick that up, Jeremy." Ada's voice boomed. She stood on the front porch. Even in the poor lighting I could sense her glare.

The man looked down at his boots and then up at the three of us. "Sure thing, Ada."

He made no move to pick it up. "Hey, son," he said again, as if the first time had been for practice.

Sawyer took a step back.

"Why are you here, Jeremy?" Ada began to walk down the driveway.

"You can stay there," Jeremy said and turned back to Sawyer. "Miss me, buddy? Come give your old dad a hug."

Sawyer put Marlow behind him and turned to me. "You both should go home."

I nodded. I took Marlow with me and looked over my shoulder. Neither Sawyer nor his father moved. They remained in their stances, staring at one another.

The next morning, the red truck was gone. I didn't ask Sawyer about what happened. I didn't ask who the man was because it would have felt like a lie. A lie because I knew exactly who the man was and why Ada was so angry.

But I didn't know if Sawyer was.

Later that week, Mom came home weary and spoke in a monotone. "What do you girls want for dinner?"

"Hard day?" Moni asked, looking up from folding laundry at the kitchen table.

"Too hard. I was slammed at work. I think I'll have to go in early tomorrow to get a head start on another project." She rubbed her temples. "What was I saying?"

"It's okay, I make dinner."

"Oh, Halmoni. You already do so much. I can pull something together."

We sat down a half hour later, without Dad, who was late. There was much back and forth between Marlow and me over what dinner should be. I suggested macaroni and cheese while she kept pushing for cut-up hot dogs and mustard. When she saw the macaroni and cheese with reheated broccoli on the side, she pursed her lips immediately.

Mom recognized the look and sighed. "Marlow, please. Not tonight. I have way too much going on. Please. Let's eat and have a nice meal."

Marlow picked up her fork and then dropped it. Rebellion won over.

"I wanted cut hot dogs and honey mustard."

"Well, we aren't eating that," Mom snapped.

I had heard this song and dance many times before. Usually, Marlow would give up after coaxing from Moni.

She spun her fork and then shook her head.

"Marlow, you're not a baby anymore. You are eight, going on nine. Now please eat."

She was met with silence, which was worse than a retort.

Mom's mouth tightened. Her forehead flushed.

I observed with a knot in my stomach as Marlow picked up her fork once more. She took a forkful of noodle and shoved it in her mouth, chewing rapidly. Her mouth moving in exaggerated motions, twisting her nose into grotesque distorted shapes.

"Marlow."

She kept going. Moving faster and faster until she spit. Regurgitated macaroni flew onto her plate and onto the middle of the table.

I had never seen Mom move at such lightning speed, scooping up the chewed-up noodle and shoving it into Marlow's mouth.

"Put it back," she said darkly. "Put it all back how it was before!" she shouted this time.

Marlow pushed her chair back and wiped at her mouth. She smiled at Mom.

"Go to your room," Mom snarled.

She stared down at her own plate as Marlow ran out. Her hand on the side of her head as she stabbed macaroni noodles until they piled up on her fork.

We ate the rest of dinner quietly, Moni only asking if I wanted more or if anyone wanted fruit. The garage door rumbled, Dad came in, keys clanked, and he cleared his throat.

"Where's Marlow?" he asked right away.

Mom pointed up.

Dad looked at Moni.

"She not hungry."

"So she's in her room?"

Mom stood up. "I wrapped a plate on the counter for you."

"Hold on. You can't just starve one of our daughters."

"Who said anything about using that word?" Mom scraped her plate into the garbage disposal.

Dad sighed. "Maybe that's a strong word. But let's at least try before taking that measure."

The dish hit the bottom of the sink hard. "I meant the other word," Mom said loudly.

I didn't like the way Dad's face looked after she said it. A rapid aging combined with a raw anger that pulsated in his eyes.

"You're really going to do this again?" he said in a whisper.

Mom crossed her arms, her mouth nearly twisted in amusement. Daring. Taunting. Baiting.

"I have to look at her every day, don't I?"

I'm not sure if it was Moni or Dad who asked me to leave the kitchen. But dinner was over, and Moni made sure we slept in her room that night.

She let us each hold a flashlight as she draped a blanket over us, her face glowing. The shadows on the walls were comforting, not frightening. We were in our own world. A cave that even the troubling noises below could not infiltrate. At least that was our hope . . .

"I tell you old Korean story now," she said, bringing us in closer with her arms.

Angry voices floated up. A crash and then silence. Another shout. Moni talked louder in Korean:

"*It is a traditional one. It is called The Ungrateful Tiger. But—I am going to tell it to you how my father told it to me. And his father told it to him. A little different than most tell it. A little wiser of a version, I think.*

"*A tiger menaced a village. One day, the villagers decided to make a trap. They dug a deep pit and covered it with leaves. They put a delicious piece of meat on top.*

"*And they waited.*"

A furious female scream shot through from downstairs. Moni leaned in closer. So close her face was inches from ours, the words from her story hot as they came out.

"*The tiger fell for the trap. Down, down, down he went. He was stuck and cried out for help. He called out for days but of course no one cared. Finally, a boy stopped to listen.*

"'*Promise you won't eat me? I will help you then.*'

"'*Yes, yes, I promise!*' *pleaded the tiger.*

"*The boy lowered a great stick down. The tiger leapt up.*

"'*Aha! Now I am free. And I have a delicious snack too. My lucky day.*'

"*The boy was in despair. 'But you promised you would not eat me!*'"

A loud thud and then shouting. She wiped away the wetness on our faces and a tear of her own. She put her head down and then looked up, straight into our eyes. Determined, her love was soaring. Boundless.

"'*Silly boy. Everyone knows a tiger is always hungry,*' *said the tiger, licking his chops.*

"'*Wait! Let us ask this passing rabbit whether you should eat me,*' *the boy pleaded.*

"'Fine,' said the tiger, loving this game.

"The rabbit paused to survey the situation. 'Hmmm. I think I must see what happened exactly in order to make my decision.'

"The tiger eagerly leaped back into the pit to show him just that. When he realized he was stuck, he roared with rage."

She pulled us in to her chest and held on tight. We burrowed in deeper, and she heaved a deep sigh.

"Now, my babies . . . pay attention and remember this. You can't trap a tiger just by catching him. You have to make him think he has won."

She kissed the tops of our heads.

"Only then have you truly trapped him."

CHAPTER 20

ISLA

1997

I was going to be eleven in a few weeks. Mom kept asking me what costume she should put together, but I didn't know what to ask for. I was too young for anything glamorous but too old to be cutesy. I was in the wonderful limbo of preteenhood, where I fit into nothing and would continue to be ill defined, slowly becoming an interloper in the land of childhood purity.

Sawyer and I were placed in the same class that year—which would have been great had we not been awarded the most crotchety of all fifth-grade teachers, Mrs. Stanhope. She had a perpetual sourpuss expression and sniffed harshly at any hint of a giggle or smile in class. The only student she liked was Oliver, which was odd because he was the worst student. I always thought she took pity on him because he was so small and pale. Even The Stanhope, as most called her—like a ship that was fated to destroy us—had some minuscule amount of feelings.

Sawyer elbowed me before math one day. "I forgot my math sheet."

I widened my eyes. "What? Did you not do it?"

My alarm was not unwarranted. Mrs. Stanhope did not spare any shame for those who forgot their homework.

"I *did* it. But I fell asleep at the kitchen table finishing it last night. I must have forgotten to put it in my backpack." He glumly shook his head as if resigned to his fate. "I bet it's still sitting there."

I glanced up at Mrs. Stanhope, who was twitching her shoulders and clapping her hands to get our attention. This would not be good.

"Try checking your bag again," I urged, keeping my eyes on her.

"Trust me, I turned it inside out looking. It's not there. Stanhope's going to eat me alive," he muttered.

Oliver nudged me. "What's wrong with him?"

"Forgot his math homework."

"Oh . . . The Stanhope—"

"I know. Why do you call her that? She *loves* you."

He tilted his head with a bewildered gaze. "Dunno. It's fun saying it, I guess."

Mrs. Stanhope clapped her hands again, this time with such forcefulness the room went dead. She smirked.

"Take out your division homework. Place it on your desk in front of you."

Papers rustled, kids scrambled, slamming loose-leaf sheets down as if they were tickets that would save them from being tossed off the train. She scanned each row, her eyes squinting. I sat on my hands. I couldn't get myself to take mine out. I couldn't move.

She stopped in front of Sawyer.

"Mr. Ford. Where is yours?"

"I forgot it," he said without missing a beat.

Her eagle eyes darted to me. "And you, Ms. Baek?"

Sawyer snapped to look at me and then down at the surface of my desk, blank and smooth.

"I forgot too," I heard myself say.

She cleared her throat, and I could have sworn she uttered a low growl.

"That is unlike either of you."

She tapped her foot. We were not her typical troublemakers. I even wondered if she was going to give us some reprieve.

"But . . . nonetheless. If you can't complete the assignment, then you *can't* be in my classroom. Stand up and gather your things. Hurry, you are wasting everyone else's time."

She sent both of us to detention.

Sawyer refused to look at me. It was the first time he had ever ignored me. His face was ruddy and seemed warm.

When detention was over, I pulled his arm outside the room. "What's with you?"

He ripped his hand down. "Don't."

"What?" I halted, stunned.

"Don't ever do that again, Isla. That was stupid."

"Huh? I was just trying to lessen the blow on you."

"It was stupid. Don't ever do anything like that again." He hoisted his bag over his shoulder and walked away. The bell rang.

Oliver caught up with me as I lost sight of Sawyer in the sea of kids that spilled out of each classroom, like zombies piling on each other for their first bite.

"Sawyer already left?"

"Yeah . . ." I fiddled with the strap dangling from my backpack.

"Weird. He always walks out with us."

"He's mad at me—I don't get it."

Oliver looked up at me. His tiny face suddenly looked so wise. "He cares. He's one of those people who actually cares. You know what I mean?"

Dad picked up Marlow and me after school. She proudly handed him a collage of cutout butterflies and ink stamps. He looked at it briefly and placed it on the front seat.

"That's nice, honey," he said quickly.

"Daddy? Can we stop and get a secret doughnut?"

Secret doughnuts were our thing on Dad's pickup days. Usually it was midweek and it was a pick-me-up for the three of us. A doughnut run that Mom never knew about.

"Not today—"

"But, Daddy. I made that for you in art today." She regressed to a babyish voice as she reminded him of this.

"Yes, I said it was nice, Marlow. But we're in a hurry."

It was not often Dad brushed Marlow aside like that. He usually took extra care to answer her questions, to affirm her need to please constantly. But today he was not having it.

"Why the rush, Dad?" I asked.

"I have to pick up Moni's prescription before the pharmacy closes. And I still have a pretty thick stack of papers to grade."

"Why not have Mom pick it up?"

I saw his face tighten in the mirror. "Because Mom is busy at work too."

"Oh." I gently kicked the seat with my foot.

"Isla? Really?"

"Sorry."

We followed Dad into the pharmacy. He practically dragged Marlow, holding her hand, rushing in through the glass sliding doors. The pharmacy was hectic, other after-work and pick-up parents rushing in to get their meds. We stood in line, a relatively long one that had already formed. Dad looked at his watch and then leaned forward to check out the counter. A woman holding a toddler in front of us bounced the girl from hip to hip as the child coughed and wiped the back of her hand across her face, strings of snot streaking like gluey cobwebs. A teenager behind us bobbed his head to music, stereo headphones covering his ears, the only person in line who was anything close to relaxed.

As we neared the front, Marlow spotted a display for gummies. Within seconds, she was next to it, examining a package of sour worms.

"Marlow—Marlow! Get back here," Dad hissed. He strode over to her. "Put that back."

She began to hang the bright-green package of candy on its hook. A man in a cobalt-blue jacket stepped in front of me in line.

"What are you doing?" Dad demanded.

"You stepped out of the line. I'm taking your place," the man answered in a clipped tone. He nodded once as if that was the end of it.

Dad stared at him. "Are you trying to say you *cut* in line?"

"No. I meant what I said."

The man folded his arms across his belly and looked straight ahead, as if Dad didn't exist.

"Sir, you clearly cut in front of me and my daughters. I suggest you go to the back of the line."

The woman with the sick toddler, who was now wailing, shifted her again in her arms, her forehead starting to sweat. The teenager behind us continued to bob his head, oblivious to the commotion around him.

"Are you kidding me?" Dad's mouth was open, his palms up with incredulity.

"Nope," the man said, rocking back on his heels. "Not this time . . . *pal.*"

I could see Dad's face go white. He clenched his hands and his dark eyes looked like storm clouds. But there was something else. A vibration of shame in his cheekbones from his own reticence.

Marlow slipped in front of Dad. Somehow reappearing as if it were the first time we had ever cast eyes on her. She held the green package of gummy worms against her chest.

"You can't talk like that," she said to the man's back.

The man didn't notice her at first.

"You can't *talk* like that," she said loudly.

He scoffed, turning only his head to give her a sideways glance. "What now?"

She clutched the package harder. "Bad names. You called him a very bad name."

Dad began to duck down toward Marlow to bring her back, his right hand reaching her shoulder. I could see his lips part to respond, the beginning of an apology, perhaps. But he stopped as she slowly stared into his face.

The corners of his mouth went up, as if something had just occurred to him. A rush of objections somehow found him in that moment.

"How dare you say that . . ." he said quietly.

"Huh?"

"How dare you call me that."

The man let his hands go to his sides and turned to Dad. "Call you what?"

Dad breathed out heavily. "How dare you call me a . . . chink."

"I'm sorry?"

"What makes you think it's okay to say that?" Dad said loudly. He pulled both Marlow and me in close to him.

The man's chin tucked in, and he gawked. He looked Dad up and down. "You nuts? I never said such a thing."

"I can't believe this," Dad said, shaking his head. "Even in the nineties, here we still are. People like you who drag us all back a hundred steps."

A pharmacist in a white lab coat approached us. "What seems to be the problem here?"

"Him." Dad pointed at the man.

"Actually, it's you. You seem to be a nutjob," the man scoffed.

"I need to get back to the counter," the pharmacist huffed impatiently. "What is the problem, gentlemen?"

"He cut in front of me and my daughters. And then called me a very derogatory word. I heard him, he said it under his breath. Right in front of my daughters too!"

The pharmacist waved his hands down. "Please calm down, sir. Is this true?" He turned toward the man, who shook his head adamantly.

"No. Absolutely not. He is completely making this up!"

The pharmacist turned to the woman and her toddler. "Ma'am, I'm so sorry to bother you. But did you hear this man use a derogatory word against this man?"

The toddler screamed and yanked at her ear. "I really—I'm sorry but I wasn't paying any attention. I'm sorry." Her child coughed again, right in her mouth.

"And you?"

He tapped the teenager behind us who looked around, still bobbing to his music. He noticed us and took off one earpiece. "What? What'd I do?"

"Nothing." The pharmacist sighed.

"What exactly did he say to you?"

Dad hung his head down. Solemn. "Fucking chink," he uttered quietly.

The words seemed to throw a strong wave at the pharmacist, who stepped back, eyes widening.

"I did not!" the man refuted.

The pharmacist looked down at Marlow and me, as if noticing us for the first time. He rubbed his hair and then put his hands together toward the man.

"Sir, I'm sorry but you're going to have to leave the pharmacy."

The man chuckled with anger. "You have got to be joking—"

"I'm not. We don't condone that kind of language here."

"Fucking—"

"Leave. Please."

This time the pharmacist stood up taller.

Every part of Dad remained motionless. Except his eyes. They followed the man as he threw his hands up, swore again, and left.

On the drive home, Dad looked at us both solidly in the mirror.

"Girls, it was the right thing to do."

He was met with silence.

"What that man did . . . it was wrong to begin with. I did what had to be done."

I held the prescription for Moni on my lap. The white paper crinkled as it shifted when we got to a stoplight. Marlow ripped open the green package, sliding a pink-and-blue worm into her mouth as she stared out the window.

CHAPTER 21

ISLA

1998

Three years.

That was the last time we had been to the cabin.

Dad had rented it out each summer we stayed away. I'd heard him and Mom talk about even selling it, that there was no point in keeping it since we never went there.

I figured it was because they didn't want to traumatize Marlow by taking her back to the place she was likely abandoned. Dad—ever the scholar, rule-abider, and cerebral one—took Marlow to Dr. Ciruelos for an assessment.

"Let's see what she thinks. Besides, Marlow stopped going regularly once she started second grade. She should see her, talk to her. Maybe there are things we could be doing better."

"She seems to be doing fine. I don't need a doctor to tell me that at this point," Mom countered, slicing a cucumber before dinner.

He slid his hand to the small of her back. "I know you miss it. The lake, the air up there. C'mon. This way we can make a more informed decision."

Dr. Ciruelos deemed Marlow an "exceptionally bright young girl." There was no reason she couldn't enjoy time up at the lake cabin. It had been three years and she still hadn't shown any signs of regaining her memory, let alone the events of the night she was found. The likelihood of it triggering anything was low. And to top it all off, she was clearly a "well-adjusted child."

It didn't surprise me . . . that Marlow's evaluation would come back as anything less than textbook.

We packed our bags on a Thursday and left for Grand Marais the next morning. The road began to wind the closer we got to the cabin. When she presented herself, like an old friend who had finally gotten around to meeting up with you, everything looked almost exactly the same. Yet there was nothing the same about its occupants: a troop less innocent, more worn and easily bruised. We were new owners in a sense, starting over and forging an altered set of memories.

Moni wasted no time setting up the kitchen. She unloaded large coolers full of meat, vegetables, and random containers of spices. A Cool Whip tub filled with red pepper flakes, a plastic yogurt cup holding a scant amount of white sugar. No container ever went to waste in our household, thanks to her knack for utility.

I wasted no time with Marlow. We ran straight out to the dock, sliding our sundresses over our heads, bathing suits exposed. I dived in first. The slippery feel of cool water seduced me. I surfaced and marveled at the endless horizon of Lake Superior, a lake without shores. I felt dizzy thinking about how long it would take to swim to the other side. Marlow's face appeared as she giggled and tongued her loose bottom tooth.

We treaded water and then lay back, kicking our legs up and then sinking together.

"Do you think the tooth fairy comes out here?" she asked me.

I looked back at the dock where Mom and Dad were embraced, looking out at us, his arms all around her as if he were twine that tied around the scroll of her waist. Maybe this was what we needed. Maybe this was how it would shift back to the way things were.

"Isla?"

Marlow waved her arms back and forth in the water, watching it loop in and out between her fingers.

"I think the tooth fairy travels." I smiled and then dunked her in.

The first night, Moni prepared short ribs drenched in soy sauce, sesame oil, brown sugar, and a little pear for softness. She laid them on a long plate for Dad to place on the searing grill. The *kalbi* was tender, sweet with a charcoal aftertaste, as we ripped the meat off the bone easily with our teeth. The pile of bones that collected in the middle of us all made me feel like a caveman, and hungry for more.

"*Omma*, this is delicious," Dad praised her after his third piece.

Marlow shared my old bed with me. It seemed so much smaller, our heads close together. Through the window we watched the fireflies glow above the grass until our eyes grew heavy.

In the morning, Mom and Dad took each of us in a kayak. Moni waved to us in the big red Adirondack chair she had settled in, mug of steaming coffee in her other hand. The mist on the water made us feel lost and delighted all at once. We floated above the lake, gliding like water bugs, graceful and serene, the slight ripples evidence of our lightness. We cast a few lines with our poles before Mom got a bite. She reeled in a spotty trout, gripping its midsection as it thrashed to break free.

The fishing knife glinted as she gripped the ivory bone handle. She struggled to cut the line, nicking the fleshy head once. Blood trickled down her palm as she marveled at it.

No one else caught anything that morning.

We returned to the dock to find sunshine and hot rays that baked my skin. I spent the afternoon on my stomach in an inner tube, lazily flapping my arms. Moni scolded me for being out so long, the top of my back a little sunburned. She smoothed aloe on it and ordered me to sit in the shade while she went inside to take a nap.

I sat under a tree with Marlow by my side. We played the game of closing our eyes and having the other one crawl up the inside of her arm with two fingers, like a spider, guessing when they reached the exact middle. We giggled and elbowed each other whenever we were way off.

It was my turn to close my eyes when I heard another male voice talking to Dad.

"Been a few years hasn't it, Patrick?"

"It has. How you been, Vince? Or wait—should I still call you Sheriff?"

"Nah. I'm off duty."

I had never seen him out of his uniform. He wore khaki cargo shorts that went practically over his knees and a short-sleeved yellow polo.

"Can I get you anything to drink?" Mom offered.

"I'm okay, thanks. Just thought I would say hello. Heard you were back in town."

"Yes, we finally decided to make it back up here. It's funny, I always forget how beautiful this place is."

The three grown-ups turned to look at Marlow and me under the tree. She was the real reason he was here. The miracle girl who was now part of a family.

"Wow. She's grown so much. You folks did a good thing," Sheriff Vandenberg said, one hand on his hip, the other in his pocket.

Marlow stood up slowly. She stared back at him, her eyes hardened.

"Hi there, Marlow. You remember me?" He waved.

She did not flinch.

He took his hand out of his pocket and rubbed his fingers against each other. He seemed unnerved by her presence.

"Marlow. Where are your manners? Say hello," said Dad with a small, embarrassed chuckle.

She kept her eyes locked on him for another moment and then broke into a pageant smile. "Hello."

"Sheriff Vandenberg is the one who helped us . . . and you as well. The night we found you. You may not remember, Marlow," Mom said carefully.

"And that's okay," added Dad.

Sheriff Vandenberg sniffed. "Of course." He glanced at Mom and Dad. "Glad to see you so well."

Mom and Dad led him back inside, their talk about how nice the season had been so far and other polite chatter floating behind them. Marlow sank back down next to me and went right back to playing our game, although she was quieter. A subdued Marlow. She placed two fingers in her mouth and pulled them out, a small tooth propped in between them.

A few more days into our cabin trip, Marlow asked about Covet Falls during breakfast.

Dad paused and took a bite of his eggs. "What made you think of Covet Falls?"

"Isla said you used to hike there with her. Isn't it close to our cabin?"

He shot me a quick look before answering. "Yes. But that was when I only had one little girl to look after. There are lots of slippery rocks you could fall on. Both of you, that is." He pointed his fork at me and then reached for the hot sauce.

"We'll be good. And really careful. Won't we?" She looked at me pleadingly.

"I don't remember it being that dangerous," I chimed in.

"You were littler then."

"Oh, come on, Daddy. I want to see the falls too!" Marlow begged.

Moni reached across the table for the jar of blueberry preserves. "Take her. She's only going to keep asking," she said in Korean.

Dad sighed. "Fine."

I looked over at Mom, who had been reading the newspaper. She said nothing and kept taking small, succinct bites of her bagel.

We trekked out a little after breakfast. Marlow didn't complain once during the hike. We heard the falls before we saw them—a dull roar that increased in volume like a crowd growing more excited and noisy as they waited for the headliners to hit the stage.

Our spot was still there. A flat perch above the falls that gave you the sensation you were ready to dive down into the raging waters.

The falls were bigger than ever that summer. A heavy rainy season during late spring and early summer had created record levels of water. I had never seen it so full and boisterous, as if it were showing off for Marlow, the girl who so desperately wanted to see it.

She said nothing.

The waters raged, a thunderous boom. Yet she remained silent. A wordless observer with little expression on her face.

Dad studied her carefully and then clapped his hands lightly. "Okay. Should we unpack the lunch? Too early? How about some snacks?"

Marlow's eyes shifted to him, as if to scoff at his casual and nearly comic transition, before turning back to stare down at Covet Falls.

"Isla, will you help me lay out the blanket, please?"

I threw the flannel blanket in the air, letting it float upward and then settle down.

"Did you put the drinks in your pack like I asked you to?"

"What? I thought you were getting those."

"Please tell me this is one of your jokes," he groaned.

"I'm not joking."

"Isla. I know I reminded you. Twice."

"Dad, I would remember something like that. You know me. What?"

He spun around. "Where's Marlow?"

"What?" I asked again.

"Marlow. I don't see her."

She was gone.

"She can't have gone far . . ."

Dad had not yet gone into panic mode, but I would witness it shortly. "Marlow? Marlow!"

We searched for her near the falls for the next hour. Dad finally decided it was best to go back to the cabin and call for help.

Mom ran out the front door. She must have been waiting for us.

"Seriously, Patrick! What the hell?"

"Did you see Marlow?" he demanded.

"What were you doing out there?"

"Stella. Listen to me, did you see Marlow come back here?"

She threw her arms up in the air. "Yes! Why do you think I'm so pissed? She came running across the lawn about twenty minutes ago."

"Well, where is she?"

Mom pointed to the large shed that fronted the lakeside edge of the property. Its wood did not match that of our cabin. "Such an eyesore," she had complained before, wanting to tear it down and rebuild it. But Dad said the size of it made it worth keeping. It was a place to put our kayaks, camping equipment, and anything else for storage.

We opened the shed door to find her crouched in the corner. Hair and clothes damp, she must have gotten in water somewhere at some point. Her knees were tucked into her body, a position similar to that when we first found her.

She looked up at the three of us, her chin shaking. The most peculiar look was in her eyes, as if she were meeting us for the first time and wondering who the hell we were to be staring at her like that.

A disbelief. A questioning gape.

Or maybe it was something else. Something else that simmered and shook. The beginnings of a rage.

CHAPTER 22

THE INTERVIEW

2021

[Studio]

MARLOW FIN: Is this the part where I tell you that, on the advice of my attorney, I can't speak about that night?

JODI LEE: You could.

[Pause]

MARLOW FIN: Don't worry, Jodi. I wouldn't do that to you. *[Winks]* This is why we're here, am I right?

JODI LEE: I believe this is what America and the world want to know. They want to hear what you have to say. Not the news headlines, tabloids, blogs, tweets. Cut through all the noise and let us hear your voice. They want to hear your story. Hear your words.

MARLOW FIN: My compelling, quotable, and headline-making words.

JODI LEE: A moment ago you stated that you have read the September 8, 2020, police report many times. How many times, would you say?

MARLOW FIN: Enough. Does it really need a number?

JODI LEE: The incident occurred at your family's lakeside cabin in Grand Marais, Minnesota. This place has great significance, of course.

MARLOW FIN: Yes. It's where I was found.

JODI LEE: The beginning of our story, you could say?

MARLOW FIN: Once upon a time.

JODI LEE: The police report was released to the public. Every detail has been out there for quite a while now. You can imagine how disturbing some of them were to many folks. An officer slipping in a pool of blood?

MARLOW FIN: I try not to think about it. You have to remember . . . I saw that blood. I lived it. There are some things you can't unsee. This is one of them. But you failed to mention one thing.

JODI LEE: What did I fail to mention?

MARLOW FIN: The officer, yes, he slipped. Yes, his foot was in blood. However, the area was also wet. This is a shed my family used very close to the lake. We stored kayaks and fishing equipment in there, so it got wet sometimes.

JODI LEE: You're saying he did not slip in blood?

MARLOW FIN: I'm saying he did not slip in only blood. There was water as well.

JODI LEE: Why is it that you feel this has to be pointed out?

MARLOW FIN: Because semantics matter. I'm here to tell the truth about what really happened. This is one of the facts of the case. I was there. There was not a pool of pure blood.

JODI LEE: You're saying it was only some blood.

MARLOW FIN: Yes.

JODI LEE: Can you describe to me what you saw when you first walked into the shed that morning?

MARLOW FIN: From the entryway of the shed you can see the far left-hand corner. This corner is closest to the window. In that corner, on the floorboards, was blood. The area was wet, and the blood had mixed with the water. It was enough to catch your eye.

JODI LEE: Enough to call 911?

MARLOW FIN: Certainly.

JODI LEE: You were the one who came upon the scene. You were also the one who made the 911 phone call in the early morning hours of September 8, 2020?

MARLOW FIN: I did.

JODI LEE: Do you mind if I play it for you?

[Voice-over]

JODI LEE: It was at this point that Marlow got up to stop the interview. She consulted with her attorney and then agreed to sit down and listen to the 911 audio. However, she would only do this if the cameras stopped rolling. In order to continue with the interview, we complied with her request. Here is the actual 911 audio that was played.

[911 audio and transcript, Cook County Sheriff's Department]

> *Dispatcher: 911, what is your emergency?*
> *Caller: Something has . . . happened. I couldn't find anyone when I woke up this morning.*
> *Dispatcher: Can I get your name, ma'am?*
> *Caller: I don't know where anyone is. I checked everywhere.*
> *Dispatcher: Can you please give me your name, ma'am?*
> *Caller: Marlow.*
> *Dispatcher: Okay, Marlow. Now tell me what happened.*
> *Caller: There's blood.*
> *Dispatcher: I'm sorry?*

Caller: I found blood . . . in the shed. Please send help.

Dispatcher: Okay, Marlow. I need a little more information and I can do that. Can you please tell me your location?

Caller: Our family's lake cabin. The one closest to Covet Falls. 6101 Juniper Lane.

Dispatcher: And you said you are alone?

Caller: I think so.

Dispatcher: Stay on the line with me, Marlow. I'm sending police and paramedics.

Caller: Why do you think they all left me?

Dispatcher: . . . I need you to stay on the line.

Caller: I have to go now. I have to go check the shed again.

Dispatcher: No, no, Marlow. Stay calm and with me on the phone.

Caller: I am calm.

Dispatcher: Yes. But do not hang up. Can you tell me what you saw?

Caller: I already told you.

Dispatcher: Do you know who could have gotten hurt? Who was with you?

Caller: Yes. I have to go now.

[CALL DISCONNECTS]

[Voice-over]

JODI LEE: After the 911 audio was finished, Marlow requested a brief break. There were some additional discussions with her team. When she was ready, she sat down with me again and we continued our interview.

[Studio]

JODI LEE: Are you okay? Do you need some water?

MARLOW FIN: I'm fine. Thank you for letting me take a break.

JODI LEE: It's hard listening to that?

MARLOW FIN: [*Nods*]

JODI LEE: Just for the record, that is your voice on that 911 call.

MARLOW FIN: I won't dispute that. That is my voice. I made that call.

JODI LEE: There has been a lot of talk that you sound . . . a little off on that phone call. That may be the nicest way to put it, and I apologize if it's off-putting. But you don't really sound all that concerned.

MARLOW FIN: I'd love for someone to give me the handbook on finding blood. What's the normal protocol and reaction for it?

JODI LEE: I think that's understandable. There is nothing normal about that kind of situation. Were you in shock?

MARLOW FIN: I was not myself. I was still trying to process what had happened.

JODI LEE: When you saw the blood, did you shout? Scream?

MARLOW FIN: I—it was nothing. I did nothing. I said nothing. It was [*draws hand over face*]. I can't explain why that was my reaction but it was.

JODI LEE: Why were you at the cabin that Labor Day weekend?

MARLOW FIN: Why does anyone go to their family's lake cabin that time of year?

JODI LEE: Police say that you came uninvited. That you showed up to the surprise of everyone else there.

MARLOW FIN: I arrived at the cabin before anyone else did. It has been in our family for years. I spent summers there as a child. I didn't think anyone would think twice if I showed up Labor Day weekend.

JODI LEE: The results of the DNA analysis on the blood came back rather quickly. I believe it was announced a week later. Do you dispute DNA blood analysis?

MARLOW FIN: I don't deny the science.

JODI LEE: The results came back with 99.9 percent certainty. The blood was that of your sister, Isla.

MARLOW FIN: Yes, it was her blood.

JODI LEE: Here's the question, then. Here is what everyone wants to ask you. What everyone has been thinking.

Marlow, did you kill your sister, Isla?

CHAPTER 23

ISLA

1998

We returned from our time at the cabin to one of the hottest Augusts in Minnesota history. Temperatures hit well over ninety for eleven days straight.

The neighborhood never went a day without an HVAC truck in someone's driveway. Air conditioners busted left and right like kernels of microwave popcorn. It was our turn on a Friday morning. We woke up to thick air and a stale stillness. It was only seven in the morning and already it felt like high noon.

"*Omma*, you should go to your friend Mrs. Hwang's. She has a condo in Minneapolis, right? It's too dangerous for you to stay here in this heat. Stella can drive you on her way in to work."

Moni huffed. "I fine right here. I'm not bother Mrs. Hwang. She has enough trouble, her son is in town. I wait for air conditioning fix."

"The HVAC guy can't come until tomorrow afternoon at the earliest."

Mom finished her coffee and buttoned the top of her blouse. "Really, Moni. It's not safe. I can take you on my way in, no problem."

"And where kids go?"

"With me," said Dad. "I'm off today. We're going to spend as much time as we can at the pool. Right, girls?"

"Can we ask Sawyer to come?" I asked.

"That would be okay. As long as Ada knows."

Marlow said nothing as she dipped her spoon into her cereal. She poured milk slowly back into her bowl and closely watched each drop.

After more coaxing, Moni went with Mom and the rest of us went to the pool. It was already crowded when we got there. Heads bobbed up and down like a game of Whac-A-Mole. Every inch of the scattered chaise longues was covered in bunched-up towels, beach bags, flip-flops, and snacks. My foot crunched over an abandoned package of Cheetos as we searched for the unicorn of an empty chair.

Sawyer located an abandoned one in the corner behind the lifeguard station. He sat on it, as if claiming his discovery.

"Nice work, bud," Dad said, unloading the bag and towels onto the cheap blue-and-white plastic strips of the chaise.

Sawyer suppressed a large smile, his mouth puckering and releasing, almost embarrassed at his reaction to pleasing Dad. "It's no problem."

I impatiently rubbed sunscreen over my face and arms at Dad's insistent orders. The sweat that had already formed on my skin repelled some of the white cream in messy, watery swirls.

The pool was too crowded to jump into. I placed my hand on the silver metal railing and felt immediate relief from my toes hitting the first step under the frigid chlorinated water. Kids screamed and splashed as teen lifeguards in uniform red suits blew whistles and shouted at them with annoyance and boredom.

A lifeguard with white-blond hair wearing blue Oakleys seemed to look straight at me as I entered. Yet he moved on and continued scanning the pool like a radar tower. He had months of a summer tan layered on his body. I suddenly felt weird in my tie-dye one-piece, as if I were underdressed, my midsection a solid block.

Sawyer poked me from behind. "What are you waiting for?" He looked at me and then up at the lifeguard, who stared at us both.

We splashed in together. I surfaced and wiped at my nose. Dad entered the pool with Marlow on the opposite end. I waved at him, and he nodded.

A little girl with hot-pink floaties frantically paddled next to me, elbowing me in the ribs. There was hardly any room to swim. We were a bucket of ping-pong balls dumped into an air duct, darting all over each other. But it was hard to care, as cold and alleviating as the water was.

Marlow came to life in the water. She was a different girl from the one at breakfast, splashing at Dad and giggling.

"Daddy, throw me off your shoulders!" Her voice was babyish again.

"What's that, sweetie?" He held a finger up to his ear.

There was so much shrieking and laughter, it was hard to hear anything. I tried floating on my back, but bumped into an elderly woman who held a chubby toddler in her arms.

"You know . . . like a rocket!" Marlow shouted, gesturing up with her hands.

He nodded and went under the water, holding his hands for her by his collarbones. She balanced on top, and he shot her up high. It was a small miracle she didn't land on anyone.

Dad came up, shaking his head. "Maybe this isn't a good idea, Marlow. It's really crowded."

She shook her head. "Please! One more time. Once more and we'll stop."

He looked around and nodded quickly. "All right. Last time."

He went under again.

Sawyer slapped some water near my face. I gasped and then slapped water right back, watching it fly into his mouth. He sputtered and laughed.

Marlow floated toward Dad's head, getting ready to crouch. But this time, she clenched her knees together. I could see the deliberate clamp she made around his neck. She crossed her legs and wrapped them around him. Dad's hands came up, waving and hitting the surface. She laughed and held on tighter, bouncing hard to keep him down.

Half of his mouth came up, enough to utter two syllables: "Marlow." She laughed at this and then pushed down again.

His head came up. "Marlow!" he gurgled.

Sawyer and I stopped our water slapping. The blond lifeguard in the Oakleys blew his whistle at her. She didn't take notice. He stood up out of his chair, ready to dive in. The more she laughed, the harder Dad struggled.

She released.

He exploded up, coughing and blinking his eyes furiously. He took in two deep breaths before he shouted at her. "Marlow! What were you doing?"

She smiled. "Did I win?"

"Win what?" His tone was angry.

"The game. I kept you under didn't I?"

"Marlow. That wasn't a game. And that was *not* funny."

"I'm sorry, Daddy. I thought we were having fun," she said, treading water, her hair a silky curtain floating around her.

Dad pinched at his nose with his thumb on one side. "Don't ever . . . don't *ever* do that again. You got me?"

She nodded.

He pointed to me and Sawyer. "You two. Watch her, I need to catch my breath."

Dad swam to the side of the pool and climbed out. I watched him lie on the chaise, his feet pointed outward. He looked different. Older.

We stopped on the way home to pick up a few pints of ice cream. Dad drove swiftly to avoid excessive melting. Moni had opted to stay overnight at Mrs. Hwang's and Mom called to say she was working late, so it was frozen pizza for dinner. Afterward, Dad scooped strawberry and chocolate into each of our bowls and we quietly ate to the sound of our spoons clinking against the white ceramic.

Mom got home as we were finishing. Dad offered her a bowl of strawberry. She sat down and looked around at each of us. We were still so quiet. She shared a longer look with Dad. He said nothing and put his head back down for another bite.

She stood up from the table and left. Her ice cream bowl was still there in the morning, a pink puddle with hardened edges.

CHAPTER 24

WREN

1980s

The lecture hall stirred and settled as Professor Patrick Baek walked in. Wren slipped into the very back row, the wooden seat creaking despite her careful movements.

She felt as though everyone would notice right away. One wrong turn of the head and the other students would know she didn't belong there.

She had followed him for a week.

As he had left the restaurant with his wife that evening, she heard him drop the name of the university, a small yet prestigious liberal arts school. She wandered its campus the next day until she spotted him, exiting a building with a few colleagues. Such poise he held in the shoulders of his brown sport coat. He laughed at something one of them said and seemed to look right at her as they strode down the sidewalk.

Watching him was her drug. He was a high she couldn't get enough of. She imagined how he would go home to his wife, who would be more than perfect. She would be electrifying. She would have interesting stories for him to listen to after such a long day, a flawlessly prepared dinner for him to sit down to. And then that safe bubble they created when they were together would protect them from withering the way the whites of an apple do so quickly. Theirs was a partnership that remained golden.

She could do that. She could play that part for him.

A couple questions to passing students and it was easy to find out what he taught. A girl even offered to point out where the lecture hall was for his linguistics class that morning. She opted out that first day. She didn't want to overindulge. But by the second week, she found herself listening to him speak about the difference between phonetics and phonology.

His dark hair glistened that morning, still wet from whatever hurried shower he may have taken before arriving. She had never seen skin so immaculate. It was the pureness of it . . . the cleanliness. It was so far away from what she felt.

"Why do words sound the way they do? What started it all? These are some of the questions I'm going to help you answer this semester."

A palpable energy spun from every one of his words. She wanted to reach out and grab at them, like a little girl catching fireflies at dusk.

She had not one idea what he was trying to convey, and she didn't care. His grip of the room, the attention he demanded, gave her an unsteady sensation; yet the funny thing was, she had never felt so sure of anything before. This was where she was supposed to be. Her impulsive roving had rolled to a stop, like a train that finally found its station.

After each lecture, it wasn't uncommon for a cluster of students to approach him, most of them female. She would linger in the back, observing him as he listened intently to their questions and then used his hands expressively as he answered. She would work up the courage to take the stairs down to the front of the lecture hall. But by the time this happened, he would be packing up his papers and snapping his briefcase shut.

After more than a month had passed, a sense of urgency abruptly overcame her and she was the first one to approach him.

"Ahh, the quiet one in the back. I don't think I've ever caught your name?"

He didn't look up as he said this, thumbing through a handout. She felt all ability to speak rush away from her, down her throat like a drain. Her silence made him glance up. Their eyes met and she felt an intense heat course through her nerves.

"Wren," she finally answered.

"This is the first time I've heard you speak in this class."

"I'm more of a listener, I guess."

He smiled and she thought it was one she would do anything to see again. Not because of his striking appearance. That was the least of it. It was the idea that she could have roots, that she felt the need to stay put once and for all.

"Don't apologize for being a listener. That's a skill most of us never really acquire."

She nodded and he placed both hands on his desk, tapping it lightly.

"So . . . Wren. What is it that I can do to help you?"

This was the part she hadn't thought about. She should've prepared a question to ask him that would show how attentively she had listened, how much *she* was there for *him*.

"I . . . I was wondering . . ."

"Yes, Wren?"

She wondered right then if he would actually remember her name. Or if he was really good at making people—people like her—feel important.

"I was wondering if you had any additional textbook recommendations?"

He smirked. "You want *more* readings?"

"Why, yes."

"My assigned reading is getting too light for you, huh?"

He was smiling and she sighed slightly.

"It's just—I find it all so very fascinating. I would really love your advice on what else to read."

He seemed put off for a split second. As if she was burdening him with more to do. But it was quickly hidden with another grin.

"Sure. Absolutely. I'll bring you a list next week. Does that sound okay, Wren?"

It was all she needed to hear.

He made good on his promise. He didn't forget. When she descended the steps again, he held up a handwritten list—in pencil on a piece of lined paper. He waved it like a prize and winked.

"I expect you to read this, Wren. *All* of this."

Another wink. It was their little joke. Their own secret.

She spent the whole week reading as much as she could from the list that she could find in the library. She wanted to impress him. But she couldn't contain herself until the next class. She went to his office instead. The door was slightly ajar. She was about to knock when she saw a flash of red.

A curtain of wavy tendrils passed by. A girl sat on his desk and leaned forward. He looked so engrossed as the girl whispered something in his ear. His hand reached up and brushed one of the curls.

Wren dropped one of the books she was going to show him. She didn't remember the walk home. Only that she found herself in Julien's apartment. She wanted warmth. She wanted a blanket to get rid of the sting that invaded her every thought. Her body. She wanted her body to feel anything or anyone.

As he started to kiss her, she pushed him back abruptly.

This wasn't the way.

She was determined to stay the course. The seat creaked again at the lecture the next morning. But this time she was glad. This time she wanted to make noise.

CHAPTER 25

ISLA

2001

Mom handed me a white paper shopping bag. She looked away as if something was about to pop out of it. I half expected to see a snake slither out, but instead found a row of pink training bras still on their plastic hangers.

"Is this absolutely necessary?" I held one of them up and rubbed the material as if it were rough and unwearable.

"Isla, you can't . . . jiggle around anymore. Especially with school starting."

"Did you just use the word jiggle to describe me?"

"You know what I mean." Her eyes drifted to my chest and then looked away.

I had studied myself in the bathroom mirror the night before, foggy from my shower. The area around my belly button was soft. I poked it with a few fingers, feathery and light with my touch. My legs had widened at the top, dimpled around the thighs like the surface of a golf ball. Puberty had added weight to every part of me.

Weight.

Was it such a bad thing? Such a bad word? There was more that covered my bones, more that protected me from hurtful, confusing words.

Chubby. Puffy. Thick. Each one pricked my ears. Grown-ups always thought you weren't listening. Always thought you weren't *really* able to grasp what they were whispering about.

I hid behind worn, wide-legged jeans and No Fear T-shirts that were two sizes too big. A tent that covered me and drew over all that I did not want exposed. I had round owl glasses that I was constantly pushing up, wrinkling my nose to see better. I was not young enough to be a cute little girl, but not old enough to be even considered pretty. The "awkward" phase is what they called it. As if I didn't feel abnormal enough, it had to be labeled with such a word. "She'll blossom, you wait and see. My youngest was like her."

Blossom? Was I a flower? When would this blossoming finally happen?

Mom began to fold the shopping bag and held it against her chest, her expression softening.

"We could go shopping for some new clothes? Maybe something more, well—just you and me could go?"

Something more attractive. Something more like what Marlow would wear?

As though on cue, Marlow slipped into my room.

Nothing Marlow wore could hide her beauty.

I remember the morning when it confronted us all. She came down to breakfast and straight into the net of "the moment." When the culmination of all the little changes collected, to the point where it was enough to make us all realize she was not a little girl anymore. Her shape was one that did not draw in comments. The reactions were silent. Words were not appropriate in response to her outline, her legs that sprouted out so quickly Mom had to buy her new clothes twice in a month. She was a gazelle. The ideal form of what men and women feasted their eyes upon.

She was now of another world.

I saw the look in Dad's eyes. The near embarrassment of staring at her. The quick lowering of his eyes down to his newspaper.

It was hard not to stare at her. She was twelve and could pass easily for a teenager. She had a confidence in her posture that I never would. I don't think her skin had the ability to ever grow a pimple, let alone any sort of blemish. It contained a remarkable smoothness that made me want to run my finger over her forearm to see if it was real. To say she had grown into a beauty was ridiculous. She had always been one.

Yet I found it all so peculiar. The prowess she suddenly wielded over everyone. The measurement of her waist. Her breasts. Her legs. Her neck. Her cheekbones. Her eyes. Her lips. The exact formation and outcome of every cell was worth so much. The weight.

The weight she now carried.

"You want to borrow something of mine?" Marlow asked, her head resting on part of my bedroom doorframe.

Her hair was slicked back into a low ponytail; it wrapped around her neck and down over her shoulder. She looked so grown up and yet so eager, so ready to be of use no matter how small. I almost lied and told her I would love to borrow something.

I could see Mom shift her shoulders uncomfortably. Ever since Marlow got her period before me, she looked at her as if she were something that had malfunctioned. She displayed an uneasy energy around her that she wasn't able to hide.

Mom shook her head. "I don't think your size would work."

"What about some of my sweaters? Isla, you'd look great in the tan—"

"Thanks, Marlow. But I'll take her to the mall before school starts Monday."

Her words were polite, affable—how one would speak to a bank teller. This was the bar she had somehow set for them, mother and daughter.

Soon, Marlow would be navigating the halls of Henley Middle School, a place I felt I had finally conquered in some limited capacity. I would be one of the older kids, two grades ahead of her, and she would be starting at square one.

By the second day of school, Marlow had already intoxicated the entire student body with her presence. She was a sweeping force, putting Moses parting the Red Sea to shame with her ability to silence any section of the hallway she passed. Kids went out of their way to make room for her, as if their touch would taint her. I wasn't surprised. Not really, anyway. I would feel a familiar sting anytime I heard whispers that grew into loud voices. *No way, they're sisters? How is that even possible? Didn't you hear how they found her?*

In the past, I would at least have had Sawyer to lean on. We would have sat back together, making our own jokes as we took in Marlow's newfound fame. But everything about him was different. Quieter. Bigger. Cloudier. He had shot up a full head taller than me, and his hair had started to darken and thicken. It was shaggy and covered his ears and sometimes his eyes. I wanted to brush it away badly, but touching him now was a foreign thing. It seemed to have dawned on him over the summer, as his limbs sprouted out longer and skinnier than ever, that it didn't bode well for him to have females as his closest friends.

The changes were small at first. A breakfast skipped at our house because of an early soccer practice; he'd grabbed a granola bar instead. Going over to the Bollinger twins' house to study for the exam, since "Topher was really good at math and everything." Lingering longer at his locker until I went on without him to the bus.

"Sorry, I forgot something," he would say when he finally caught up, an apologetic smile mixed with a little shame. Shame because he knew I wasn't that stupid, and for saying something so generic.

On the bus, he began to sit next to Topher, their heads bent over together. Greta would be his replacement, as she stiffly slid in next to me.

Eventually he wasn't waiting for me or walking with me at all.

Oliver would often join me instead. He never got the urge to separate himself from me like the bad part of an apple that gets lopped off.

"Why aren't you trying out for soccer like the other boys?" I asked, hands tugging at my backpack straps.

He squinted up at me. His growth spurt had not hit him like the others. "Why aren't you over there with Marlow and her groupies?"

"Fair enough," I replied as he smirked.

The following afternoon, Marlow ran up from behind and linked arms with me as a flock of sixth and seventh grade girls looked on with envy. Why was I the one who got to walk with Marlow Baek? Who was I, anyway? The pudgy girl with baggy clothes and stringy hair.

"Sawyer is just trying to be one of the guys now," she said in my ear.

"What makes you say that?"

"Isla, I know it's been bothering you."

I scoffed. "And when did you get so wise?"

"I'm not. But remember I'm here, too, you know." She elbowed me and smiled.

I nodded and looked ahead to our bus.

When we got home, I let her "experiment" with my hair. She pleated it in a long braid and then dusted my eyes with a dark turquoise shadow. I looked in the mirror. My eyes looked bruised. I wiped away at my face with Kleenex.

"Where do you even find colors like this?" I scrunched up the white tissue bleeding in bluish powder.

She bit her lip, scrutinizing her work. "Maybe I put too much on."

"You think?" I turned my face toward her, the eye shadow faded and streaky.

We both burst into a fit of laughter, the kind that made us shake and clutch our midsections. When it stopped she put her chin on my shoulder.

"You see."

"See what?"

"Your face."

"My face?" I wrinkled my brow.

"It comforts me."

I must have looked confused or even a little annoyed. She didn't say anything else. Instead, she flapped her mouth like a fish a few times, jabbing her chin into my shoulder.

"Quit, that feels so weird." I dusted her away with my hand.

She laughed and started to undo my braid.

"Let me fix this. I didn't do it right." Her fingers fell through some of the knots in my hair. It hurt but I said nothing.

Later that evening, I went across the street and knocked on the front door. I was surprised to find Ada alone.

"Sawyer is at Topher's house. Video games . . . I can't remember the name of it. Something that involves violence, I'm sure," she said in the doorway.

I must have looked disappointed, despite trying to keep what I had thought was a very straight face, because she then told me to come inside.

I followed her, the house smelling of onions and spice. She had taken down most of the dream catchers. There were only a handful by the kitchen window.

"I made some slow cooker chili. Want some?"

"No thank you. I already ate."

"Suit yourself."

She scooped some into a small bowl and motioned with her spoon for me to sit down. I sat across from her and looked up as she took a quick bite. A piece of red bean slipped out of her mouth. The light hanging over the kitchen table shone on her thick white roots, the rest of her hair still a deep, dyed red. The lines on her face had deepened, but she had always looked old to me. In that way, she had changed very little.

"You know, Sawyer doesn't really talk much. About what he went through back in Wyoming," she said, peering at me.

"I know."

"Not even with me."

She paused, letting another bite of chili sink into her mouth.

"He saw too much. Too much sickness with his mother. Boy is trying to figure some of his shit out right now. At this age . . . you know it can be especially hard. Know what I mean?"

I slowly nodded.

"He doesn't have a father. I mean—he does. But not one who will ever be there for him."

"I know what you're trying to say, Ada. Don't worry."

She put her spoon down, and a few drops of chili sauce plopped on the table.

"I just don't want you thinking he's left you behind or nothing, darling. I'm real glad, you know . . ."

Her face scrunched up and went back to normal so quickly that I nearly missed it. She stiffened her mouth and broke into a grin that was a little too wide.

"I'm real glad he has you, Isla."

CHAPTER 26

ISLA

2002

"See? I told you that color would work."

Oliver hung on my bedpost and then popped a cheese cracker into his mouth.

"Hey. Watch the crumbs."

"Stop changing the subject. You look great in forest green."

It was the night of the Henley High School spring mixer—an informal dance as a precursor to prom. Oliver had convinced me to wear a sleeveless sheath dress. It was simple but, surprisingly, gave me a feminine shape.

"Marlow!" he called.

"Shhh. Do you always have to be so loud?" I scolded.

He ignored me, and Marlow breezed in. She appeared impossibly fresh, with rosy, dewy cheeks that stood out above her fuzzy white sweater.

"Oh, Isla!" She put her hand to her cheek.

Oliver gave a thumbs-up.

I rolled my eyes. "Jesus, both of you. Stop with the dramatics."

"You look so pretty," she said, putting her hands on my arms.

I believed her for once. My body was finally starting to cooperate. The blockish and padded figure had melted slightly. I had hips and a waist. But I was no more comfortable in this body than the one before. I moved with uncertainty, a hermit crab that had found a newer, shinier shell, yet missed her old one.

"Why can't eighth graders go to this again?" Marlow sat hard on my bed.

Oliver plopped next to her. "Is it true you got asked by a junior?"

"Does it even matter? I'm not allowed," she whined.

I stared at myself in the mirror again, starting to doubt the initial rush of euphoria I'd had. Wouldn't everyone wonder why I was wearing a dress? Would I look like I was trying too hard?

"I can't wear this." I started to reach for the back to unzip.

"You're crazy!" Oliver leaped up to stop me.

"Isla, you have to be kidding me. You need to wear this!"

"What's all the yelling about?"

Sawyer entered my bedroom, and I instantly felt a rush of embarrassment, a need to cover up any exposed skin. I felt so visible and bare, a specimen under the microscope.

"What are you doing here?" I said this more as an accusation, my voice coming out irritated.

He held up his hands. "Whoa. Sorry, what? I ran into Moni earlier this week and she told me to come over to eat something before the dance."

"And?"

"And? I wasn't going to miss out on that. Do you know how often Ada actually cooks real food?"

He quickly looked me up and down and then turned away. "You look really nice, Isla," he said to the wall.

I didn't respond. He'd always had manners. Why *wouldn't* he say something so polite? So respectful? I would have rather he'd thrown a barbed comment at me—something that didn't resemble the stale dialogue of coworkers in an office.

Downstairs, Moni had bowls of hot rice she had stir-fried with chopped-up kimchi, spam, and egg.

"Korean junk food," she said, chastising the dish.

"Moni, stop saying that," Marlow said. "It's delicious."

Moni spooned more rice into Sawyer's bowl. She patted his head. "You need eat more. Too skinny."

He smiled fondly and patted her hand. The rice couldn't go fast enough into his growing and stretching teenage body.

It suddenly felt like we were little kids again—Moni doting over us all, clucking and spooning more food into our mouths. The wave of nostalgia almost made me dizzy. It was broken when Sawyer scooted his chair back, thanking Moni and saying something about having to meet up with Topher and his older cousin for a ride.

Later, when the gym was packed full of high school kids, sweat, hormones, and nerves, I told Oliver I needed fresh air. We stood with a line of other freshmen in the back, spectators of the bobbing and grinding in front of us that was to be construed as dancing.

"I can't take another second of this!" I yelled into his ear.

He nodded and proceeded to dance in place all by himself. I had to admire his lack of inhibitions. Sometimes I wondered if he was simply that unaware—that he was blessed with a naivety when it came to other people's judgment.

I burst out the side doors. The heat of the gym had somehow shrunk the stiff material of my dress. It felt tight, and no longer moved with my body. I tugged at the bottom hem and sighed at the instant quiet—only disturbed slightly by the distant humming and buzzing of the dance music.

"You couldn't stand it either, huh?"

Sawyer stood to my right, leaning against the brick wall.

His sudden presence wasn't startling to me. "Stand?"

"It was getting hard to breathe, even." He moved down and rested his head next to me.

"For me it was more the smell of all the kids who I suspect don't shower, collecting in one space."

He laughed. "You have a way with words, Isla."

"Where's Topher?" I asked, looking around.

"He ditched me for a chick in his study hall about twenty minutes ago."

"What a guy."

"He's not too bad. Most of the time."

I nodded neutrally. We leaned together against that brick wall, the silence feeling neither long nor short. But a quiet that didn't bother us.

He suddenly laughed again, this time harder.

"What's so funny?" I half grinned.

"I was just thinking about that one summer we tried to sell Moni's scarves on the street corner."

"When we were trying to save up for a puppy?"

He rubbed the back of his head, smiling. "Yes. And how mad she got."

"And how Ada got even madder when we tried it again, with her garden tools."

I began to laugh so hard with him, my eyes squinted shut. He chuckled hard, his shoulders heaving up and down. When I opened them, he was staring at me. I wiped a tear away.

"I don't remember the last time I laughed that hard," he said.

"Yeah . . ." I found my voice drifting off. My hand instinctively reached up and started to pull on my hair, stroking it a few times as it draped down my shoulder.

Sawyer leaned forward, like he wanted to reach out and touch my hair, an urge in his eyes, maybe even a bit of longing. His mouth closed and he retracted.

"See you back in there?" He pointed over his shoulder with his thumb. It was awkward and endearing all at once.

I mimicked his movement and he laughed again.

In the morning, I pulled open my desk drawer that jammed and never opened all the way. I reached in the back and felt around until it hit my hand. I rolled it forward with the tips of my fingers and held it up.

The shiny knight figurine. He had dropped it that first day we met, the day he moved in across the street. It had fallen in the grass, and I don't know why but I took it. Every day since then I had meant to give it back. But I would tell myself, one more day. One more day and I'll return it to him.

"What's that?"

I snapped the knight into my hand and whirled around to find Marlow standing in my room.

"Nothing. I'm cleaning out my drawer," I answered hastily.

"Really. What is it?"

She started to move behind me, but I stuffed it in my back pocket and sat on the bed.

"Marlow. It's really nothing. Can you leave now?"

She giggled. "Why are you being so secretive? I thought we didn't have secrets."

I felt warm, my face reddening as if I had opened an oven.

"Just . . . leave it. Okay?"

She looked down at my lap, as if trying to determine if she should wrestle me for it. "Do you like keeping secrets from me?"

Her face looked serious, forlorn even.

"No . . . this isn't—Marlow, this isn't a secret. Can you please respect me and give me *some* privacy?" I snapped.

She stared at me, then backed away, shrugging, and left my room.

Sawyer and Oliver came over for dinner again Sunday night. Mom laughed as Dad shook his head.

"Don't you kids get fed at home?" Dad joked.

"Yes, Mr. Baek. But who wants to eat at home when you can eat at Moni's?" Oliver slurped in a few *japchae* noodles and sank his fork into a mushroom.

Moni beamed as she brought over more dishes. "No, Moni food not that good. You only that hungry."

We went to the basement after everyone had finished eating. Oliver and I played ping-pong while Marlow brought a stack of CDs down from her room.

"I missed the dance. So I'm bringing one here." She put a disc in the boom box and hit the "Play" button. Savage Garden's "Truly, Madly, Deeply" floated out of the speakers.

"It wasn't a dance," said Oliver, hitting the ball with his paddle. It bounced on my side and off the table.

"Crap."

"My point!" He shot his hands in the air.

Marlow moved her hips back and forth. "It *was* a dance. Did they play music?"

"Shitty music," he argued.

Sawyer sank into the sofa and patted his stomach. "I always get stuffed when I come over here."

"Perfect!" Marlow said, turning to him with her hands out. "You can dance it off."

He groaned. "Oh, no, no. And especially no to that song," he said, pointing to the speakers as though they were guilty.

"C'mon. Show me how to dance." She leaned down and pulled him up.

"You know how to dance."

"Fine. Then dance with me."

I bent under the ping-pong table to look for the stray ball. When I stood up, she had her arms wrapped around his neck, and his hands were on her waist.

"See? Not so bad." She leaned her head into his chest.

Oliver twirled his paddle a few times and shrugged. The music kept playing but it seemed to grow louder and louder. I rolled the ball in my hand.

"Maybe we should play something else. Where do you keep your board games again, Isla?" Oliver scratched the back of his head and looked around.

"In the spare room closet." I pointed and kept watching them.

Marlow swayed and burrowed her head even more. And then she pulled up and looked him straight in the eyes. She put her hand at the nape of his neck and moved her lips up to his. Her tongue slid in. His eyes were closed, but hers were open. They turned to me and never wavered as her mouth moved on top of his.

She was punishing me.

Sawyer pushed her back. His hands fell down heavily. "Marlow . . ."

"Just practicing." She giggled, as if it had all been a joke. A big, sick joke only she was in on.

In my room that night, I pulled the drawer open and tossed the knight figurine inside. It rolled into its place in the back.

CHAPTER 27

ISLA

2004

It was late fall and most of the leaves had found their new home on the ground. I remember the swish, swish, crunch of Marlow's steps. The black boots she wore had chunky heels that created wide imprints through the red and gold colors.

I had decided to take photos of her for my senior art project. At first, she loved the idea, exclaiming how she couldn't wait to pose. But once in front of the camera, she became timid, nervous even.

I had never seen Marlow like this.

I clutched the Nikon I borrowed from the classroom, bouncing its heftiness in my hands as I tested the lighting with a few shots.

"What is this for again?" she asked, annoyed. A gust whipped some hair into her mouth, and she sputtered it away.

"My art class final. We have to use a medium we haven't done yet. Photography is the one I chose," I explained, snapping more shots.

"A few pictures of me and you can call it your final?"

"Well . . . I have to do a little more than that. It's part of a bigger composition."

She paused to tie her cream sweater around her waist and adjust her sterling silver cross necklace. The delicate chain made her collarbone look even smoother.

"Are we done yet?" she whined.

"Marlow," I said through a sigh.

"Fine."

She stood straight up and flapped her arms once.

"Maybe try walking toward me," I suggested, keeping one hand on the camera as the other waved.

She took a few steps and then shook her head.

"What's wrong?"

The wind blew her hair across her face again. When it fell away, I saw that she looked so . . . sad. As lost as she did the night we found her.

"I don't want you to . . ." she whispered.

"Yes?" I urged impatiently.

Her eyes looked impossibly big, and her lips pressed together.

I let the camera fall to my side. I spoke gentler this time. "Marlow. It's only me. Isla. Remember?"

She nodded, an electric relief taking over as she shook her hands out.

"I'll try to make it quick. Okay?"

She walked away from me and then turned back, looking over her shoulder. The fleshiness of her upper lip looked so pink. It seemed to curl up and almost touch the end of her nose as she smiled and laughed at me. She seemed to melt into some other form of herself. Another Marlow who loved the camera.

"Should I twirl?" She placed her hands down at her sides and spun.

Even behind the small, dirty lens of the old camera, it was hard not to recognize the splendor she held in every movement of her frame.

"Sure," I said. "Go for it."

She suddenly turned straight toward me and widened her stance. She spread one hand over her face, her eye caught between her index and middle fingers.

"What do you think? Good enough for *Vogue*?" she quipped.

I snapped a few photos.

"Isla?"

"Just keep going," I said.

Later that week, in the darkroom, I finally got around to developing the roll of film I took of her. I submerged the pearly-white photo paper. It shimmered under the red light. I let it go back and forth gently until it floated up like a drowned body emerging from the sea.

She formed.

Her mouth first and then her eyes. I stared down at her, unaware of how long it had been until I pulled the photo out with tongs and clipped it up.

I didn't know. Or maybe I did know. This was the picture that would change everything.

CHAPTER 28

ISLA

2005

I opened my mouth to taste the snowflakes, each one a slippery drop on my tongue. My hair was covered in them, a net of lace. I adjusted my yellow knit hat and shook my head.

"Marlow, you're going to make us late again!" Oliver called out, his arm draped over the open passenger door.

"You know she isn't coming down until she's ready. Why go through this every time?"

"Because I like shouting at her," he said, putting his hand up as if it were an obvious answer.

I reached in to turn the heat on, twisting the dial extra hard to the right to get it going, a quirk of the old Jeep that Dad had passed down to me when he got a new car. He had handed over the keys, proud and nervous.

"Take care of her, Isla. She's had a lot of mileage but she's still a good one," he had said with a little sadness. I wasn't sure if it was because he was attached to the Jeep or because it meant I was growing up. It had taken much convincing, even though I was newly eighteen, to complete that transaction.

"Marlow!" Oliver shouted again, this time tossing his head back and shimmying. He gave me a cheeky smile as I rolled my eyes.

The front door flung open and Marlow stood there, statuesque and leggy. She had on light-gray leather boots that went above the knees, and a soft, white beret. Her cheeks were flushed pink and her wavy hair cascaded down her chest.

"Oliver. You little shit," she said, swinging the door closed behind her.

"Yes, but I'm *your* little shit." He ducked to get in the Jeep.

"Why do you get to ride shotgun?" Marlow whined.

I got inside to warm up and looked in the rearview mirror to see Sawyer coming toward us. He walked with such purpose now. Not the lagging little boy or the sulky preteen, but sturdy with each step. He wore his hair shorter, and it made him look older. I wasn't sure if I would recognize him in a crowd, the way his shoulders had become so broad and full. He had spent part of the summer detasseling corn for a friend of Ada's. There was a certainty he wore on his face, a watchfulness I wasn't familiar with.

"Scoot over, boots," he said, nudging Marlow.

"Making fun of my boots now, huh?" She hopped closer to Oliver's side.

"I would never make fun of you, Marlow." Sawyer held his backpack in his lap and then set it on the floor.

She smiled and elbowed him.

I readjusted the mirror and reversed the Jeep.

When we arrived at school, I could see her in the corner of the mirror, adjusting her hat and fluffing her hair. She was a girl who already knew how to make an entrance. High school had come even easier to Marlow. It was her playground, and she was the muse for both the male and female student bodies. I imagined it felt like walking on water for her, the rest of us underneath, some near the surface, some trying not to drown, floundering as she traipsed above. A water nymph content and unaware of any troubles below.

In fourth period art class, Mr. Bahar motioned for me to come over to his desk. I had always liked him as a teacher. He never got in anyone's face or micromanaged. He liked to sit back and see what kind of art we would produce without much prodding. This was a class where it was the student's space, not the teacher's.

"Isla, I was very impressed with your final submission last semester."

I immediately tried to brush it off. "Oh really? It was just a few photographs."

"No really, Isla." He swept a finger over his mustache. "The composition was excellent. The juxtaposition between the subject as a young child to the present is stunning . . . eerie, even."

"It was a few photos I took of my sister. Thank you but—"

"I submitted your piece to the Midwest High School Regional Art Contest. Each school is only allowed one submission. I hope you don't mind. The deadline was during winter break and I wasn't able to contact you at that time. If it makes you uncomfortable, I can withdraw it on your behalf. But this piece . . . it really resonates, Isla."

I stared at the dark hairs above his lip. They moved up and down as he spoke.

"Isla?"

"Are you sure?"

"Am I—"

"There are so many other pieces you could have chosen. We have a lot of talented artists in this class. You really thought mine . . ."

"Know. I *know* you have a brilliant eye, my dear."

He was so kind, so real in his belief in my piece. I couldn't break that. I began to nod. "Okay, then. It's fine."

"Glorious."

Mr. Bahar used words like that. Ones that made you feel buoyant as he said them.

"The gallery show is in two weeks. You can go see it on display for yourself. I can give you more details as they come. Isla, you should be very proud of yourself."

I felt anything but proud.

It was only me and Sawyer on the way home. Marlow had cheerleading practice and Oliver a clarinet lesson. The Jeep rattled slightly before I turned it off in our driveway. Snow started to fall again, this time faster and with urgency. The windshield was covered in seconds, a blinding white sheet.

We sat in silence. I motioned to get out, but he stopped me by talking.

"This may sound like a complete lie. But . . ." He tapped his window. "I'm really going to miss this snow when I'm out west this fall."

"Yes. That sounds like a complete lie," I said immediately.

He laughed. "Seriously. This has been my home since I was eight."

"I think you'll be fine. Give it a week in that California sun and we'll probably never see you again."

"Yeah . . . I'll miss Moni's food."

"She will miss feeding you. It's pretty much her favorite hobby."

"I'll probably starve out there."

"Probably." I placed my hands on the steering wheel even though the Jeep was off. "Did Ada finally warm up to you taking that scholarship?"

He shrugged. "She has to. It was the best one that was offered. I can't stay here for her."

"I'm sure she knows that."

"I hope so."

He turned his shoulders to face me. "You decide on which school yet?"

It was my turn to shrug. "I'm getting there. But Chicago for sure."

We had already had this conversation before. Him leaving for California, which schools we had been looking at, what scholarships he had been offered. Our questions merely followed the footsteps of a familiar path, afraid to stray elsewhere.

"Will you miss me?" he suddenly asked.

I felt my mouth form a protective smirk and couldn't help but laugh. "What?"

His face reddened and I wanted to reach out and apologize by placing my hand on his cheek. I curled up my fingers instead in my lap.

He faced forward again, concentrating hard on the snow.

"It's going to be so strange. I've seen you almost every day for the last ten years. Moni, your parents . . . Marlow. Even more than my own grandmother. It's home here, you know? You're . . ."

He didn't finish his sentence and looked at me again. My face had started to grow cold sitting there. The snow had thickened on all the windows around us. It was so quiet. We were buried deep in the ground, in a tomb of radiant white, encased away from everything else. A trembling began in the pit of my stomach. He reached out and took my hand, pressing it between his as if to will warmth into it. I looked down at our hands together and back up at him. What was it he had said that made the trembling stop? Was it her name? I shook my head faintly—I doubt he could even detect it—and then placed my other hand on the door handle.

"Isla—"

I opened it and snow slipped down into the Jeep and onto my coat. "My art final."

"I don't—"

"My teacher submitted it to regionals. There's a gallery show coming up. We should all go." I sounded like a stranger.

He nodded slowly and then got out.

A few weeks later, I attended the gallery showing with Mom and Moni. I never mentioned it to Marlow or brought it up again to Sawyer. We drove down together to the Minneapolis Convention Center, Moni already proud, holding my hand in the car.

The three of us stood in front of my piece, a framed matte board with two black-and-white photos placed at different angles. The first: one of the earliest pictures Dad took of Marlow. She was six, with that empty look on her face she wore, standing on a stool in the bathroom, looking over her shoulder. A toothbrush was clutched in one hand. The other: the one I took of her the previous fall, with her hand spread over her face. The curve of her cheekbones looked as though they were carved out, her eyes light and engrossed.

You couldn't take your eyes off her.

Each second came something new that you hadn't noticed before. A pang inside you that someone could really have this much control over your very eyes. She was art that didn't exist yet. A medium all her own.

Between the two photos, I had inserted a clipping of an old newspaper article about her from 1995, a tiny blip in the paper about the girl found in the woods. A few lines of red paint crisscrossed the article.

When we were finished looking at my piece, Mom and Moni floated to other displays. I stayed near mine, as if it needed to be watched over.

A bald man in a formfitting charcoal sweater stopped in front of Marlow's picture. He bent forward, his nose almost touching the black matte board. He didn't move, with the exception of his hand rubbing the base of his neck, as if to soothe himself from his visceral reaction.

I could see the whites of his eyes, glistening. Wet.

CHAPTER 29

THE INTERVIEW

2021

[Studio]

MARLOW FIN: Kill.

JODI LEE: Yes?

MARLOW FIN: Kill. That is a very, very strong word.

JODI LEE: Perhaps I should rephrase my question, then. Did you have anything to do with the murder of your sister, Isla?

MARLOW FIN: We don't know what happened to Isla. Whether she is alive or dead. Whether she was killed or if there was an accident. All we know is she is gone.

JODI LEE: Have you seen your sister since the night of September 7, 2020?

MARLOW FIN: No, I have not.

JODI LEE: What do you think happened to her?

[Roll package, footage of police at crime scene]

JODI LEE: It was a year ago Labor Day weekend that Marlow's sister was last seen by anyone. On the morning of September 8, 2020, police arrived after receiving a 911 call from Marlow. Her haunting words have been played over and over again by the media:

I found blood . . . in the shed. Please send help.

Two Cook County police officers were dispatched to the family's lakeside home near Grand Marais. Marlow was found almost immediately. But there was something off.

[Secondary Studio, interview with Officer Randall Bittner]

JODI LEE: You were the first one to arrive at the scene?

OFFICER BITTNER: Yes, ma'am. I was followed closely by another officer and then Sheriff Vandenberg.

JODI LEE: Did you know of any preexisting history between the Baek family and Sheriff Vandenberg?

OFFICER BITTNER: It was pretty much known around our force that he was there when Marlow Fin was found all those years ago in the woods. Especially when she became a celebrity.

JODI LEE: Did you notice his reaction when he arrived?

OFFICER BITTNER: Stunned. He didn't really know what to say when we found her.

JODI LEE: You found Marlow first, correct?

OFFICER BITTNER: Correct.

JODI LEE: Can you tell me what you saw?

OFFICER BITTNER: Ms. Fin was crouched over by the edge of the lake near the shed. She didn't say anything to me even though I called out to her several times before approaching. By the time I reached her, she abruptly stood up.

JODI LEE: Did this alarm you?

OFFICER BITTNER: Somewhat.

JODI LEE: Was your gun drawn?

OFFICER BITTNER: My hand was on my holster for a moment. But her hands went up. Almost as if she knew what I was going to say next. I slowly approached her and asked her to turn around. She complied and that's when I noticed the blood.

JODI LEE: You saw blood right away?

OFFICER BITTNER: Yes. She was wearing a white dress, sort of a nightgown. And there was a very apparent spot on the lower area of the skirt.

JODI LEE: How big was this spot of blood?

OFFICER BITTNER: I'd say bigger than a quarter.

JODI LEE: Blood that was later matched to her sister, Isla.

OFFICER BITTNER: Correct. Forensics matched her DNA to that spot of blood on the dress.

JODI LEE: What happened next?

OFFICER BITTNER: I instructed Ms. Fin to sit down on the grass with her hands behind her head. She complied. I waited for backup, and she was taken into the squad car.

JODI LEE: Was she handcuffed?

OFFICER BITTNER: No, ma'am.

JODI LEE: Is that standard? Wouldn't most people in that situation be handcuffed? Some are saying she has been given special treatment due to her celebrity.

OFFICER BITTNER: She had complied up until then and she didn't show signs of posing a danger to herself or others. She was secured in the squad car.

JODI LEE: At this point, you have a backup officer. Sheriff Vandenberg has also arrived on scene. Did any of you try speaking to Marlow?

OFFICER BITTNER: My backup stayed in the squad car with her while Sheriff Vandenberg and I scoped out the premises. We checked the entire cabin and then the shed.

JODI LEE: Tell me what you saw in that shed.

OFFICER BITTNER: At first there was nothing notable. A few kayaks, camping and fishing equipment. There was water on various parts of the floorboards. I suspect it was because the water level was very high that summer. There were record rainfalls, flooding. Sheriff Vandenberg and I proceeded to inspect the inside. And that's when I slipped.

JODI LEE: The headlines said you slipped in a pool of blood.

OFFICE BITTNER: Yes, it was a pool of liquid. But it was a mixture of blood and water.

JODI LEE: Would you say it was a lot of blood?

OFFICE BITTNER: I would not describe it to that extent. But we were immediately concerned and called for additional backup.

JODI LEE: Who talked to Marlow first following the shed inspection?

OFFICER BITTNER: That would be myself and Sheriff Vandenberg. We returned to the squad car, and she was very quiet. I would even describe her as catatonic. Sheriff Vandenberg tried asking her if she knew where she was. Who he was and if she remembered him. That woke her up and she started talking.

JODI LEE: Talking . . . about?

OFFICER BITTNER: The blood. She kept repeating how she found the blood.

[Roll package, footage of protestors]

JODI LEE: Marlow was immediately taken in for police questioning. She denied having anything to do with the disappearance of Isla, and at some point during her interrogation asked for attorney representation. Nearly a year has passed since then, and there have yet to be any charges made. The investigation is ongoing but many are calling for Marlow's arrest.

Protestors line up almost daily outside her main residence in Brentwood, California. Although it's reported that she's residing elsewhere at an undisclosed location. Their voices demand that she be held accountable. Her status as a celebrity should not be a factor. But accountable for what, exactly?

I spoke with former Minnesota district attorney Shareef Meadows about this case for the legal angle.

[Secondary Studio, interview with Shareef Meadows]

JODI LEE: There was blood found in the shed matching Isla's. Blood found on Marlow's dress at the scene matching Isla's. The suspicious 911 call. Her strange behavior before, during, and after questioning. Now everyone is asking why? Why hasn't an arrest been made?

ATTORNEY MEADOWS: No body, no crime, Jodi. You've probably heard that saying. But there are some things to clarify about this—it's not all-encompassing or entirely factual, legally. Without a body it is very difficult to make a case for murder. A grand jury is not likely to indict Marlow if there isn't a body to show an actual homicide has occurred. Isla has not been declared legally dead in the state of Minnesota.

Now, have there been murder charges, even convictions, without a body? Sure. In this case, it remains to be seen if any further evidence could surface or if the DA's office makes a move.

JODI LEE: But some are arguing that it doesn't really take a detective to draw some conclusions here. Isla goes missing the exact same time her blood is found in the shed. The last person to see her alive is Marlow. Doesn't that add up to a charge?

ATTORNEY MEADOWS: Listen. I understand the frustration of the public. A woman goes missing and they want answers. But we aren't going to get our answers by arresting someone without proper evidence.

This is a highly publicized case. Beyond that, even. There is a national and even international interest as to the fate of Marlow and her sister. The prosecution is not going to be rash or take any of this lightly. If or when they go after her, they have to be sure.

[Studio]

JODI LEE: Marlow?

MARLOW FIN: What do I think happened to Isla . . .

JODI LEE: You say that we don't know if she is alive or dead. But you were the last one to see her. It begs the question—what do you think happened to your sister?

MARLOW FIN: I wish . . .

[Pause]

JODI LEE: What is it that you wish?

MARLOW FIN: I wish I could call her. Without thinking twice, just pick up the phone and call her and know she'll answer. And tell me everything is okay. That's what I wish.

But in my heart, I know that this is the reality. This is the truth. Something terrible happened to my sister.

And I want to find out the truth as much as everyone else does. I think people forget that she is my sister. She is my family. She isn't some face in the news. I keep my feelings and emotions close to my heart. I always have because I don't feel the whole world deserves to see every part of me.

But I want to find out what happened to my sister. I want— *[voice breaks]*

JODI LEE: I see tears. This is the first time we've seen real emotion from you.

MARLOW FIN: *[Nods]* Yes.

JODI LEE: I hate to sound so crass. But I know there are people out there who are probably thinking, okay—we got some tears. But so what? She's an actress. A terrific one, award winning. Why should anyone believe these tears?

MARLOW FIN: Frankly, I don't give a shit if anyone does or not. Does it matter? Whether anyone else believes me? That won't bring her back. That won't reveal the truth.

[*Swipes at eyes*]

This is not the first time someone I love has disappeared on me.

JODI LEE: It's not? Who else has disappeared from your life?

MARLOW: My mother. My real mother.

CHAPTER 30

ISLA

2005

Oliver nervously tapped the table and flapped the plastic diner menu. It was covered in foggy fingerprints, smeared ketchup, and some other unidentifiable sauce.

I hadn't seen him since his weekend visit to the dorms my first month on campus. He had opted to stay in the Twin Cities area at one of the technical schools. He had a talent with computers and didn't see the point in wasting time for four years listening to lectures on microeconomics or other topics he called "drivel and bullshit."

Bluey's was a diner in Henley, famous for its 1950s-style getup, jukeboxes, and milkshakes poured on glasses set atop the heads of its restaurant-goers. I had ordered a strawberry malt, secretly enjoying the old thrill I'd felt as a kid, while a waitress stood on a chair and poured it onto my head. One tiny splatter landed in my hair, and I licked it off.

"Oh God, the Henley fries. Remember those?"

"A little too spicy for me."

"But the gravy and the cheese." I practically squealed. "I'm getting too excited." I slapped my menu down. "So, tell me. What's new with Oliver?"

He swallowed and drummed the table again.

"Is this a nervous Oliver? I don't think I've seen this before."

He smiled weakly. "Well, there's always a first."

"Okay. I mentioned Henley fries and I didn't even get a peep. Seriously . . . what's wrong?"

His face had narrowed even more as he got older. Angular and elflike, he looked especially fragile when he pursed his lips.

"I . . . didn't you get my instant message the other night?"

"Oh—my screen froze. I had to reboot my computer and it was taking too long so I went to bed. The internet connection is the worst on my part of campus. Why . . . what did it say?"

He looked stricken, as if I had given him bad news.

"Oliver. You okay?" I asked softly.

"No. Yes. I will be," he said shaking his head in circles.

The truth was, I had an idea of what he wanted to say. But he deserved to speak when he wanted to. And how he wanted to.

"So . . . I haven't really dated yet. At school this fall."

"Neither have I." I sipped my malt.

"Right. But for me it isn't about girls."

He paused and stared at me, his eyes widened as if holding his breath.

"Has it ever been?"

He started to grin. "I think . . . you know what I'm getting at?"

"Oh, Oliver." I put my hand on his and squeezed tight. "You're my best friend. This isn't news to me. Nor does it have anything to do with just how weird I think you are."

He burst out laughing, throwing his head back and flashing his usual grin at me.

His relief soothed us both in that moment. Yet the idea that he doubted my reaction even a little made my heart ache.

We arrived back at the house to find Marlow packing for another trip, this time to Los Angeles.

Her life had become a whirlwind, a tornado of change and triumph. The agent who signed her from the gallery photo was evidently a big name in the modeling world.

Oliver had the same unbridled enthusiasm for this news as I had for Henley fries. "He's huge, Isla. Like he's made some of the household names. Cindy Crawford. Linda Evangelista. Kate Moss . . . Gisele!"

Two months after signing, Marlow was flown to New York City for a photo shoot with *Seventeen* magazine. Her pictures were so impressive, the editor decided to use one of them for the June cover. It was bizarre seeing her face, an apple-pie teenage smile plastered across her mouth, staring back at me from the newsstand near the checkout aisle when I went with Moni to get the carrots Mom forgot.

Dad had bought ten copies and brought them home, tucked under his arm, and then fanned them on the kitchen counter. Mom flipped the chicken breasts on the stove and said nothing. Her eyes avoided the covers, as if she'd be looking directly in the sun if she did.

Marlow plucked up one of the magazines and held it, jumping up and down with delight. She stopped to run her fingers over the glossy cover and gazed at her image, as though she were looking at her own face for the first time, in awe, foreign to every facet of it. Was this really her? Did she really look like this?

She stood in front of her closet, legs spread out and hands on her hips, posing before pulling out a high stack of camisoles, all various shades of beige.

"How many camisoles do you really need?" I asked, running my hands along the sides of them.

"At the go-sees, the clients like models looking minimal."

I raised my eyebrows. "Go-sees?"

"You know, when you go see a potential job, an audition? They want hair pulled back, little to no makeup."

Oliver peered at her face. "Are you even wearing makeup right now? I can never tell."

She playfully pushed his cheek away. "Ugh. I can smell the diner on you."

"How many weeks of school are you missing?"

"So far only one. We're trying to keep things on the weekends." She began to place some of her other clothing stacks in the suitcase. She looked at me out of the corner of her eye. "Sawyer home for fall break?"

His name made the corners of my heart ping.

I shrugged. "I doubt it. It's a long way just for a weekend."

"So you've talked to him?"

I nodded slowly. "Here and there."

We'd had merely two conversations over chat. They had been brief, transactional. A cordial fulfillment in making sure the other one was "okay" at college.

"Go get 'em, kiddo," Oliver said, holding his arms out to Marlow. She folded him in, towering over his small frame. She looked like the older sister coddling a younger brother.

"I'll try."

I could see her eyes shift to me. Waiting for me to make the same move, but I sat next to her suitcase and pulled the zipper up and down.

"I'll miss you, Isla," she said quietly over Oliver's shoulder. Her lips looked so round and pillowy. When she said the word *you*, they puffed out like the top of an apricot.

She left with Dad in the morning for the airport, an ungodly early flight. The house was quiet when I came down in my T-shirt and robe, the coffeepot still on from Dad hurriedly making a cup before they left. I poured myself one and sat in the living room and looked up to see Sawyer's window. I couldn't remember the last time I saw the light on, like a single pane of fire. High school was not that long ago, but moving away had pushed it into another lifetime.

I heard the slow, searing sound of tires and thought maybe Dad was already back. But instead, a car pulled in Ada's driveway. I didn't recognize it and then realized it was a white taxi.

He quickly climbed out and paid the driver through the window. I opened my mouth, as though if I said something he could hear me. My robe fell to my sides, and I reached down to pull it back tight over my body. When I looked back up, he had gone inside. The lights turned on, Ada likely greeting him.

I turned away from the window and went to the kitchen. I didn't like feeling like a voyeur to his life. Not with him. Dad returned and got ready to head to campus for a Saturday class. Moni came downstairs and shared a cinnamon roll with me before going out for her morning walk.

"Do you want me to go with you?"

I put my hand on her forearm. She looked especially small since I had gone away to college. I never realized how delicate she was until then.

"You think Moni is old lady?" She grinned and waved me off.

I folded my arms across my chest, watching her shuffle down to the sidewalk, her hands behind her back, a slight hunch.

I passed the morning reading a book in bed, pretending he hadn't returned home. The taxi wasn't real. Him getting out of it wasn't real.

Moni returned, asking what I wanted for lunch. If there was anything special she could cook for me. I told her anything she made would be special and she proceeded to boil water for *kalguksu*, a hot noodle soup. She handed me green onions and I washed them and began to chop.

"Oh," she said holding up a finger. "I see Ada on walk. She said she want talk with you."

I paused with the knife in my hand. "Ada?"

"Yes. She stop me on way in."

"Are you sure that's what she wanted? For me to go to her?"

"Yes. Now don't cut piece so small." She fluttered her hand over the cutting board.

I remember burning my mouth on the noodles, not letting them cool as I hurriedly ate lunch. I heard Moni mutter under her breath with a *tsk tsk tsk*, saying I ate too fast for a woman. I helped clean up after and threw a sweater and coat on.

When I knocked on the door, Ada answered looking weary. Like she hadn't slept since I last saw her.

"Ada . . . Moni told me—"

She bobbed her head. "Yes. Yes. Come in, darling."

I followed her inside to find the house empty.

"Sawyer is back home. I don't know if you knew."

"I saw a taxi this morning. I assumed he was here to see you for fall break."

She rubbed the back of her neck. "He wasn't supposed to come back."

"Oh . . . then why—"

"His father died, Isla."

In that moment, I realized I forgot he ever had a father. That the thin man in the red truck all those years ago ever existed, that he was the man who should have been here for him to call Dad.

"He got the phone call from some idiot distant cousin back in Helena two days ago. It should have been me to tell him. That bastard basically drank himself to death. He was a sorry excuse, but he still was his father."

I could only shake my head.

Sawyer. Where are you?

Ada rocked on her heels. "Well . . . he came home after he heard. I don't know why or what good that was going to do. But I suppose he felt like he couldn't stay where he was. I talked to him for a little bit when he walked in. And then he just . . . took off."

"Took off?"

"That's why I told your grandmother to send you over here. I know you probably have a better idea of where he ran off to than I ever could."

"But—"

"I have to cover an overnight shift at the factory soon. He's nearly a grown man so I'm not worried but then again—I am. You know what I mean, dear?"

"Yes."

"Try to see if you can spot him." She paused and smiled warmly. "It sure is good to see you, though."

I didn't have to stop and think it over. There were no phone calls to be made. No car needed to drive around in a search. I knew where he would be.

I knew him better than myself.

Our field was stiff with long grass and dried leaves. He looked so tall, his back to me, hands in his pockets. The edges of his ears were reddened from the cold fall air. I wanted to reach out and cover them with my hands, shelter them.

"Sawyer," I said.

He didn't turn around, not right away. He seemed to be waiting for something. When he finally did, he looked at me with lost eyes. It made the surface of my skin ache.

"Ada send you?"

"Sort of. Why didn't you come over? I heard . . ." I looked down at the ground. I didn't want to see any more pain.

"Yeah. All these years and he's gone. Just like that."

"I'm so sorry, Sawyer."

He shook his head. "Nothing to be sorry about. He was never there."

He dug his boot into the grass. "God. Remember how much time we spent here, the three of us? I bet it was hours and hours. Just staring up. Not caring about anything else . . ."

I stepped closer. "I know he wasn't around for you." I spoke carefully. "But he was your father. It must hurt."

"You know," he started to say.

It was right then I could see the glisten in his eyes.

"Had I walked past him going down the street, I doubt he would have recognized me. Maybe I wouldn't have recognized him . . ." He shook his head and heaved a sigh. "He was a lousy father to me. I could handle that. I had to, there was no choice. But to my mother . . ."

"It's okay to be upset. Sawyer—"

"Did you know he went out with his friends? The night she died?" his voice wavered. "He left me alone with her. She was the sickest she had ever been. Instead of being with us, he went to the bar."

I closed my eyes and put my hands on his shoulders.

"I was a little boy. I was left alone to watch my mother die."

His lower jaw trembled and he turned away, pressing both hands to his temples. His elbows jutted out and he nearly growled.

"I hated him for that."

He threw his arms down and I let him just breathe. We stood in silence, listening to the swallows as they dived in and out of the trees.

"When I found out he was gone, I didn't expect to feel anything. I didn't want to give him that. He wasn't owed anything else from me."

The tension in his face softened, and his wet eyes grew clear.

"And then I thought of you."

His hand reached out and touched the ends of my hair.

"I didn't want anyone else but you."

When he bent down toward me, our mouths went warm and soft. I let him pull my head in, his fingers digging in gently. I tucked so perfectly under him as we wrapped around each other, pulling one another in more and more.

He watched me later in his room as I pulled the sweater over my head. I had never felt someone's eyes look over my body with such wonder. I felt his hands run over my skin and I remember holding my breath when he slid on top of me. His head burrowed in my neck.

"Isla," he said just once.

We closed our eyes together and, in the morning, I pulled the blanket up tight to my chin. I looked over to find him gone.

CHAPTER 31

ISLA

2006

It always begins with a phone call.

When the ordinary suddenly seems such a precious gift, you would willingly have a hundred of those moments over anything past that phone call.

I was in a bathrobe when I got the phone call. Fresh out of a college dorm shower, my feet in flip-flops a size too big for me. The landline in my room rang. I hadn't gotten a single call from that phone until then. Only my parents had that number. *You know, in case of an emergency,* I had said, jotting it down for them.

In case of an emergency.

"Isla?" Dad's voice asked. A question that made no sense.

"Yes?"

"It's Dad."

"What's wrong?" I immediately asked.

He paused, which made it worse. I wish he had spit it out, like a spoonful of soup that was too hot.

"Dad. What happened? Is it Marlow?"

"No."

"Then what?"

He sounded so shaky, even in the few words he'd spoken. I wanted to hang up on him. I wanted to mute his fragility and the way it made the bottom of my throat expand and tighten.

"It's Moni."

"Where is she?" I asked.

"Huh?" He was taken off guard.

"Where did they take her?"

Dad didn't answer right away. When he did, I felt a slight hope, even relief. "The hospital. ICU."

At least she wasn't gone. At least she was still in a place where work could be done.

"Why?"

"She had a massive heart attack, Isla. Mom found her this morning in the bathroom."

"Is she going to be okay?"

I hung up. I couldn't listen to my father cry like that.

She remained in the ICU for two more days. Dad would call me with updates, asking me if I wanted to drive down and see her. Telling me he would come get me if I was too upset to drive.

I went to my classes, took vigorous notes, and even ate meals regularly. I had a sudden, voracious appetite. The more terrified I was at the thought of seeing her, the hungrier I became. I went to the dining hall and made two waffles for breakfast, stuffing large bites in while the syrup dripped down the sides of my mouth. Was I crying yet? I couldn't feel any wetness. Just the syrup. I slid my fingers down my cheeks and rubbed them together with disappointing stickiness. Where were the tears?

Dad called again.

"Isla . . . honey. I know it's hard, believe me. I don't know how"—his voice cracked—"but she would want you here."

I left the dorms and sat in my car. I put the keys in the ignition and then put my head back. Every time I closed my eyes, I pictured her covered in tubes. Puffy from the IV fluids. The mechanical sounds all around her, the cyclic beeps that dehumanized her. I couldn't see her like that. I wanted to see her how I last saw her. Holding my hand, her palm soft and smooth, head bent down at her church. She had insisted I go with her before I went back for the semester. The pastor had said a prayer, but I wasn't listening at all to it. I was listening to her steady breathing, louder than I remembered it being but still gentle. Her light-pink dress suit made her look angelic, youthful. My hand rested in hers and she let it stay there.

I let the tears slide down, a warm relief. As if she had forgiven me with each one that hit my upper lip, a salty blip. When I returned to my room, the phone rang.

"She's . . . she's starting to pull through. I don't want to get your hopes up but—the doctors say she may have turned a corner."

I didn't have to see Dad's face. I knew he was smiling.

CHAPTER 32

ISLA

2006

Marlow clapped her hands with delight as she blew the candles out. For a second, I saw her as a little girl, the pleasing eagerness all over again.

The smoke circled my nostrils and made me hungrier for the cheap, chocolate grocery store cake.

"It's not my birthday, though," she said, tapping both hands over her cheeks.

"We celebrate you," chimed Moni.

I slid the knife over the thick blue-and-white frosting, cutting into the "G" in "Good Luck Marlow!"

It was her last night at home. She was moving to Europe for the summer. The *Vogue* cover in January had made history; she was the youngest American ever to grace it. She was the epitome of a natural beauty. The photo chosen for the cover was a close-up of her face, hair brushed across her forehead, hand loosely curled under her chin. There was nothing else for her to lean on in the photo. No heavy makeup, couture outfit, or jewelry. Only her presence could tell the story. She was completely isolated in it, a lone figure who invited herself inside everyone who cast their eyes on her.

The five of us sat around the table, each with a spongy, dark piece of cake, the sugar thick in the back of our throats. With her gone, the outline of our family, the rope that had encircled us, would be breaking.

Dad did his fatherly rites and hugged her, wished her well, telling her how proud she had made all of us. I watched Mom do the same, but hers was rigid and obligatory. She looked so . . . relieved that she was going to be out of sight for a while, a reprieve from the tension she carried in her forehead whenever Marlow entered the room.

Moni pulled Marlow aside and put her hands on her face. She whispered in Korean, as Marlow nodded. They embraced and Marlow's lip quivered.

She was not the same Moni. Not the one we had before the heart attack back in March. This one was fainter, her edges no longer sharp and quick. She conserved herself for the essentials and did not cook as often. She had survived but she had been replaced. Death was too strong of a word but, in a way, there had been one. A small loss that each one of us felt.

A week after Moni had started to recover in the ICU, I got an email from Sawyer. It was the first time he had made any sort of communication with me since that night. I felt numb when I saw the email appear in my inbox. I placed the cursor over it, ready to delete it. Whatever he had to say would not be enough.

But I read it.

Isla,

I heard from Ada about Moni. I'm so sorry. I hope she is getting better every day. Please know that she and your family are in my prayers. I hope you are okay considering. I don't know what else to write. I'm sorry.

I'm sorry.

When I had finished reading it once, I deleted it. I didn't want to read it over and over again. I didn't want to agonize over every word, wondering if he had agonized as much over writing each one. *I'm sorry. I'm sorry.* He had written it twice. Was one for Moni and one for me? Was I owed more than that?

I spent the rest of the semester keeping my head in my art history textbooks, studying slides with intensity—the glazed pigments of Botticelli and the dead yet smug eyes of Jan van Eyck's subjects. I was deep in everything fifteenth-century art and wanted nothing to do with the edged words of his email.

Oliver brought a joint one weekend. I took it without hesitation, burning my throat and coughing from the excess. Sometime after, I heard Oliver say something about Sawyer, how he had started seeing some Cal Tech girl. I took another hit, my head and body agile as I swung my arms to the music and tossed my head. I felt the tongue of my RA, who I had been friendly with, his mouth forceful. My head suddenly throbbed and I sat up quickly. Oliver ran after me, patting my back and saying something about how he thought the guy was a creep. The next day, the RA asked me if I wanted to go get something to eat sometime.

We went to a movie after meeting up a few times. Once for coffee, the other for sandwiches. We sat in the back of the second-run theater, where tickets were half off. He was deeply engrossed in Angelina Jolie as we watched her and Ethan Hawke in a car chase scene in *Taking Lives*. I went to go get extra butter for the popcorn. I watched as the yellow liquid oozed over the kernels, dissolving the ones at the top.

There were a few more dates after that. He slept over a couple times and then the semester was over. We had each other's numbers and he called me once. He texted a week after I was home for the summer. I didn't respond. I never saw the RA again; he dropped out that fall.

I got a summer internship at a gallery in Saint Paul thanks to one of Dad's colleagues in the fine arts department. When I wasn't there, I was spending as much time with Moni as I could. Helping her water her plants and holding her arm as we went on her daily walk.

I sat on the front porch one afternoon in early August. I thought about whether I wanted to stay in the dorms or move to my own apartment. I sipped on an iced tea, the outside of the glass getting slippery from the humidity. I wiped my hand on my shorts when he appeared across the street. I didn't know when he had gotten home or why he was here.

He asked to see Moni and I let him go inside. A half hour passed and then he came back out.

"She looks . . . better than I thought. I don't know if that's a good thing. But, well . . ." He sat down next to me.

"Isla."

He said my name like it hurt. Like a question.

I looked across at Ada's house. The siding was starting to fade, the wood splinters visible even from where I sat.

"Moni told me you got a great internship. I'm happy for you."

I nodded. "She always thought you were such a nice boy." I set my glass on the concrete.

"Yeah . . . so did I."

I felt him start to lean forward to get up, but he settled back down.

"I wanted to say so much that night, Isla. I really did. But it never came out. And then I looked over at you and you looked so . . . so right. I couldn't disturb it. I—"

"I heard you're with someone out west. Cal Tech, was it?"

My words stuffed all of his back into the bottle. He slid his hands over the porch step and stood up.

"She's studying to be a chemical engineer. Smarter than me." He let out a laugh that had no verve behind it.

"I doubt it. You're pretty damn smart, Sawyer."

He gently pounded a fist in his hand. "You've always been a part of my life, Isla."

"I know." I turned away. "I know." I couldn't face him anymore.

He walked back across the street. Somehow, with the way the back of his head curved, his outline bending, he was a stranger to me.

CHAPTER 33

WREN

1980s

Tonight, their windows glowed like fire, as if a torch had been lit and every move was on fully ignited display.

The weekly class had grown too meager for Wren.

She spent most evenings waiting for the world to settle down. To go quiet and dark so she could observe them hidden in the shadows, each of their windows a different television show for her to watch.

Some nights, the wife would be away. Perhaps out on a business trip. Or he would be absent, an obligation with the university. But tonight—tonight they were together.

They ate quietly this time. There was no banter, or heads thrown back with laughter, a glass of wine in hand. He seemed disinterested and read the paper. She barely touched her plate and got up by herself. There was no fighting. But it seemed worse. It seemed to Wren that someone had dimmed their shared brightness.

She kept her eyes on the wife as she went up the stairs and then saw her reappear in the bedroom. She sat at her vanity and didn't move until finally reaching up with her hand, tracing her throat and then placing her head down. Her back heaved up and down as if she were crying. But Wren wasn't certain. She wanted to be there, in that room, to know for sure.

She needed more.

The lecture hall was sparse the next morning. Many of the students had ditched to leave early for Thanksgiving break. She felt exposed and kept her head lower than usual. Patrick seemed less enthused as he went through the motions and followed the syllabus. There was no spark behind his remarks. He was drone-like and disinterested. As soon as the class was over, he hurriedly packed up and made his way to the exit. She had barely gotten up from her seat. She rushed out, bumping into a few other students, and dropped her pencil. She didn't bother to retrieve it. Scrambling, she burst out the doors to the steps and found him already striding across the quad, dead leaves spraying left and right.

She trailed behind closer than she usually did, afraid of losing him again. He entered a campus coffee shop.

His wife was waiting in a window seat. She looked weak. Neither of them got anything to drink. They stared at their hands and then out the window. Their mouths moved a few times. She couldn't make out any words. He got up and left, his face taut, eyes narrowed.

Wren let him walk away. She didn't want to see him like that. She stood still and watched him until he turned the corner of the building and was out of sight. The wind picked up, but she didn't care to move. She wondered if he would come back, try to make whatever had happened with his wife better. Restored. She needed them to be right again.

"Excuse me," a quiet voice spoke near her ear.

She was slow to turn around. There was no reason for anyone on this campus to talk to her. At first, she thought it was a mistake. Someone else was being called upon.

"I'm sorry to bother you but . . ."

She turned around and could see the redness around her eyes—a confirmation of what she had speculated the night before. Those were the eyes of someone who had done more than their fair share of crying.

"Can I ask you something?"

Wren stumbled back once. She felt as though she were an escaped prisoner who had finally been caught on the outside. The midday light was suddenly so bright and harsh, she nearly placed her arms up to shield herself from it.

"I need to go," she said.

She began to run but the woman called after her. "Wait, please! Don't go."

Her mind stopped before her body. What would be the point of running? She had been caught. She would have to face them regardless. Admit to her shameless obsessions. She exhaled and turned back. The woman looked relieved.

Wren opened her mouth to explain herself. Apologize. But her voice had turned into a rusted wheel that wouldn't turn.

The woman stared at her as if she were seeing a painting up close for the very first time. She slowly smiled. It was sad.

"My name is Stella. And I have something to offer you . . . if you're willing to listen."

CHAPTER 34
THE INTERVIEW

2021

[Studio]

JODI LEE: Are you saying, Marlow, that you remember your real mother?

MARLOW FIN: [*Takes a deep breath*] I don't know if remember is the right word for it. It's more like . . . like I can sense her. You know how they say a newborn recognizes the smell of his mother? It's like that. I just recognize something.

She left an imprint on me that can never be taken away. She existed at some point . . . she had to have. Even though I was abandoned, I am still her daughter.

JODI LEE: Do you ever think about your real mother?

MARLOW FIN: All the time.

JODI LEE: What about her?

MARLOW FIN: What she probably looked like. If she has the same mannerisms as me. If I would recognize her if I saw her walking down the street. There have been times I've seen a woman who looks like what I've pictured, and I have to keep myself from stopping her.

JODI LEE: And does it stir up any memory of her? These visualizations?

MARLOW FIN: I started to hear a voice. Someone saying "baby, baby, baby." It repeats in my head like a mantra. I don't recognize the voice, but it sounds very comforting in my head. Like she's telling me everything is going to be okay.

I know it sounds like I'm nuts. Jesus, she says she hears voices, right? But it's singular. Repetitive. At a subconscious level. It really tripped me up when I was modeling overseas. I mean, I did think I was going crazy at the time. I was using pretty hardcore. No, that's not true—very hardcore is more accurate. I didn't want to admit to anyone that I was lonely.

JODI LEE: Why? You were well into your career by then, right? Why did you feel lonely?

MARLOW FIN: You have so much constant attention on you, people literally swarming around you, touching your hair, your face, strangers seeing you naked as you change between locations. It's a bee-hive you can't get out of. Even with all of that right in your face, you feel like you are completely and utterly alone in a room. Who actually gets you? Who actually gives a damn about you?

JODI LEE: I think plenty of people did, Marlow, and still do. Yours was a face that couldn't be shown enough. You were on top of the world.

MARLOW FIN: Was I, though?

I must have been that spun out because my agent sent me to this hypnotist in Sweden. She took me deep. Like deeper than I thought I could ever go. And that voice? It became clearer. Everything became clearer.

JODI LEE: But yet it all still remains a mystery. The origins of Marlow Fin.

MARLOW FIN: [*Closes eyes for a moment, breathing in*]

JODI LEE: Are you all right?

MARLOW: Mmm-hmm.

JODI LEE: What would you do, then, if you were ever able to uncover that mystery?

MARLOW FIN: What mystery?

JODI LEE: The mystery of how the little girl ended up all alone in the woods.

MARLOW FIN: [*Smiles*] We'll have to wait and see, I guess.

JODI LEE: And the mystery of your sister, Isla . . .

MARLOW FIN: [*Shakes head*] You know what I don't get, Jodi?

JODI LEE: What is that?

MARLOW FIN: There has been so much attention and focus on me. What was I doing before that night? What did I do while I was there at the cabin? What happened the next morning? The scrutiny is real.

But what about Isla? Where is she? Has anyone seen my sister?

JODI LEE: We all want to know the answer to that, too, Marlow.

MARLOW FIN: And here's the other thing. What about questioning other people besides me?

JODI LEE: Meaning?

MARLOW FIN: We're forgetting I wasn't the only person with Isla. Why isn't everyone questioning the one other person who was there that night?

CHAPTER 35

ISLA

2010

"They've invited everyone on their list. All their top models. Movie producers and directors. I heard even Leonardo DiCaprio," Marlow had gushed into the phone.

She had just turned twenty-one, and her agency was throwing her a huge birthday bash in New York City. She had called me at work immediately when she got the news.

"Isn't that like his thing? To date models?" I had asked earnestly.

She laughed. "I miss you, Isla."

Her party was set for that Friday night. I was at work. I had secured a position as assistant to a gallery owner in downtown Minneapolis, which really meant a glorified internship, finding myself most days cleaning the office and stuffing envelopes.

It was late as I locked up the gallery. She pulled up in a gaudy silver Mercedes, honked, and rolled her window down. She wore a Bohemian circlet; a row of tiny, beaded white flowers danced across her forehead. Her hair was straightened, so long that it almost went to her waist.

"What—what are you doing here, Marlow?" I asked with more suspicion than surprise.

"Celebrating my birthday. Bought myself something." She rubbed the steering wheel and grinned widely.

"You're supposed to be in New York City! They probably spent a lot of money setting up that party, Marlow."

"Do you really think I wanted to celebrate it that way?"

"Let me think . . . yes!" I looked around as if my response deserved a larger audience.

"Screw it. They're doing it for them, not me."

"Marlow . . ."

"Ugh." She threw her head back. The circlet slipped down and then came back up again. "Get in."

She tossed a black dress over the car console at me as I got in.

She insisted that I change into the dress she got for me. It would have looked better on her. She was all lines that visually pleased, and I was all ones that didn't. But I was leaner then, by my standards, and she made me feel like I could own it.

That was the thing about Marlow. She could do that to you in a second, her focus so concise. Her path could only be in line to you, barreling hard and fast. There was no time to breathe or think when she wanted it. An unaffected watchfulness. She was unpolluted, unmanufactured with every sleight of hand.

She was beyond the realm of control.

I sat back that night, as if I were placed in an amusement park ride, putting my hands up and never opening my eyes.

At first, she drove to an obscenely expensive restaurant. She looked down at the embossed menu and back up at me and stood up. Not because she couldn't afford it but because it was decidedly beneath her. We picked up pizzas instead, plus a case of expensive champagne, and camped in a penthouse suite downtown. I remember watching her devour each slice with such abandonment as the champagne fizzed in my mouth. I spit it out when we laughed so hard we doubled over with tears.

We washed our faces before we settled under the sprawling white comforter. I always thought she looked the most beautiful when she had nothing else on her face. The freckles scattered across her nose made her look untouched.

Her hand reached out to me under the covers and then traced the outline of my face.

"I love this face."

"Why? Isn't it your face everyone adores?"

"No."

"Shut up, Marlow," I said, then laughed.

She squeezed my shoulder. "Thank you. Thank you," she whispered.

"For what?"

When I woke up, she had already left for the airport. The next time I saw her was on the cover of that summer's *Vogue* issue. Back when I could look at her face with admiration rather than the noxious pain that would form behind my eyes.

When I could look at her without tightening my hands. When she hadn't taken everything from me.

CHAPTER 36

ISLA

2010

"Can you please switch out number four with number three? I think the lighting is much better in that corner for it."

I stood back and watched as the short guy with a long ponytail from the setup crew quickly switched the two paintings.

"Shit. That looks worse. Sorry. Can you please switch it back?"

I gritted and bared my teeth apologetically. He shrugged and obliged.

"Thank you . . . okay. I think that's it. Yes, we're done."

It had been about a year since I had started as an assistant to the downtown gallery owner, and she finally entrusted me with curating a show. Not just any show, but a Saturday evening one featuring her newest client, an up-and-coming encaustic painter who experimented with mixed media. I actually loved her work, and making sure it presented well gave me both a thrill and nervousness that the job had yet to bring out in me.

I went into the bathroom and hung up the garment bag with the black dress Marlow had given me a few months back, when she ditched her agency birthday bash. I smoothed the front and leaned forward in the mirror to apply a dark coral lipstick.

A few hours later, the show was winding down. I finally allowed myself a glass of champagne, too nervous earlier to want anything that would inhibit my ability to answer anyone's questions. The owner gave me a thumbs-up down by her waist and winked. I felt my shoulders release. It must have been a good sales night. I let the bubbles settle on my tongue and took another sip, this one longer.

My black heel bounced off a stagnant foot.

"I'm so sorry," I said without really looking up. I had dribbled a little down my chin. I swiped at it with my free hand.

"Are you?" he asked.

I hadn't seen him since that afternoon on our porch. I had heard how he was doing through bits of information that floated in and out around me to form some sort of a story. He had graduated a semester early and stayed out in California. At some point, he joined an architecture firm in San Diego. I sometimes wondered if he was still with that other girl, the two of them going to the beach together, him touching her hair like he did mine.

He had no tan like I'd always imagined he would. A light stubble covered the lower half of his face, making him look distinguished, professional. It felt like he was playing a part, that this couldn't possibly be the boy from my childhood.

"You're taller," was all I could muster.

"Yes."

His mouth twitched upward. I had already amused him.

"Why are you even—"

"I moved back. I wanted to be closer to Ada. She's not as young as she once was, you know."

"Really? That red hair could have fooled me."

"She dyed it blue recently. I've been back a few weeks. I started at a firm not too far from here, actually."

He looked over his shoulder as if he could see it from there, and then all around the gallery.

"This is . . ."

I put my hand up, waiting for it. "Amazing? Awe-inspiring? The most spectacular art show you've ever seen?"

"No. I wouldn't say that," he said, still contemplating each piece.

"Sawyer!"

I nearly rolled my eyes. How quickly it felt like old times. How quickly my heart was beginning to slip into place.

He looked back at me and stared with glowing eyes. "It's exactly how it should be."

I swallowed and felt my nostrils flare.

"It's you . . . I see you in it," he said.

I wasn't going to pretend. I wasn't going to hide away from the immediate burn that coursed through my chest when he said those words.

I smiled and held his gaze. I held up my glass. "Well . . . thank you."

He took my hand, and I don't remember when he let it go.

We met for lunches downtown over the next week near his office. Sushi one day and then hot dogs from a stand another as we sat outside in the early spring sun. He was careful with me, as if I were an icicle in his hand that had to be preserved, and he kept everything light whenever possible. He began to spend time at my condo, making dinners and failing miserably because neither of us bothered to actually pay attention. We could only focus on each other. We laughed about the ridiculous things we did as children all those summers, quiet when we realized it would never be that way again. That those days had passed, locked and sealed from us. We'd never touch them again.

We were no longer children.

But we had that summer to become something else. There was no greater time in my life. No other series of moments, no cherished slide-show, that could compare to the bliss he gave me. I felt every line, dent, and shape of his lips when he kissed me. He pulled me close with such urgency, his nose burrowed into me and clinging hard, a deeper demand this time. He was a man sure of what he needed. The reassurances that we thought were lost came back to us. We sank into each other that summer, two stones in the water that fell into the same current.

In the mornings, we would lie next to each other. Staring at the other's fingers, hands, and limbs, as if each of us had been born just then, new and unexamined. His hands ran over me with such fascination while I fluttered under him, sometimes having to catch my breath from it all.

We drove up to the North Shore for a weekend. The cabin seemed so different with him next to me. The rooms were brighter and the windows so clear, there was no barrier between us and the lake. He followed me as I led him through the woods, showing him my favorite paths. In the evening, I lay on him, my arms sprawled up as we felt the heat of the fire. We read and fell asleep in the afternoon. I woke up and traced his jaw and then took his hand. He followed me, the sun rushing down over the water, hurrying to escape. I dived in without any clothes and he was there next to me, wrapping around me as I held on to the dock. The water lapped under our chins, and I came. He carried me back. We were both so cold and yet there was nothing to complain about. Nothing to be afraid of. Nothing to taunt us.

The summer ended. I looked up to see it was raining. I caught the drops in my mouth as he whispered in my ear once more. *Marry me.*

This is where I should have said *the end*.

Where it should have ended.

CHAPTER 37

ISLA

2012

She returned to us as lovely as ever, a woman who carried herself with an impossible height of finesse. Her career was equally at new heights—the "it girl," as they called her. Every magazine cover was her, the hot new movie role was her, the giant billboard in Times Square was her.

Her.

Yet the shadows under her eyes, expertly concealed with makeup—she had worked with the best of the best in the world, of course—were discernible only by me. A perfect eggshell, smooth and unblemished, had now the smallest of fissures. She attempted to look as lively as possible while telling her stories to us, her mouth always shaped upward like a stenciled crescent moon, but she would look so tired in between these forced energetic charades.

She held me close and told me she was so happy for me and Sawyer, and then smoothed the sides of my hair.

"Thank you," was all I could say, as though she had offered to pass me a basket of rolls at the table.

I then asked her to be my maid of honor.

"Oh, Isla. I am so . . ." She couldn't finish, her eyes welled, and she held me again. "You are going to make the most beautiful bride."

I knew that wasn't the case. *She* would be the most beautiful bride the world had ever seen, should she ever make that leap. And I wasn't envious of that. I wanted to set it straight in my head, like a fact in a history book.

"I have so many designer connections. Monique Lhuillier is a friend of mine. And I know the head designer at Amsale. We hit up a few parties together during Paris Fashion Week. Please. Let me help you select your dress," she chattered.

I nodded, as if agreeing with her, but smiled dryly.

"I don't know if it's going to be that kind of wedding, Marlow . . . but that's very kind of you. We're going to keep it simple. The wedding is going to be here, probably. Remember that field we used to play in all the time?"

She clasped her hands together. "Yes. Our field. That's going to be stunning with all the fall colors."

Was it her field too?

"Right. We might have the ceremony there. It's going to be small. Close family and friends."

She suddenly looked exhausted. Like a toddler who needed her afternoon nap.

"You know what this means?" she asked as her eyes looked at me vacantly.

"What?"

"Sawyer is finally going to be my brother. Officially, that is."

She insisted on celebrating that night. I refused to call it a bachelorette party even though she did.

"We have to have a last hurrah."

I was somewhat swayed at this point, but I must have looked skeptical.

"After the wedding you will be all Sawyer's."

"It's a marriage. Not an ownership. I'm not a professional sports team," I smirked.

She tilted her head with solemnity. "No, but you will belong to each other. Just give me this last night."

I agreed to a dinner and then a night in at my condo. She was reluctant about the tameness but gave in.

She behaved herself at dinner. We ordered a large sushi platter and a cocktail each. The cocktail wasn't enough for her, and I watched her ask for a vodka neat. And then another. And then another. She paid the bill and left for the bathroom only to return to the table bouncier, more fluid. I told her we didn't have to keep drinking, but really meant she didn't have to keep drinking. She ignored me and continued at my place. By then, she was slurring her words and wasn't even trying to hide the hits she was taking out of her purse.

It was only ten o'clock when she began to vomit. It crept out of the corner of her mouth like seedy mustard, and she struggled to get any water in. I pulled her hair to the side and looked away when she vomited again.

"It's the withdrawal," she explained, catching her breath.

"What?"

"I tried to cut back. But I couldn't . . . not this time. And so using hard again—" She heaved but held her composure this time, holding her hand up.

Jesus, Marlow.

I pinched at my brow, exhaling slowly. "Is there . . . anything I can do to help?"

"Just don't leave me," she whispered.

She fell asleep on my couch. When I went to cover her up, she slipped her hand onto my wrist.

"Isla. I'm sorry."

Her voice was steady. She had sobered up a little by then.

"You don't have to be sorry."

I sat next to her on the couch as she remained on her side.

"Yes. I do. I ruined your bachelorette party."

I tried smiling. "You didn't ruin it. I didn't want one to begin with, remember?"

She seemed grateful for my carefully crafted response. But it was the truth. She really hadn't ruined anything. I stayed with her until she began to drift off. I shifted the couch as I stood up, and she stirred. She turned to me.

"Isla. Everybody has a secret. Right?"

She sounded so young, her voice high and breathy. She was a few blinks from falling asleep, the relaxed dream state before slipping away.

"Yes. Everybody."

"If I had a secret, would you want to know?"

"There's probably a reason it's a secret. So, no."

"Don't you want to hear it?"

I tapped the silky top of her head. "Marlow . . . it's getting late. And you really should get some sleep."

"It's about them."

"Them?"

"Mom and Dad."

She looked scared and determined all at once and then turned away, shutting her eyes. Her breathing grew heavy and I wondered if she even knew what she had said.

Her mood shifted back to all vitality the following evening, when Sawyer and Ada came over for a special dinner cooked by Moni, an occasion that had gotten rarer. I saw her pull him aside. They laughed and tossed their heads back over stories from the past. She leaned in a few times and spoke in a low voice, practically a whisper. Her hand would touch his arm and he would nod to whatever she said.

I poured another glass of red wine and let it flood between my teeth as I watched them.

I had invited Oliver over for the dinner as well. He positioned his elbow out and rested it on my shoulder.

"You know he loves you like nothing I've ever seen, right?"

I stood up straighter and held my glass with both hands. "I know. That's why I'm marrying him."

Marlow giggled loudly. I took another sip.

We watched them for a moment before Oliver put his hand over his mouth and muffled a chuckle. "Did I ever tell you about the time when you got the flu? I think we were like, nine or ten? You had it pretty bad, remember?"

"Yeah—Dad said I was one temperature check away from going to the hospital. Why?" I said, my eyes keeping in place.

"Well, Sawyer . . . he was so worried about you. He made us ride our bikes all the way to the library. And he asked them to pull out all the medical reference books for him. As if he was going to find a way to help you. Can you believe it?"

I saw Sawyer stand up and then hug her.

"He was like that. He still is like that."

"You don't have to tell me this."

Oliver circled the rim of his wineglass with his finger. He squeezed my arm and then moved on, sitting next to Ada in the living room. I could hear him ask about when she was going to finally get a Harley, followed by her cackling and slapping his arm.

After everyone had gone for the night—the leftover food tucked away in containers, Marlow passed out upstairs in her old room—I held the knight in my hand and examined it. The etchings of the slit in the visor had faded; parts of the paint had chipped off. I slid it in the pocket of my cobalt-blue dress, the one Sawyer said made me irresistible. We sat in the backyard, his hands around my waist. I still trembled under his touch. There was something delirious about the firm paddings of his hands.

"You are something, Isla Baek," he said and then kissed my ear and cheek. "Are you sure you want to marry a guy like me?"

"A guy like you?" I mocked.

He laughed gently in my ear and then stroked the insides of my arms. I held both of my hands out in closed fists.

"Pick one."

"What?"

"Just pick one."

He settled me back in his lap and leaned forward. "Does this count as my wedding gift?"

I slugged his shoulder playfully. "*Pick* one."

He tapped my right hand. I opened it to reveal an empty palm.

"All right. The other, then."

I held up the knight figurine for him to see. He sat up straighter and then plucked it gently from me. He began to laugh. Softly at first, until it rolled into an uproar and a few tears trickled down.

"Where did you find this?" he asked in disbelief.

I leaned in closer, my forehead close to his. "Truth?"

"Yes, truth."

I told him about how I found it in the grass that day. The very first day, moment, minute we met. How I don't know what came over me, but I'd picked it up and kept it all these years.

"I have returned it now to its rightful owner."

He stared at it again and then pulled me in. "I'll always keep it here. That way you won't steal it from me again." He tucked it in his pocket. He kissed my neck and then mouth, longer and deeper. "I love it." He took my hand. "I love you, Isla."

We were married a few weeks later, our wedding day a glowing fall afternoon. He wore a navy suit and I a simple cream silk dress. I held a small bouquet of peach peonies and walked down our field to him. The tops of the tall grass swayed for us, and he bit the bottom of his lip when we joined hands and drank me in, as if he did not want the image of me to ever go away. I wondered if he would ever look that handsome again. I didn't want him to. I wanted to see him older. I wanted to be able to think back on him like this, how I was the lucky one.

After the ceremony, Moni came up to us both. She clutched both of our hands, feeling so strong right then, her knuckles smooth. She pulled us together and nodded.

"Have a good life together," she said in Korean and let go and turned away.

The reception was held in our backyard. We had transformed it with lights strung over the trees and bushes, a firepit in the middle. A few paparazzi had caught wind of Marlow returning home for her sister's wedding. They lingered outside in the street, waiting for a shot of her in a bridesmaid's dress.

But she was upstairs in her room again. Her morning had begun vibrantly, chitter-chattering around me as I got ready. She seemed to lose steam right before the ceremony, and I saw her throw back two glasses of champagne.

I didn't see her emerge until later in the evening when it was time for her toast. Her breath was stale and she smelled of cigarette smoke as she muttered something about how she had stepped on her dress and ripped it. I smiled at a few neighbor guests staring at her, and held her arm.

"Maybe we should go get some water?" I suggested.

She shook her head. "It's time for my speech."

"It's okay. We can do toasts later. There's no rush—"

"No. It's time."

She clapped her hands forcefully and stood in the middle of the yard. The hum of the wedding guests came to a halt. I spotted Sawyer across the lawn with Ada, who was seated in one of the white wooden folding chairs. He had taken his tie off by then, his jacket draped around Ada. I almost forgot about Marlow in that moment, as I could not have loved him more right then.

I looked up to Marlow, standing on a chair. Her heel slipped and I lurched forward to catch her but she regained her balance.

Mom and Dad stood with Moni near the makeshift bar we had created. I saw Mom grab ahold of Dad's elbow.

"Unbelievable," Marlow mumbled. She held her hands up. "It is unbelievable that two of my favorite people in the world are now man and wife . . . wait, is that sexist? Excuse me. Husband and wife. Or partners in life?"

She adjusted her bra and I wanted to close my eyes and make her disappear. Twitch my nose like Samantha from *Bewitched* and the reception could go on without her.

"I love my sister, Isla. She knows it. I hope."

Her words had become waves of slurred syllables and points of forced enunciation. She pointed to me. I couldn't do it. I couldn't feign a smile. I could only look back at her, hoping she would stop.

"I have a lot of high hopes for you two."

She crossed her arms and held out her index fingers, pointing at each of us.

"I hope that every day is better than the last. That there be more sex than fights!"

The guests laughed nervously, sympathetically. I hated that they were being polite; it made it all that much worse. I wanted to leave right then, rush across to Sawyer and tell him to take us out of here.

"But hell. We all know that isn't always the case . . . look at . . . look at the parents of the bride." She clapped her hands toward them. "Professor of linguistics? Or is it really professor of the student lay?"

She laughed hysterically and Mom bolted, charged Marlow like a linebacker, and threw her arm around her, swooping her down from the chair. I followed them inside.

Marlow continued to laugh, little bullets of heaving as she slid down the refrigerator door. Mom grabbed her by the shoulders and forced her up.

"What the hell is wrong with you," she growled, her face inches from Marlow's.

Dad forced her back. "She's not of sound mind right now, Stella. Let her sleep it off."

"No!" Mom shouted.

Marlow laughed harder.

"What's wrong, Mommy?" she asked. Her makeup had seeped under her eyes, and I had never seen her look so haggard.

"I am not your mother. I wish to hell we'd left you that night!"

I didn't have time to process her movements. Marlow lunged forward, a leap that startled every part of me, and reached for Mom's throat. Her hands looked like two metal cages, wide and snarling.

They met her throat and clung.

"Marlow!" Dad yelled.

He yanked her down and held her against him. She thrashed like a wild animal, and I wished she was a fire right then. A raging fire that I could douse with water.

Flashes blinded us from the window. Three men with cameras stood on their toes, frantically taking photos.

I looked over to the sliding glass doors. Moni leaned against them, her face so small, her hand to her mouth. She had turned into stone.

CHAPTER 38

ISLA

2014

I wish I could say time healed us. That we learned to forget all the slashing words and venom that soaked into us all. But that would be a lie.

Time seemed to only crush the pain in as if slabs of cement were stacked against us.

A year and a half went by with no sign of Marlow.

And then someone else left us.

Dad found her in the morning. She lay on the floor halfway between her bed and the bathroom. She must have tried to get up in the middle of the night and something gave. We suspected maybe another heart attack, but it didn't matter whether we ever knew. She was gone. And with her any of the last threads of decency our family had been holding on to—for her sake—had dissipated.

Young-Mi Baek. Omma. Halmoni.

Moni.

I wondered if she could hear my thoughts. If she was already somewhere trying to comfort me. Did she regret the life she had carried out in a place she never fully called home? One foot in soil that had made her but the other sunk in where she had grown her family? Did she regret giving her whole body, heart, and mind to her child? And to the children of that child? What remained was hardened skin and bones, tough from all the sacrifice. To her, living was sacrifice. But that right there held more worth—contained more significance in every part of her because of the way she lived—than anything else that could ever be created.

Did she know that? Should I have told her?

There are a million words and regrets after a loved one is gone. That is what makes them so dear. Lost to the ones who are left behind.

I liked to romanticize it all, pretend she already knew what I should have said to her. That every meal, dish, and bite I took from her hand was all that had to be said. But I didn't know if that really was the case. If that really was enough.

I placed my hands on her hard shell of a hand and kissed her cheek that had become a wall. I said goodbye and did what everyone is supposed to at a funeral. But it wasn't her. This was only an ornament in place of her.

I turned to look over my shoulder, hoping she was actually in one of the pews in the back, quietly sitting with her hands clasped, waiting for me to come sit next to her. A red ribbon marking her favorite hymnal, she would open it and point to the verse I should begin with.

Her friends from the Korean church moaned and cried lowly, a constant drone of angst. A few of them approached me and softly patted my hands. I put my head down and felt myself having a hard time breathing. Sawyer placed his arm around me; my head knocked into his shoulder.

After the burial there was a reception at our house. The kitchen smelled of weak coffee, and people milled around with plates of white cream cake. I found it so odd, as if it were a celebration. The waves of pain had started to die down inside me; my body could only take so much. At some point I had to feel nothing.

I poured myself a cup of coffee and looked over it to see a woman with red hair. She looked to be in her forties, the tops of her crisp, white collared shirt poking out of a black sweater. She looked so familiar.

Was she a former teacher? Maybe a buyer at one of the gallery shows? I followed her as she went around the corner to the living room. She went up to Dad and whispered something in his ear and he nodded, his face solemn.

She glanced up and caught me staring and looked away.

I had seen that look before. When she came out of his office. That same failure to see me. The embarrassment to look deeper into a little girl's eyes.

How dare you.

My fingers went tight on the white handle of my cup. Not because of the woman. But for him allowing her in our house. The place that really was only home when Moni was here. Such disrespect it reeked of toward Moni.

We had just buried her.

I couldn't bring myself to say anything to him. He didn't notice me standing there, my chest filling with sand. A fence had been implanted around my face and I couldn't see past it. The anger funneled down and away, spilling to someplace where it might not return to me. I didn't tell him how much he disgusted me.

Instead, I was short with everyone around me the week after. Sawyer got the brunt of it; nothing he did seemed to satisfy me. The kitchen was left too dirty, the laundry still wasn't folded. Domestic duties had swept our marriage out of the honeymoon phase. As I came home from work one evening, I snapped at him for not putting the dishes away like I had mentioned in the morning.

He said nothing. He put his hands on my shoulders as he walked past me and popped the dishwasher open. His patience only irritated me further. I didn't move as I heard the sounds of plates clattering and silverware being dropped into the drawer.

I should have apologized. But I didn't.

We lay next to each other in bed that night, reading, and he reached over and turned his light off, the sheet pulling with him. It was almost two years of being married, but the fairy tale was slightly fading. We were happy most days, but I could tell the fire we had carried together glowed less. The sex was still good but less frequent. He would come home from a long day at the office, wanting a good shower and bed. And I wouldn't contest it, needing the same thing.

I turned my light off and leaned on him, rubbing his chest. "I'm sorry. This has been a tough week for me."

He kept his eyes closed. "Isla, you don't have to be sorry. I know you. We just said goodbye to her. I don't expect you to be yourself."

I felt the need to bury myself even closer to him right then.

"Hey, hey, you're really squishing my chest." He chuckled.

I kissed him and settled back in.

Sometime in the middle of the night I woke up. A sensation of pressure in my throat had stirred me. I swallowed and then felt the tears go down my face into the pillow. My hair felt wet, and I lay there motionless, hands joined across my chest. I hadn't cried for her until then. That would make it all too real.

But it had happened. She was gone. And I cried.

I got up extra early and made Sawyer his favorite breakfast, a few over-easy eggs and some toast he could dip in the yolk. I sliced a few bites of cantaloupe and arranged them in a design on a plate. I loved watching him eat. His satisfied bites were everything that morning and it made me think of Moni. Was this how she thrived? Was I carrying on a part of her?

As swiftly as Marlow had come back home for the funeral and left, she was back again later that week. She had spent the previous year in rehab and had declared herself a new person. She had changed her look, cutting her hair into a clean, shoulder-length bob, dyed light, and wore natural-toned makeup. Part of her new persona included a budding music career. She had a show at a lounge downtown and had invited all of us to attend. The tickets were limited, and people in the Twin Cities were scrambling to get one—to see Marlow Fin sing live and in person. Mom and Dad declined their invitation . . . or was it just Mom?

Mom had said very little to her at the funeral. Acknowledging her but treating her like a distant family member she was required to be polite to. Marlow had no reaction to this, making me think rehab had perhaps been a good thing for her, that maybe she really had changed.

Sawyer and I arrived a little late; my meeting with the gallery's latest clients had run long. We ducked into a few chairs in the back of the lounge and ordered beers. She walked up onto the blue-lit stage. Her long, white jumper dress made her look like a Grecian column. She nodded to the acoustic guitarist and drummer behind her. The drummer tapped the hi-hat a few times and bobbed his head with the beat, cueing them. Simple chords came in and she braced herself to join, closing her eyes.

Her voice was weightless and clear. Like bells in a high tower.

It seemed unnatural that someone that beautiful could also produce something equally beautiful out of sound.

The room expanded with her singing, a slow and moody melody. The lounge seemed to become the size of an open amphitheater, and her presence pushed us all away. She was a tiny figurine that twirled on a pedestal and sang for us.

I leaned over to Sawyer to ask what he thought but stopped myself.

He was entranced, wearing a thrilled smile I hadn't seen cross his lips in some time. His hand went up to his chin and he fell forward, as if that would allow him to listen even better.

I moved my eyes back up to her, and she was singing to us. No, she wasn't looking at me. She was looking straight at him. I swore I detected a pleased smile as she took note of his deep enjoyment. Or could it have been because she thought he was proud of her?

Was it something else . . . a coy jab toward me?

I could never tell. I could never tell what Marlow wanted with me.

CHAPTER 39

THE INTERVIEW

2021

[Studio]

JODI LEE: The one other person who was there that night . . . are you referring to your father, Patrick Baek?

MARLOW FIN: Yes. Thank you.

JODI LEE: Your father was also brought in for questioning the following afternoon. He was located at his home in Henley and brought in for questioning. Not as a suspect, but as a person of interest.

[Roll package, footage of Patrick Baek leaving police station]

JODI LEE: Patrick Baek, the father of Marlow and Isla, was the only other member of the family present that Labor Day weekend. Earlier in the day he drove himself and Isla up to their lake cabin when they came across Marlow waiting for them. He described Marlow as acting strange. According to him, there were some verbal arguments in the evening. He left both women and decided to drive back home that night.

[Police video recording of Patrick Baek questioning]

SHERIFF VANDENBERG: Now Patrick, I know this is difficult. Isla is missing and I can understand you are a bit in shock.

PATRICK BAEK: That would be an understatement.

SHERIFF VANDENBERG: But can you tell me a little bit more about what happened right before you decided to leave?

PATRICK BAEK: Marlow had drunk a little too much after dinner. There was some arguing between her and Isla. I tried to step in and handle it. You know, do the dad thing and get them to calm down. But for some reason that made them get angry with me. So I knew we weren't going to get anywhere. I decided it was best for me to leave.

SHERIFF VANDENBERG: Was anyone else present at the cabin? Earlier throughout the day or in the evening?

PATRICK BAEK: No. It was just me and my two daughters.

SHERIFF VANDENBERG: But what about Isla? Weren't you her ride to the cabin?

PATRICK BAEK: I made sure she was okay with me leaving. That she could drive them down in Marlow's car in the morning. She was completely coherent. She was fine and reassured me . . . she . . .

SHERIFF VANDENBERG: Do you need a minute, Patrick?

PATRICK BAEK: No. No. Let's get this over with. I need to be with my wife.

SHERIFF VANDENBERG: Do you know what they were arguing about?

PATRICK BAEK: Sister stuff. Trivial stuff that really doesn't seem to matter now.

SHERIFF VANDENBERG: What time did you leave the cabin?

PATRICK BAEK: It was around midnight.

SHERIFF VANDENBERG: Did you stop anywhere on the drive back? Talk to anyone?

PATRICK BAEK: I stopped at a gas station in Pine City. It's a little over halfway back to the Twin Cities area. There's a Holiday Station there I frequent whenever I make trips to the cabin. I got gas, went inside to pay. I bought a coffee. The store clerk didn't say much, just thank you and have a good night.

SHERIFF VANDENBERG: And what time was this, would you say?

PATRICK BAEK: A little after three in the morning.

[Voice-over]

JODI LEE: The police were able to corroborate Patrick Baek's account of what happened after he left the cabin on the night of September 7, 2020. The credit card statement confirmed he did, in fact, stop at the Holiday Gas Station in Pine City, Minnesota. Security footage at the gas station was time-stamped, showing he was in the store at 3:23 a.m.

[Police video recording of Patrick Baek questioning]

SHERIFF VANDENBERG: Do you have anything to do with your daughter Isla's disappearance?

PATRICK BAEK: No. Absolutely not. I have nothing to do with the disappearance of my daughter. But why are we already calling it that, Vince? It hasn't been that long. What aren't you telling me?

SHERIFF VANDENBERG: I'll get to that, Patrick. I promise. But you haven't heard from her since last night? Had any contact with her?

PATRICK BAEK: No. Nothing. I've called her phone a million times. So has Stella. You have to tell me now, Vince. No one has told us. *[Voice shaking]* What did you find?

SHERIFF VANDENBERG: There was . . . there was some blood in the shed. That's all I can tell you at this time. But we will have it—

PATRICK BAEK: Oh Jesus . . . oh God. *[Gasps, starts to cry]*

SHERIFF VANDENBERG: I'm sorry, Patrick. To be the one to have to . . .

PATRICK BAEK: My little girl. *[Crying]*

[Studio]

JODI LEE: Did you ever watch the video of your father's questioning?

MARLOW FIN: Yes. Most of it, anyway.

JODI LEE: When you watched it, did you find his demeanor normal?

MARLOW FIN: As normal as someone can be in that scenario, I suppose.

JODI LEE: What about your demeanor? There has been some speculation that your behavior during your questioning was strange.

MARLOW FIN: Well, it was an interrogation. Not a questioning. I sat through a far longer ordeal than my father did. And why does everyone keep saying that . . . *strange*? What does that mean, anyway?

JODI LEE: Experts in the legal community and law enforcement say you behaved oddly after you were brought in, even for someone who had been through trauma. Slightly erratic even when answering questions.

MARLOW FIN: I was in shock over Isla. I still am.

JODI LEE: What do you miss most about her?

MARLOW FIN: I miss being sisters with her. That's what I miss.

JODI LEE: Do you believe you had a good relationship as sisters?

MARLOW FIN: Yes. I do. No relationship is ever perfect. But we had a really special bond.

JODI LEE: What about your other relationships?

MARLOW FIN: Such as?

JODI LEE: What was your relationship with Sawyer Ford?

CHAPTER 40

ISLA

2015

"Did you touch her?" I asked, my head down and my hands tucked under my legs.

"Isla."

"Did you touch her?"

"Nothing happened."

He tried to sit next to me on the bed, but his hands didn't bring any warmth with them as they felt for my shoulders. I stood up and went to our bedroom window and leaned against the frame. It felt juvenile despite the circumstances.

I hated that he was even saying those words to me. *Nothing happened.* An answer that required a question insinuating something had.

Six hours. It had been six hours since the photos were released online. The story hit the waves of tweets and retweets just in time for the evening news cycle. Every outlet was reporting on the photos. I let myself watch them as they came, the headlines and fodder, talking heads giving opinions about people they had never met. I was a child peeking between her fingers, looking at something she shouldn't be seeing.

My phone vibrated and glowed and I glanced to see her name, calling me again. I flipped it over on the windowsill.

"Please. Come talk to me," Sawyer pleaded.

"I can't. Not right now," I answered shakily.

My hand felt the smooth, white wooden surface.

A month ago, we had sanded and painted all the frames on the second level of our house. It was our first house. Small but every bit of what we needed for us. It was our "for now house." For now, until we needed a bigger place. For now, until we found our dream home. For now, until we decided to have a family . . . It was old and had an original kitchen sink from the 1930s, but Sawyer loved the old fixtures. The crystal doorknobs and crown moldings that were still in place from whatever family had first built it. He said he liked the idea of there being history, the feeling that others had lived there before us. I told him he was too hokey and then he laughed at me and drew me in.

"I love that it's ours. That's what I love the most," he said, kissing the top of my head.

We repainted the upstairs room a clean eggshell and then tackled the frames. Our bedroom was bright and vibrant, the daylight dreamy. When we finished sanding for the day, he made us a clam pasta dish.

"Where did you learn to make this?"

"Didn't I ever tell you I had a roommate out in California who was in culinary school?"

"Well, thank you, roommate!" I exclaimed, sucking in a salty and briny noodle.

The dishes were nearly empty, minus a few scattered shells, when he began to kiss my belly and nuzzle my breasts. I giggled, my hair sweaty and full of dust, and he sat me on his lap as we fucked slowly at first and then urgently. I breathed hard when we finished, and stayed on top of him, his head resting in the nape of my neck as I stroked his hair.

Afterward, he had sat in bed with his laptop. I felt myself drifting off, the sounds of the keyboard clacking away. I looked over and he closed his laptop suddenly.

"What was that?" I asked sleepily, making the question sound more innocent than it really was.

"What was what?" He set the laptop on his nightstand and reached for his water.

"That picture. I saw one when I looked over."

"Picture? I was drafting a proposal for work."

I thought I saw her. Her unnerving eyes looking at me for a split second. As if to taunt me from his screen.

Or maybe I had imagined it. There was no picture and some sick, tortured part of me wished there had been.

"Really?"

"Really."

He turned to his side.

"Well, can I see it, then?"

"What? Jesus, Isla. I'm tired. Can we please go to bed now?"

Maybe I was being irrational. Maybe he was really tired. But why couldn't he show it to me, appease the pestering wife? Isn't that what husbands were supposed to do?

I went to bed that night picturing what it would look like if I were to see them with each other. Whether he would be better with her, her legs so lean and back arched perfectly. A body that he wasn't so familiar with. Whether she would feel better, and how I would feel when I saw them together.

The weeks after were our usual routine of coffee, work, dinner, sleep, alarm, and repeat. We bustled around each other but not with each other. His kisses were short and to the point. I would try to get him to linger, but he was already someplace else. I didn't have to look at his face to know he wasn't fully there.

"Are they really slamming you with projects?" I asked over dinner one night.

"Why do you ask?"

I took a bite of the curried chicken I'd made. "You seem kind of tired. Quiet."

"I've been working seventy-hour weeks. I'm always tired."

He ate on autopilot and then put his plate by the sink.

"Sorry, I'm on a deadline. Client wants another draft of blueprints." He said this looking down at his phone, scrolling, typing, and went to the study.

He didn't mean to be cold, I told myself as I cleared my own plate and began to load the dishwasher. *He's stressed, just let it be.*

A few days later, he was packing his carry-on for work. I took note of the nice shirts he was placing inside it, the ones he usually saved for special occasions.

"Where to this time?" I asked, lightly running my hand over the collar of one.

"LA. Another architecture firm wants to work jointly on one of our national clients. They're sending me," he answered, without looking up, as he tucked in more clothes.

"Do you know when you'll be back?"

I pressed my mouth closed and shook my head before asking more questions.

"Hey . . . are you okay?" He closed his carry-on.

"Yes. Fine. I'm just going to miss you."

"I'll be back in two days," he said softly before placing his hand on mine. "It's a short trip. Maybe we can do a weekend getaway when I get back? An extended weekend?"

"Sounds great." I kissed his cheek as if putting a button on the whole matter.

I kept busy at the gallery the next day, staying late. But I hurried home the following afternoon knowing he would be coming from the airport soon.

I checked the roast in the oven and then went to the counter to stir the butter into the steaming potatoes I had strained. My fingers lingered too close to the steam, and I jumped back.

"Dammit." I flung open the freezer and held some ice cubes on my hand.

My phone rang and I answered, thinking it was him.

"You landed already? I haven't finished making dinner yet—"

"Isla. It's me. Oliver."

I tucked the phone against my ear and shoulder, rubbing the ice on my fingers. "Oh, Oliver! Sorry, for some reason I thought you were Sawyer."

My laugh wasn't matched.

"I take it by the sound of your voice you haven't heard," he said quietly.

I let the ice slide into the sink. "Heard what?"

"Oh, honey . . . I hate that I'm the one bringing this up. I called because I wanted to make sure you were okay. I'm sure it's only the way they take those photos. Those stupid paparazzi—"

"Oliver. Tell me."

I heard him take a deep breath.

"There were some photos put online . . . an hour ago maybe? I was at work and this dingbat from human resources was gossiping about it when she walked by my desk. I went to go see what the fuss was and . . ."

I dropped the phone. I ran upstairs to my computer and pulled up the first news website I could think of. And there it was. At the very top.

MARLOW FIN SPOTTED COZY WITH BROTHER-IN-LAW

I scrolled down and saw the images. Marlow, in a tight maroon dress, as Sawyer walked next to her, his hand on the small of her back. They walked close, their heads down together as they ducked into the entrance of a hotel lobby.

This is your doing. You imagined it, remember?

I kept clicking, image after image, a frame-by-frame take on what couldn't have been more than ten seconds of them walking. I zoomed in, panicky. The two of them, going into a hotel together. It couldn't have looked worse. I had done this to myself. All the imaginings and one-sided suspicion. I had manifested my own worst nightmare.

You did this.

He walked in and called my name like I was a lost pet. He never did that when he came home. This time it was as if he didn't know whether I would be there.

"Isla," he said when he came upstairs.

I looked up at him from our bed, my face shiny and red.

"What the fuck, Sawyer?"

He pleaded with me immediately. Explained that they met for dinner since he was in town. That it was nothing more than them going inside for that dinner.

"I don't believe you," I said, a knee-jerk reaction. Isn't that what the wife was supposed to say when something like this happened? But who the hell would this happen to?

You, this happens to you.

"What?" He was incredulous.

"Have you seen the pictures?" My voice raised.

"Yes. Yes, Isla! And I'm telling you, they make it look bad for no reason. The scum who call themselves photographers look for angles like that. All I did was walk into a restaurant with her."

But I knew there had to be more. With Marlow, there was more.

I stood up. "Did she try to kiss you?"

His hands, which had been so animated in front of him as he spoke, dropped down.

"Answer me. Did she try to kiss you?"

He couldn't lie to me. I knew whatever he answered would be the truth.

"Yes." His jaw set and he began to shake his head.

I could only see Marlow right then. Marlow's face. Marlow's lips.

Marlow, you did this.

He went on to insist he pulled back before anything happened. That it was nonsensical; he had always thought of her as a baby sister.

I let him go on. I let him hold me and then tell me he was sorry I had to go through this. That Marlow was lonely. She'd always been a

217

bit troubled, and she felt terrible immediately. Begged him not to say anything to me.

I felt numb when I should have stayed furious.

He fell asleep before I did. I went back to the computer and looked at each photo again. Analyzing them as if I had an exam in the morning. I peered at one and put my nose up to the screen. His hand was in his pocket. The side he always kept the knight figurine in. I pressed even harder trying to see.

Was he holding on to it? Did he think of me when he held on to it as he touched her?

CHAPTER 41

THE INTERVIEW

2021

[Studio]

MARLOW FIN: My relationship with him? [*Scoffs*]

JODI LEE: Your brother-in-law, Sawyer Ford. You knew him since you were a little girl, correct?

MARLOW FIN: [*Nods*] Hmmm.

JODI LEE: You seem upset, Marlow.

MARLOW FIN: I'm fine.

JODI LEE: Maybe we should start with men in general, then. You have a history of relationships with quite a few famous men. Hollywood A-Listers, moguls, athletes. For someone who didn't like the extra media attention, that probably didn't help?

MARLOW FIN: Men in general. [*Shakes head*]

JODI LEE: Is that a bad thing?

MARLOW FIN: Yes, Jodi. It is. You were doing so well and then you go there.

JODI LEE: Are you uncomfortable discussing your past relationships?

MARLOW FIN: Not at all. It has nothing to do with being uncomfortable. But why not ask about my relationship with women in general too?

JODI LEE: I stand to be corrected. Do you have a preference?

MARLOW FIN: I don't really have a preference. First of all, I think that's a terrible word, as if someone has a choice. There is no choice when it comes to how your body chooses to respond biologically and how your emotions choose to react.

JODI LEE: That wasn't what I was implying.

MARLOW FIN: I see.

I've had significant relationships with both men and women. More men. Am I talking about emotional and sexual relationships? Yes. And I'm not the least bit uncomfortable or afraid to talk about Marlow Fin and men, since you asked.

JODI LEE: All right then . . .

MARLOW FIN: I'll tell you about my relationship with men. It's like drowning.

JODI LEE: Drowning? How is that?

MARLOW FIN: I despise most men. They have too much power simply for having a Y chromosome. And yet I was given the ability to attract most of them. Some would call it a power of my own. What did I do with it? I used it. I fucking used it and pretty much sucked those reserves dry. I threw myself in the water. And now that I realize I betrayed myself, I can't get out. That's why . . . that's why I'm drowning.

JODI LEE: Are you still drowning, Marlow?

MARLOW FIN: Absolutely.

JODI LEE: That's all very interesting. But here is something that doesn't make sense. If you despise men so much, why all those relationships? Why engage?

MARLOW FIN: You can despise and still be intrigued. I won't lie to you. I certainly had my fun.

JODI LEE: [*Leans forward*] Are you going to be okay if I bring up Sawyer again?

MARLOW FIN: I'll try to be fine.

JODI LEE: He was your brother-in-law, but he was also your childhood friend?

MARLOW FIN: He was more than just a friend. He was my brother before it was ever legally recognized by some marriage license. Some of the best memories of my life . . . no, they were definitely the best times of my life, were with him and Isla. Those summers together— no one can ever taint that.

JODI LEE: Can you tell me about those summers?

MARLOW FIN: [*Silence*]

JODI LEE: Marlow?

MARLOW FIN: Magic.

JODI LEE: Your sister, Isla, would eventually marry him in 2012. We discussed a certain event at the wedding earlier. Did it make you envious when they got married?

MARLOW FIN: No. I was happy for them. They were the two most important people in my life, other than Moni.

JODI LEE: Can you explain, then, why you were photographed going into a Beverly Hills hotel with him a few years later?

[Roll package, photographs of Marlow and Sawyer]

JODI LEE: They were the photos that shocked the world. Marlow Fin and her own brother-in-law, walking closely together into a hotel lobby in the fall of 2015. Marlow's reps would later deny any reports of infidelity on his part. However, a few witnesses inside the hotel would state they saw them kissing. Others claimed they went up to a room together, although this was widely disputed. All accounts were denied by her reps.

[Studio]

MARLOW FIN: Jodi, this will be the first and last time I ever address this. My brother-in-law was in town for his job. I was the one who reached out to him to see if he wanted to meet for lunch or dinner.

JODI LEE: How did you know he was going to be in town?

MARLOW FIN: My agent was married to the owner of the LA company he was meeting with at the time. She mentioned it to me earlier in the week. I hadn't seen him in a while and thought it would be fun to catch up.

JODI LEE: So, did you call him? Text him?

MARLOW FIN: I sent him a text.

JODI LEE: Did you text often before all this?

MARLOW FIN: No. We really only connected when I went back home, which was rare.

JODI LEE: He must have agreed right away?

MARLOW FIN: No, actually. He wasn't sure if there would be time. But when his meeting ended early, he sent me a text letting me know dinner could work.

JODI LEE: If it was only dinner with a family member, then why the hand-holding? Why the close physical contact?

MARLOW FIN: We didn't hold hands. He escorted me inside. I think he may have placed his hand on my back. That's it.

JODI LEE: Have you seen the pictures?

MARLOW FIN: I've only looked at them once, very briefly.

JODI LEE: And what did you see when you looked at those pictures?

MARLOW FIN: Two people going inside a hotel.

JODI LEE: Did you kiss him?

MARLOW FIN: No.

JODI LEE: Did you try to kiss him?

MARLOW FIN: Yes.

JODI LEE: You are admitting to me right now that you did in fact try to kiss your sister's husband, Sawyer. A man you just called a brother a few moments ago?

MARLOW FIN: I'm not proud of it. But I am being honest when I say I was looking for closeness in that moment. I was utterly alone.

JODI LEE: But is that really a valid justification?

MARLOW FIN: No, it is not. I never said it was justified.

JODI LEE: Did you ever try to kiss him on another occasion? Engage in any other acts of physical intimacy?

MARLOW FIN: No. He was better than that. Better than me. The choice I made at that dinner, and those pictures, cost me dearly.

JODI LEE: Do you say that because of the fallout with your sister, Isla, was a result of it all?

MARLOW FIN: There wasn't anything I could say or do afterward that would make it any better.

JODI LEE: Did Sawyer try to engage in anything physical with you that night?

MARLOW FIN: He was the one who pulled away.

JODI LEE: What did he say to you when he did that?

MARLOW FIN: I honestly don't remember. I was too embarrassed. My heart just dropped. It was like my body was acting before my mind could react. I think I tried to call Isla but he told me not to.

JODI LEE: What happened with Isla and you after the story and photographs broke?

MARLOW FIN: She did not speak to me for the next few years. I tried almost daily to reach her. But she refused. The next time I talked to her was . . . [*Pause*]

JODI LEE: You were saying?

MARLOW FIN: Oh . . . I can't believe that was when we finally spoke again . . .

JODI LEE: Marlow?

MARLOW FIN: I'm here. I'm still here.

JODI LEE: Okay. Please let us know if you need a break.

MARLOW FIN: No. Continue.

JODI LEE: There is another date I want to discuss. I want you to share with everyone what happened on December 16, 2017. Do you remember anything from that day?

MARLOW FIN: [*Shakes head*]

JODI LEE: You don't remember?

MARLOW FIN: I do. I do remember. That's why it's so difficult to even talk . . .

JODI LEE: We can take a brief break if you—

MARLOW FIN: Do you remember when I told you there were two dark holes in my life? The two darkest moments? The first I already shared with you.

JODI LEE: Yes. I do.

MARLOW FIN: Well, that date you mention? That's it . . . that's the second one.

JODI LEE: Can you tell the viewers, in your own words, what happened on that December day?

MARLOW FIN: [*Stands up out of chair, panicked*] I can't do this. I have to go. I have to leave.

CHAPTER 42

WREN

1980s

Wren stared at the hairline fracture in the teacup. She had noticed it earlier but now it seemed to be getting wider. She placed her finger on it and felt for the roughness. The apple turnover had gone cold on the green-patterned china plate.

"Have you had time . . . to think about it?"

The restaurant was noisy, but Stella's voice was hushed. She looked around as if every person was pretending not to listen to their conversation. This was their second time meeting each other in a week. But this time, she seemed eager for an answer. Every press of her lips and sweep of her hair was filled with apprehension. Impatience was starting to creep up in her voice, like the edges of wet paper curling up.

"Yes. I have," she answered carefully as she pushed at the turnover with her fork.

The truth was, she hadn't.

She didn't know what to do with a request like the one that had slipped from Stella's mouth, as if dark eels had tumbled out toward her, writhing and invading her body. It was a question that frightened and thrilled her all at once. She tried to forgot about it when she left that first meeting, the weight of its deliberation too heavy. But now—here it was again, and the only thing she knew was this was something to either immediately cast out or grab at with both hands.

They both looked out the window together. Snow had begun to fall and tap the glass with melted dots. As they turned back, she caught her gaze.

"Your eyes. They're . . . remarkable," Stella said before quickly breaking away and taking a sip of her tea. "But I'm sure you've heard that before." She placed her hand on the middle of the table, her head slightly downcast.

The snow fell harder, colder as the flakes grew in size.

"I have a confession to make," she suddenly said.

Wren looked up. "Confession?"

"Yes." She took a sip of her tea and kept the cup close to her face. "That first time we spoke. That wasn't the first time I saw you." She set the cup down. "I noticed you before that. You struck me as someone I knew. I don't know how else to explain it. So . . . I followed you."

"What . . . why?"

"I really don't know. But then the more I followed you, the more I realized you were actually following someone else." She stared hard. "I think you know what I'm talking about."

Her face felt cold.

"You know . . . I understand this isn't easy for you—or anyone for that matter—to answer. But please know . . . please know that whatever you decide I am grateful you are even considering it."

She blinked quickly a few times and placed a finger under her nose as if to hold in whatever was on the brink of escaping.

Wren picked up her fork and pierced the crust of the turnover. Flakes burst onto the white tablecloth. She chewed the large bite and kept her eyes on the plate. A bus pulled up in front of the window. The sound of its engine sputtering suddenly gave her a headache. She thought of how she could get on it and leave town. Leave this restaurant and what this woman was asking of her. But it was all so exhausting.

"It would mean so much . . ." Stella's voice trailed off.

"I'll do it," Wren said.

"You'll—you'll what?" Stella looked down at the turnover first and then into her eyes.

"Yes. My answer is yes."

CHAPTER 43

ISLA

2016

I found little ways to show my anger toward Sawyer over the months following the Marlow photo incident. Maybe it wasn't entirely anger, but the refusal to let our life together continue unscathed. How could it ever be the same? If it was, it would mean what we had together was not as cherished as I had believed it to be—not worth being rocked by it all, too ordinary to stop its monotonous flow. I wanted him to know how much it hurt me. How much *they* had hurt me. If she wasn't going to be here to see it, then he would have to pay the price.

Someone else has to feel the hurt.

They were so slight at first, I wondered if he even noticed.

His side of the bed left unmade. The less desirable cut of steak for dinner. His clothes unfolded in a heap after being in the dryer. The milk that he needed for his coffee left out to spoil.

There was a spiteful, unpleasant side of me I never knew existed. Creeping out in each and every move.

If he was aware of any of my childish actions, he didn't show it. I turned up the dial.

I slept on the far edge of the bed, far from where we used to face each other before we fell asleep, breathing in tandem.

I stopped writing notes in his lunch. They used to be a morning ritual, a smile on my face as I wrote with blue pen on yellow Post-it Notes, sometimes silly jokes only he would get or a simple reminder that I loved him. The pen and Post-it pad remained untouched in the drawer.

When he kissed me, I would pull away abruptly at the last second, just enough so he would feel my haste.

His silence in response to my little acts of war only increased the animosity that was beginning to grow inside me, a pot on the cusp of bubbling over that needed to be tamed. I hated the way we felt like roommates, milling around each other but never engaging. Suddenly it had become my fault, my doing that we had fallen into this loop of impassiveness. My one-sided games had turned on me. And yet I wanted to scream at him for doing this to *us*. He was the guilty party, yet here I was . . . the only one in pain.

He surprised me one night after dinner. We had another one of our nearly silent meals. I got up and took our plates to the sink when he spoke.

"You have to stop doing this, Isla." His voice broke through, and I froze for a second.

"What do you mean?" I shook the plates into the garbage. A few peas spilled onto the floor.

"I don't think I have to explain. You've been punishing me these last few months. And do I deserve it? Yes. But at some point, we've got to try to move on."

I whirled around. "Why is it that I have to be the one to fix this? You're the one who did this to us."

My words instantly made me feel more childish than ever.

He put his head down and rubbed the sides of it.

"How many more times do I have to say I'm sorry? Because whatever the number is, I don't think it will ever be enough."

It suddenly dawned on me that I had perhaps pushed too far. That I had been too harsh for his actual actions.

Who am I trying to punish?

"Are you saying that you don't want to move on?"

He stared at me blankly. "I'm saying . . . I don't know. I don't know what to do to make this right—"

"What do you want, Sawyer?" I asked loudly.

"What do I—"

"Yes. What is it that you want? Out of this. Us." I motioned all around, as if the kitchen deserved a tour.

"I want . . ." He sighed. "I want for you to be happy."

He got up and went outside, the front door shutting firmly.

I held the plate down at my side, my shoulder drooping from the weight of it. I left the kitchen just as we were. Dirty, messy, and lived in. I went to our room and slept, waking up the next day to find him already gone to work.

The bedroom felt as cold as my insides. I rubbed my arms and tried to remember the last time we had woken up without a dull, aching dread. Wondering how much longer we could go on like this before it set in permanently, a suction on our marriage that could never be lifted.

He came home that night later than usual. I had already gone upstairs to take a shower. I didn't hear him come in or go up the stairs. When I stepped out of the shower, he startled me, but I made no noise. He stood straight on and stared at me. I had never felt so exposed, so unconditionally naked. The water dripped down my nose and I wiped at it and then instinctively covered my breasts.

"Don't," he said quietly.

I pulled my hands down. He looked over every inch of my bare body, as if it were the first time he was seeing it. I was almost thirty and had already begun to feel the differences from my twenty-year-old self. This body was now a little softer, a little worn. There was less tautness but more that curved. Did he see those changes? Was he taking note of it all?

He looked straight into my eyes, and it made sense, like a math equation that had finally been solved.

I was seen.

His hands went from the sides of my waist up to my neck and he pulled me in.

"It's you. It will always be you," he said, his lips moving against mine.

I gripped his shoulders and he held me up and hoisted me onto the counter. We breathed in and out together with such force, incensed with each other and loving each other all at once. He let go when he came, and I yelled out once. He was shaking and we stayed together, my wet hair cold, strands falling onto his back.

I wish I had never let go.

Four months later we bought an old farmhouse outside the Cities. The day the real estate agent showed it to us, the white paint faded and in shambles, the front porch swing halfway hanging, we looked at each other and knew.

This would not be another "for now" house. This was our house.

A tiny ocular window high up in the front, with blue and yellow panes of stained glass, shone with possibilities. We spent the next couple months pouring everything we had into restoring the house. The bones remained but so much had to be renewed. We stripped all the walls of the old wallpaper, dried out and peeling. We replaced it with a fresh coat of paint, put shiplap in the entryway, and added a thick marble slab for the kitchen counter. There was still so much to be done but we had all the time in the world to finish it . . . or so we thought. That's what everyone always thinks, a little white lie that slips deeper and deeper into darkness.

Somehow, we had also restored ourselves. We weren't the same Isla and Sawyer. That would never be possible. But we had come out together still clinging, still hoping for a life well lived.

One with each other.

CHAPTER 44

ISLA

1996

There was once a little girl who stole a knight.

The little boy learned her name and then dropped it in the grass. He ran away and she bent down to get a closer look. The grass was soft and dewy from the morning, her fingers nearly slipped picking it up, heavy in her small hand. A tiny knight that she would keep close.

Someday I will return you. Someday I will take you back.

She went home and tucked it away safely in her drawer where it stayed most of the time. But every once in a while she would take it out and hold it up in the light, letting it dance in the air, and then place it back, hidden.

The boy grew and so did she. Their innocence dwindled with each passing day, as though exposure from the burdens around them ate away a thin layer at a time. He would have heartache and she just as much pain, but they would reach out to each other, their fingers barely touching and then pulled apart, the wind carrying them this way and that. Until they finally dropped into their own worlds, and he was no longer the little boy.

She would return the stolen knight, and it was his promise to her that it would never leave him. And she would wait.

Wait for his return. Wait for her stolen knight.

But would she remember? Would she remember all there was to her knight?

The way he hummed when he ate something that satisfied him. The way his head tipped down to look over his dark-framed reading glasses in bed with a book. The crooked smile he saved for her before he would lean in and kiss her cheek. The watch he wore throughout all of high school and college. How the brown leather was worn, faded and tearing at the edges, the way he twisted the face even though it didn't rotate.

The way his brow formed, so hopeful and yet nervous, when he asked her to marry him. The earthy smell of rain as his knee bumped into her toes and how he lifted her off the ground so easily when he whispered it once more in her ear and she said yes. *Yes, yes,* she breathed into his ear and then he clung tight to her, making her feel more wanted and needed than she ever would again in her life. The feel of his touch as his fingers ran through the sides of her hair, drops of rain sliding through it as every inch of her spine went cool and shuddered and craved.

But there would be things she forgot to remember. She was a collector of water with her bare hands. It slipped through her fingers with every try. The exact color of his hair. The panic of not really being able to see it, guessing whether it was brighter or more golden. Was it like that in the light? Was it darker when she touched it? Why couldn't she be certain when she closed her eyes and searched for it?

She would be angry with herself for what she couldn't remember, angry that she didn't think to keep everything in, steep every second like a tea bag in hot water, getting stronger and thicker with each twirl of the string.

She would remember so little of the countless moments she had with him.

But she would remember everything about the day her knight left.

CHAPTER 45

ISLA

December 16, 2017

Sawyer looked out the window and paused.

"What?" I asked, looking out with him, trying to see what he saw.

"It's snowing," he said.

Sometimes when I wake up now, I am right back in our farmhouse on that December day with the white quilted bed and black iron headboard, the smell of the paint we had just brushed over the bedroom walls. I should have told myself to shut my eyes and go back to sleep. Told him to stay with me and never leave that bed. Never let another minute continue, to make time stand still.

But it didn't.

We got out of that bed together.

He went downstairs and made coffee like he always did. I heard the sound of water running as he rinsed the pot and filter. My feet stretched out onto the cold wood floor. It was a Saturday and the first thing I thought was I hadn't gotten a Christmas present for him yet.

"I think I'm going to drive to Rosedale Mall," I said over my plate of scrambled eggs and croissant Sawyer had made for me.

He took a long sip of his coffee. "Want me to tag along?"

I shrugged coyly. "If you want."

He smiled. "All right." It faded slightly. "I have to spend a few hours on the Kolstead plan, though. It has to get finished before Christmas. Are you sure you want to go alone?"

"Sawyer, I'll be fine."

"I know but I don't like you driving around alone in this weather."

I glanced outside. "It's barely snowing."

He looked uncertain. I reached across the kitchen table and held his hand.

"I'll be fine," I said once more.

"I love you, Isla," he said.

His voice had a strange sadness to it. I tightened my grip on his hand.

We cleaned up the kitchen together and I changed to go out. I pulled my heavy winter coat on and passed the study on the way. He was bent over, intent on his work.

"I won't take too long. Maybe we can have leftover soup for lunch?"

Ordinary . . . our words to each other were so ordinary.

He didn't turn around but sat up, maybe unaware I was right behind him.

"That sounds good," he answered.

The back of his head stared at me, and I didn't step into the study to give him a kiss or wrap my arms around his shoulders. I left instead for the mall, in a hurry to beat the increasing snowfall. In a hurry to get a good parking spot. In a hurry to beat the lunchtime crowd. In a hurry for anything else but him.

By the time I parked in the mall lot, the entire ground was covered in white. My maroon rubber boots hit the pavement, spreading the wet, sticky snow around my feet. For a second, I considered getting back in the car and forgetting the whole thing. The idea of milling through a crowd of other last-minute Christmas shoppers felt so unappealing, like another bite of a rich and heavy dish when you were already beyond stuffed. What was I thinking going out like this? I suddenly wanted to be back at the farmhouse. I would pull the cold pot of leftover soup out of the refrigerator and heat it on the gas burner. Sawyer would tell me how good it smelled once it started to boil, and we would eat it together with a few pillowy rolls. He would stretch out on the couch with me afterward as we talked, his voice deep and hushed over me until we fell asleep. The fireplace would grow too hot, and he would turn it off and rejoin me, pulling the worn, red wool blanket over us, my head rising and falling with his chest. I would dream and we would wake up to a white and swirling snowstorm.

I locked the car door and crunched my way into the mall. It was only a little after ten, but I immediately got sucked into the crowd of obsessed shoppers, a worker bee thrown into the drone of hasty work.

I stopped in front of a pop-up Christmas decoration store, and a tiny silver reindeer ornament caught my eye. It was what Sawyer would have pointed at. He would have loved the simplicity of it. I went inside and pulled it from the display Christmas tree, the fake bristles scratching my hand.

I held up the smooth, metallic ornament in the light, studying it. Imagining it on our tree in front of the window. Perfect for our first Christmas in the house.

Perfect.

I smiled and went to the cash register and asked the store clerk if I could get the ornament engraved. I made arrangements to come back when they were finished with it in an hour. I was about to leave the store when my phone vibrated. I should have ignored it. I should have left it alone. But I did what I had done a thousand times before. I looked to find a text.

Isla. Need your help. Plz Call.

I felt a lurch in my body, a reaction to seeing her name on my phone. I hadn't had any contact with her since before the photo incident. She had tried several times to contact me. But they had grown fewer and further between, until I assumed she had moved on with her life.

My throat became dry. I stopped at a coffee shop to get a drink and eagerly drank the bottle of water I purchased.

My phone rang. It was her. I closed my eyes and held my finger above the decline button. It was red and provoking as I let it hover.

She's your sister. It's almost Christmas.

I thought about Moni right then. Her gentle face and how she would have given me a small smile and an encouraging nod.

"Hello?" I answered as if it were an unknown number.

There was silence.

"Marlow," I said quietly.

"You answered." Her voice was muffled and slurry.

"Yes. You said you needed help?"

I heard a muted noise, perhaps her clearing her throat.

"Are you okay?"

"Fine. I'm fine," she said loudly.

I cocked my head away from the phone and took a deep breath. "What is it that you need help with, Marlow?"

"My flight got canceled. I need someone to pick me up."

"Your flight? Where are you?"

"I'm at the MSP airport," she heaved out quickly.

"You're in town?" The thought of her being physically close made my stomach tighten.

"Yes. I can't get on the plane."

"I thought you said it was canceled?"

"Well . . . they won't let me on it." Her drawling words and randomly loud pitches were enough to clue me in.

"Can you get a cab? Doesn't your agency usually have a car service?"

"I can't find my wallet. I think I left it on the plane."

"So, you *did* get on the plane, Marlow?" I asked impatiently.

She heaved a giant sigh, as if she had already explained it to me. "I was on the plane. But then they made me leave . . . I need you to pick me up, Isla. I need your help."

"Marlow, I can't just . . ." I looked over to the Christmas store, remembering I had to pick up the engraved ornament.

"Please. Please, Isla," she begged.

I paced around. "Give me a minute. I need to think."

"I need to go home . . . I need to go home, Isla." I could hear the tears in her voice, real pain and panic.

I closed my eyes and could see her, a glistened face and twisted mouth.

She's your sister. Marlow is your sister.

"Okay . . . I can't get you right now. Can you wait just a little bit?"

"No, no! I can't stay here anymore," she said frantically. "These people . . . they keep staring at me. I need to go home now, I—"

"All right. It's okay. You're going to be okay, Marlow," I tried to speak soothingly into the phone. "Have you tried Dad?"

"I don't want him to see me like this. I don't want—"

"Marlow, why can't he—"

"Just listen to me. *Please* help me."

"Sawyer, then," I blurted.

Why? Why do you give in to her?

"What?" She sounded more confused.

I exhaled slowly. "Sawyer can get you."

She went silent.

"Either that or you will have to wait until—"

"Okay . . . thank you, Isla."

"You're welcome," I said quickly.

I hung up and realized what I had agreed to. Was it too late to take it back? To wait for the ornament to be finished and then go get her myself?

But she sounded so desperate . . . so unhinged. If too much time passed, who knew what state she would be in, or worse, what would happen to her. I could at the very least have the decency to watch out for her safety. I kept thinking about Moni and what she would have wanted me to do . . .

I pulled my phone up again and texted Sawyer.

I know this sounds crazy, but you have to go get Marlow at the airport. Right now. She's not herself and needs help. Can you do that for me please?

A toddler in a pink puffer coat ran by me and shrieked. Her mother chased after her and the father lagged behind, holding a baby in a yellow fleece onesie. In all that had just happened with Marlow, I couldn't help but pause for a second and wonder. Could that be us? Could that be Sawyer and me years from now? In the throes of the wonderful craziness of a life together?

Okay. I'll go right now. I hope you're okay.

He didn't ask for more details. He didn't question anything.

I abruptly felt sick, a hint of nausea hit me. It came in a giant wave and then passed.

What have I done?

I had told him to go to her. I had set something in motion, my hand still shaking over whatever lever I had jerked back.

The ornament. You can't forget the ornament.

A few shoppers bumped into my shoulders as I made my way through the crowd without really seeing a single person. Time went haywire, the minutes seemed both short and long. The display in the storefront didn't look as festive and cheery anymore. The ornaments appeared dull. I handed the store clerk my credit card as he rang me up and said enthusiastically, "Happy holidays!" I looked at him and nodded as he passed me a white paper bag tied with a shiny green ribbon. I didn't look inside. Some words exited my lips, maybe a thank you, and

239

I left the store. I don't remember the drive from the mall back home, only the snowflakes sailing down to my windshield and then being swept away by the wipers.

The farmhouse was cold and dim. I looked in the study to find he had dropped his pencil, blueprints scattered across the desk. An unfinished cup of coffee. I touched his chair and I could swear it still felt warm. He hadn't wasted a second to do what I had needed. I turned the fireplace on and pulled the wool blanket over my legs and waited. The flames burned into my irises, and it seemed I had barely blinked a few times when the doorbell rang.

Why would Sawyer ring the doorbell?

I looked out the window to see a figure in front of the door. I placed my hand on the knob, letting my heart play games with me. Letting it try to reason with craziness, bartering between hope and the truth.

It's Sawyer. It's Sawyer playing a joke on me.

I swung the door open.

A man stood there. A man I had never seen before. He had on one of those fur-lined trapper hats, and it was all I could do not to find the inappropriate humor in the caricature it made him resemble. I spotted the state trooper car in the driveway and looked at him, shaking my head already, trying to make him go away.

"No," I said.

I don't remember what he said. I don't remember what I said in response. I only know that he had to hold me up; every sensation in my limbs failed me. I was no longer in my body.

Somehow, I was seated in the passenger seat of the trooper's car. A wail trapped somewhere deep inside me, ringing my insides with pain. I could practically hear Sawyer whispering with so much love in my ear that it ripped every piece of muscle in my heart.

Shhh. It's okay, Isla. It's okay.

I kept my eyes shut tight. If I opened them, it would be all too real.

Brightness blinded me as we entered the hospital. The trooper held on to my arm as I trudged next to him, looking to the left and to the right, as if he would be there. Full and intact. Warmth, blood, and flesh. There for me to grab on to and scream with relief.

But it wasn't him.

She stood there, a cut above her left eyebrow. That was it. A single cut.

"Isla," she said, reaching out, her chin already trembling.

I said nothing as she wrapped her arms around me and wept. It annoyed me. I wanted her to shut up so I could listen for my husband.

My husband. Where was he?

"He didn't feel anything. He felt no pain," she said.

I shuddered and nodded. I fell onto the cold, tiled floor.

CHAPTER 46

THE INTERVIEW

2021

[Studio]

JODI LEE: When asked about the accident on December 16, 2017, Marlow exited our interview once more, this time visibly shaken and unable to speak. Myself and our producers, of course, gave her time to calm down and collect herself. Her team did not allow our cameras to follow her, so we waited. Waited for her return to the set to finish her interview. Would we get any answers from her? Would she even come back?

[Roll package, pictures, and footage of accident scene]

JODI LEE: The accident happened nearly four years ago on a busy Minnesota highway. Sawyer Ford, the husband of Marlow's sister, Isla, picked up Marlow from the Minneapolis–Saint Paul International Airport close to noon. The weather was questionable, as it had been snowing all morning. Exactly why Sawyer was the one picking up Marlow from the airport is still not clear.

What we do know is Marlow had been kicked off an American Airlines flight bound for JFK earlier that morning. The airline declined to comment other than to say she was in a condition "unfit for flying," although a state trooper report would later indicate Marlow appeared intoxicated at the time of the accident. Sawyer was nearing his exit when he lost control of the Subaru Forester he was driving, likely due to the slippery road conditions. He overcorrected, causing him to hit another vehicle in the lane next to him. Both cars came to a stop. The accident was minor.

The tragedy begins here. Had that been the extent of it, Sawyer Ford would have walked away from the entire accident. Multiple witnesses who slowed down their vehicles to help said he exited his vehicle and bent down on the driver's side to inspect the damage.

Now the details become unclear. Some witnesses think they saw him slip on the snow or even trip over something. Others say he was simply bent over by the front tire. But what happened next is not for the faint of heart.

A commercial truck that was unable to stop in time struck the thirty-year-old architect and husband, killing him instantly. His body was thrown more than one hundred feet away into a ditch.

Marlow survived the accident with a single cut on her face.

CHAPTER 47

ISLA

2017

You are in our thoughts and prayers.

I must have read that over and over in the sympathy cards that arrived daily. All in white envelopes and modest patterns because what greeting card company would make colorful, celebratory ones? I would fall asleep and wake up to that phrase, an intonation I hated.

Am I? Am I really in your thoughts and prayers?

What would that do now, even if someone did make good on that promise?

He would have been so damn polite. He would have thanked everyone for the cards as if they had sent sheets of gold, and made them all feel so cared for.

Sorry, Sawyer. I'm so sorry I'm not as kind as you would have been.

There was a small service at the Lutheran church he and Ada used to go to. The only thing that made sense was to do everything I could to help Ada get through it. For someone who loved her spirit crystals and tarot cards, she was a faithful churchgoer. I sat next to her as the pastor, a man I had never spoken to before, preached to our small, mourning crowd about what a beautiful life Sawyer had, even though it had been cut short.

He knew nothing about Sawyer. He had never met him and here he was telling us about his life. I had the urge to tell him to stop, but felt Ada shake with a silent sob and clamped my mouth closed.

Oliver took my arm and helped guide me to a waiting car. I looked at him gratefully and then had to look away. His eyes were red and full of pain. He had lost a friend too.

We drove back to our neighborhood, the shiny blue urn in my lap. It pressed hard against my stomach as its weight shifted in the car. I quivered with the oddity of it and wanted to get to our field as soon as possible. Those ashes didn't belong in my embrace.

The snow had melted that morning; it had been hopelessly sunny and all wrong for a funeral. The tall grass was wet and bent. I waited for the wind to blow and catch the ashes as I held it up and poured.

Sawyer.

I closed my eyes.

I could hear our laughter as children all those years ago, our heads touching as we lay and stared up at a wide sky that had promised us so much. I opened my eyes and let the tears fall. They hit my mouth, salty and wounded, and I wanted to die right then.

Ada stepped toward me and took my hand, squeezing it. She didn't let go.

"I know, honey. I know . . . he was a good one. We all knew it."

She hadn't spoken a single word until right then, and yet they were all I needed to hear from her.

We had a reception back at the house, so similar to Moni's it made me queasy. Even the same white cake was served. Whose idea was it to get white cake? Sawyer loved chocolate. And why were there people here I had never seen before?

I did my best to thank anyone who came up to me. It was what he would have wanted, for me to be polite. But I felt like they were all spectators waiting for me to crack. Wondering how in the hell I was still standing.

I wondered the same thing.

As everyone began to mill out of the house, Oliver came up and touched my arm. "You sure you don't want me to go back with you?"

"I'll be okay. It's been a lot of people, too many people, really. Believe it or not, I could use some alone time, after planning the service and the reception."

"Positive?" His brow furrowed with concern. "I don't like you being all alone in that big old house."

I reached out and hugged him hard. "Really . . . thank you."

I pulled away and noticed her sitting outside in a car—both hands up by the dashboard as she leaned forward to stare at me.

Oliver followed my eyes and saw her get out and stand by her car door.

"Oh Jesus," he said under his breath.

She started to walk toward the open front door, and I turned away.

"Isla," she called after me.

"No." It came out as a whisper.

I ran out to the backyard and left through the gated fence. My hands shook as I got inside my car. Oliver came dashing out, my purse in his hands, Marlow trailing him. He handed it to me through the window and I gave him another grateful look as I started the engine. I turned my head so I couldn't see them, but I caught sight of him blocking her gently as I pulled out of the driveway. I looked up once in the rearview mirror.

She stood in the middle of the street, arms straight down at her sides like a soldier, watching me.

My heart raced. I didn't stop until I made it back to the farmhouse.

I slammed the door as if to seal off the rest of the world. The quiet. I needed it. I needed a moment without another "I'm so sorry." Without the smell of coffee and cheap cake. Without the drum of voices that never really got Sawyer the way I did.

Without the sight of *her*, her eyes watching me through the windshield.

And then I felt it, the sheer solitude. The silent echoes of our house that told me he would never enter again. I had been running away from my mind. I had been staving off the truth with little tricks. Convincing it that once I was alone—once the funeral and well-wishers were all over with and gone—it would return to normal.

He would return to the house we built together.

No, no, no.

He was never coming back. He was never coming home to me. I was alone but it felt unbearably loud all around. There was screaming inside me, an uncontrollable panic taking over. And I hated it. I hated it with everything I had.

How can you be gone? How is this possible?

Something else needed to be there . . . something else needed to wrap around me, or I wouldn't make it. I was sure of it.

I stripped off the ill-fitting black dress I bought two days ago and turned the faucet on in the big white tub upstairs. I slid in the hot water and let the noises drown out.

There was relief. I sucked in air slowly, and then let it out. I shut my eyes and put my head back.

I floated.

She did this. She did this to you. She did this to you both.

My chest vibrated with silent weeping. A rage so deep and violent it split me in half. My forearm draped over my face, I screamed.

"Marlow!"

The water covered my head as I sank. I screamed her name once more out into the void.

CHAPTER 48

ISLA

2017

A few months after Sawyer's funeral, I got a call from Ada.

We had kept in touch. I visited her occasionally. She was the only one left who knew Sawyer like I did. The only one who continued to talk about him as if he were still here, as if everything about him hadn't drifted away with his death. He wasn't going to be forgotten that easily.

Our meetings were the small lights in my days. I would often bring her something to eat. She loved simple foods, dense in calories—perhaps eating took too much effort and a single meal was enough. A gravy-laden meatloaf with mashed potatoes. A thick macaroni casserole. She was even less mobile now; she'd grown heavier over the years. Her hair thin and white, she had ceased dyeing it. It still surprised me each time I saw her, the lack of vibrant red, its absence even stronger than its presence had been.

She would sit in her recliner and eat her meal while I told her about my day. As repetitive and lackluster as each day was, she seemed to enjoy these dull details. I suppose it was a story she could bear to listen to, as though listening to anything else was too much for her. Another piece of unwelcome news might tip her over, like a glass that had been propped up haphazardly, ready to break.

I picked up the picture of Sawyer's mother displayed next to her one afternoon. I didn't remember her being that lovely when I first saw it all those years ago. But she radiated, and I imagined Sawyer back with her. The daughter Ada lost now with the husband I lost.

"Comforts you, doesn't it?" Ada said from her plate as she rocked the chair a little.

"Yes. It does." I placed the frame back on the table.

"I look at it each night. I wonder if they're together somewhere. My little girl finally with her baby." She paused and studied me. "How you doing lately, hon?"

"Oh, you know, Ada . . ."

"I mean really. I'm okay being like this until it's my time. I've got no complaints. But you've got some life ahead of you."

I nodded to placate her.

"Don't waste it." She waved a fork at me, and sauce dripped onto the arm of the recliner.

I moved closer to her and wiped it away with a napkin.

She rocked her chair some more, and then seemed distracted, staring into the blank television screen. I made sure she was set for the night and began to pack away her leftovers in the kitchen.

"Say . . . I meant to tell you last time," she called abruptly from the living room. "She was here."

I closed the lid on a plastic container. "Who was here?"

"Your sister."

Marlow.

I didn't say her name out loud. I raised my head. Something in my core began to tremble.

"Why? What did she want?"

"She was really quiet. Didn't say much. Knocked on my door out of the blue and I answered. She didn't even come inside. Said she was really sorry about Sawyer. That she loved him like a brother and thought I should have something."

My chest had already begun to pound. Banging on the inside, crying out to be released.

"I didn't know if I should even bring it up to you. But then I kept thinking about it. Maybe you should come over and take a look."

I found myself walking slowly toward her. Each step as if I were moving through a thick pit of waist-high sand. Each beat of my heart thumping in my ears, pulsating with dread.

I turned to face her in the recliner. She held it up with two fingers.

My throat became a drought. I reached out with cupped hands. She dropped it in them.

The knight figurine went cold with my touch.

He promised. He promised to always have it with him.

My veins went icy from the thought of it. The thought of what she could have done.

I pictured the accident. The truck loud and barreling, hard to ignore as it sped down the road. I imagined how cold his body must have been, lying in that ditch covered in snow. Where was she when he was dying, when he was taking his last breaths? The knight somehow ending up in her hand, her single cut dripping blood on its helmet.

How did you get it, Marlow? How did you take it from him?

CHAPTER 49

ISLA

2019

The farmhouse grew larger every day, the emptiness starting to take over every corner, every crack. I could sense it bulging, creaking with agitation, wanting to reach out to someone else. Someone who wasn't as empty. Someone who wasn't dead inside.

I left the position at the gallery. On my last day, the gallery owner hugged me and told me to come back whenever I was ready. I felt my chin dig into the top of her shoulder as I stiffly let her squeeze me. We both knew I wasn't coming back.

I had begun to shut myself out and away from anyone who knew me. Slowly taking each piece of plywood and hammering away, board by board, to cover up the storm I had become. If they knew my name, they would immediately think of Marlow Fin. And then the inevitable secondary realization that I was the wife of that guy she was with—the one who got crushed on the road by a delivery truck. I could see it in their eyes every time, a bullet striking me in the open wound that would never close.

Oh, you're the wife of that poor dead guy. The sister of that beautiful woman.

I wanted to shout back at them. *Yes! Yes, to everything you are wondering! Now can you please leave me alone? Can you please look at me with anything but a blinding curiosity and pity wrapped up in smugness?*

But the worst part . . . the worst part of it all was that it reminded me of who I was.

I began to think I would never be able to escape it.

A month later, I found myself walking aimlessly before the sun came up until I stopped in front of a bakery. The glass windows were incredibly clear, the store lights bright beacons. The workers inside looked happy organizing loaves of freshly baked bread into baskets, scones lined in a row, and croissants layered over each other. I pressed my hands against the glass like a child looking in, and nearly knocked on it to get their attention. This space . . . *this* . . . I could do this.

I could be quiet and work among them. They wouldn't even notice me. I could pretend nothing existed outside those walls.

I got hired for overnights, when the rest of the world was asleep. Where I could be left alone with nothing but bags of flour and yeast. The strong, sweet, and fermented smells both charmed and annoyed me. The dough mixer churned as I mechanically measured, poured. Repeated. Flour would settle in my hair, and I would go home as the sun was rising, shaking it out and feeling tired enough to sleep the rest of the day away. When everyone else was up and ready to be loved and hurt and carry on—I would be gone, cocooned away from it all.

At home, I kept the television off. My phone I only turned on for the occasional calls from the four people who I still let in. Mom, Dad, Ada, and Oliver. But my contact with even them thinned out, a horizon that would disappear when night finally fell—existing, but not for anyone to see.

There were two times I saw any sign of Marlow. Once, as I pumped gas and the screen at the station played an ad for an expensive French perfume. She was in it, a cream chiffon fabric draped around her naked body, close-ups of her fingers tracing her lips. The second, a stack of magazines dropped outside a storefront on my way home from the bakery. The cover featured her profile. She looked herself again by all standards. I wondered if she had gotten sober once more. If she was living the life she always wanted.

I put the farmhouse up for sale in the spring. There was a potential buyer within a week.

"It's a low offer but—" the real estate agent started to say.

"I'll accept it."

"Do you want to possibly see—"

"No. I'll accept it," I said firmly.

I was ready to leave the house behind.

And on a warm spring morning, I left the bakery after a particularly long overnight shift. I turned around from closing the bakery's front door, the bell jingling above me as if to summon her, and there she was. Standing in the middle of the street.

"Don't go," she said quietly.

She wore an olive jacket, the hood pulled over her head.

I looked around to see if anyone else was there. Anyone to maybe stop me from talking to her because they, too, were witnessing this and would be just as outraged at her audacity. But the streets were deserted. It was far too early in the morning.

I stepped down from the curb.

"What do you want, Marlow?"

"Can we talk?"

I stared at her for a moment.

"What for?" I finally said.

I began to turn away.

"I want you to be okay with me," she said, the words stumbling over each other, as though afraid if she didn't say them quickly enough I would leave.

"Okay with you?" I furrowed my brows with disbelief.

"Yes . . . you don't know how it's been for me."

A hint of a quiver hung in her voice and irritation flooded me.

"What does that even mean? To be okay? Is anybody ever *okay*?"

"I want us to be."

I shook my head heatedly. "Marlow. I'm never going to be okay. I'm never going to be okay with what happened."

What happened. I can't even bring myself to mention his name.

She stepped closer to me, her palms up, mouth turned down. She looked so desperate. But for what, I couldn't understand.

"I'm not asking for that."

"Then what?"

"Forgiveness."

I felt my throat tighten and it angered me further that I even felt anything for her. As if my own physical reactions had betrayed me.

"You seem . . . you seem better."

Somehow, I was able to force what was starting to bubble up back down in its tube.

Her eyes lit up. "I am. Thank you for noticing." She shifted her feet around. "So, you became a baker?"

I chuckled lightly, surprising me as it came out. "No. I'm a glorified flour measurer. Really."

"Why did you leave the gallery?"

"I needed something . . . simpler."

My lighter tone relaxed her. She put an arm out and dropped it.

"I miss . . . I miss us. Whatever used to be there and hasn't come back in a long time. I miss it."

She looked at me with soft, imploring eyes and, for a second, I almost gave way. The resentment had grown heavy. Heavy enough to drop and leave behind. But in that one fleeting moment, I realized it was not enough. Like a boat on the crest of a wave, fighting to get out of the storm, I was sucked back into raging waters.

"Too much," I whispered.

"What?"

"Too much has happened."

"Isla, please. I'm different. I'm sober. Please, let me help you."

"Help me? You want to help *me*?"

"Yes," she said, moving even closer.

"No. No. Stop." I ducked my head as if she were about to strike me. "Isla . . ."

"Don't you get it? I've lost enough. I lost him. I lost Sawyer . . ."

I felt the tears as I felt his name slip through my mouth.

Sawyer.

She put her hands together and then up under her face.

"Oh, Isla."

She looked so genuinely sympathetic. So . . . remorseful. With those limpid eyes of hers that never ended.

But the anger from earlier lashed up again in me and I remembered who I was talking to. She was good at this. She was good at making people believe every word she spoke was true. She wanted me to believe she was sorry.

"The knight figurine," I said in a low voice.

Her eyes widened with astonishment.

"Don't even pretend to be surprised. You knew I would find out." I ripped at her before she could even deny it.

"Isla, I wanted to tell you about it. But I never got the chance—"

"Why give it to Ada, then?"

She began to shake her head in protest. "Because there was no one else to give it to. *You* ran away from *me*, remember? I couldn't get within a foot of you."

"How did you get it, Marlow?" My voice hardened.

"What?"

"I said, how did you *get it*, Marlow?"

She narrowed her eyes. "What are you trying to say?"

"Did you pull it from his dead body? Had to have the one thing left that really belonged to me?"

Her beautiful brow furrowed with intensity.

"No. No, it wasn't like that—"

I stormed up to her, my face as close to hers as it had been since we were little girls. I could see the tiredness under her eyes. She was weary. But it didn't stop me.

He felt no pain.

"Did you . . ." I trailed off.

She lifted her chin. "Did I what?"

"You know, Marlow. You *know* what I'm asking."

I was shaking, I couldn't feel my arms.

"Are you really asking me this?" she said harshly.

I said nothing as I watched her eyes glaze over.

There was no room left in the cavity in my chest. It had expanded and propelled to a reckless beat.

"You said he felt no pain . . . he felt nothing."

She sighed as if tired of my games.

"How would you know that?" I asked.

"We don't have to do this." She sounded exasperated and it only made me press more, my foot hard on the pedal.

"Yes," I hissed. "Yes, we do."

"I slipped up . . . okay?" she said, throwing her arms up. "I had too much to drink. I was out of it that day . . ."

She trailed off before becoming calm, like a horse trainer whispering to a wild and unruly mare.

"It was all an accident," she said. "A horrible, horrible accident."

"Was it?"

She closed her eyes and licked her lips. "Yes. And it kills me, too, that he isn't here anymore. But, Isla. You need to finally accept this."

"I can't. I won't," I practically yelled.

She gazed hard into my eyes, searching, and then gripped under my mouth.

"Why are you doing this, Isla?" she asked sadly.

I jerked away from her grasp.

She stepped back from me with reluctance and began to walk away. But suddenly halted. Her head hung down until she turned and looked over her shoulder.

"The truth is . . ." Her chin trembled once. It quit like the power going out. "The truth is I don't remember. I can't remember."

I stood there for I don't know how long after she had gone. Waiting for my body to unfreeze. Waiting for the blood to return to circulating after going dry with the rage and fear that had encircled me.

I didn't see the young man talking to me at first. The nice kid who would sometimes wave to me as he took over my shift each morning. His blurred face formed features when I saw his mouth begin to move.

"Are you okay?"

His eyes were concerned and then shifted to acknowledgment, relief.

"Hey . . . I know who you are . . . I thought I recognized you. You're Marlow Fin's sister, right?"

CHAPTER 50

ISLA

Labor Day: September 7, 2020

He looked so much older than I remembered him to be.

His hair had thinned in the front, and age spots dotted the area around his eyes and jawline like constellations. I never thought of my father as old until that moment. I saw Moni somewhere in his face, but it faded out when he turned from the road to glance at me.

"Do you think we should stop at Betty's Pies . . . for old time sakes?"

I was in my thirties, but he was still trying to provide a consolation for his daughter, a treat to make all her troubles go away.

"If you want," I answered flatly.

"Let's stop, then. I could use a break. Stretch these old legs out."

It had been his idea to go up to the cabin for a few days.

My disposition apparently had not seemed too healthy lately. Mom had been calling me with more frequency, making our conversations even shorter.

"You know we worry about you, Isla," she said two days ago.

"I wish people would stop saying that."

"It's been nearly three years. Our hearts are broken, Sawyer was a son to us all. And they break for you but—"

"But what? Time to move on?" I said bitterly.

"Well . . . yes. You're still so young, honey. You could still have a life. You *should* have a life."

"I don't want a life without him."

She had gone silent—the purpose of my cold statement. I was tired. I was tired of having to explain my grief. It seemed nonsensical to me that anyone would question why I was still in the same state of misery. Why nothing had changed for me. Why I couldn't pick myself up and have that epiphany about starting a new life, come to terms with the fact that Sawyer's death had meaning and it was all destined to happen this way. Why I couldn't go on appreciating life even more, like some moment in a subpar movie.

Utter bullshit.

His death had no meaning. There was no greater purpose behind it. He was gone and I was left with the hollow space he left behind.

It had required an additional phone call from Mom and coaxing from Dad for me to agree to a little trip up north. "Fresh air" was the cure-all for everything. A change of scenery would apparently be the treatment I required.

I didn't agree to go to the cabin for their sake. There was only one small motivation that got me in the car with Dad—the memories of Sawyer that lingered there, like a shirt I had left behind and needed to reclaim. Of the time when we had just sunk our teeth into the flesh of being together, a ripe peach so perfect it would never get any better than that.

The bends in the shore-lined highway were familiar to me as Dad weaved in and out, his hands steady on the steering wheel, so cautious. He slowed down to park in front of Betty's Pies. As we walked up, I could see the cobalt booths through the window, the white-and-blue-checkered floors. He ordered a slice of blackberry rhubarb, and I shook my head, only wanting a coffee. We sat in one of the booths and he ate his pie almost forcefully. Had he hoped this little stop would cheer me up? I picked up my coffee and held it toward him.

"Pretty good coffee," I said, a pathetic attempt to be something of the daughter I used to be.

"Are you sure you don't want anything other than that?"

"I'm fine."

"You're missing out on Betty's famous pie. How often will you ever come here?" He looked to the front of the restaurant. "Maybe get something to go or—"

"You know I brought Sawyer up here once."

He adjusted forward in his seat. "Oh. I never knew that."

"Yes." I sat back into the booth. "Did you ever bring anyone up here?"

I didn't know what came over me. Maybe it was the coffee going straight to my head. The fatigue of trying to be present on this forced trip. Or maybe I finally had to ask him, make him admit it out loud . . . to me at least.

He warily wiped a blob of pie filling from his mouth.

"What makes you ask that?"

I lowered my head. "Come on, Dad. We all knew."

He went quiet, keeping his eyes focused on his plate, not looking up at me once. My question was being ignored. He was walking past it as if it had never been asked.

The table seemed to grow longer between us.

He took his last bite, scraping it up with a fork. "What do you want to do first when we get to the cabin?"

I slid the coffee mug from one hand to the other. It was my turn to ignore his question.

We got up and stood in line to pay. I thumbed through a rack of brochures and came across one for Covet Falls, a stunning picture of the waterfall nearly spilling out of the flap.

"Let's go for a hike."

He turned around, surprised, and looked at the pamphlet in my hand. He frowned briefly and nodded.

"Okay, Isla."

When we approached the cabin, the clouds hurriedly covered the skies over us like sheep herded together. The windows appeared so obscure and vacant, like an old tree that had been hollowed out and left to decay.

He parked the car, and we opened the trunk to retrieve our backpacks. The slow rain dropped on our heads.

"Are you sure you still want to go to the falls?"

"Yes. I'm sure."

He wiped a few drops off his face. "We'll need those rain slickers. I think they're still in the shed."

I followed him along the side of the cabin down to the dock. He fumbled with a bronze key and unlocked the padlock. I stepped inside behind him as he foraged around looking for the slickers. My elbow bumped into a few folding chairs and a large red tote fell to the ground.

He looked over his shoulder and then held up two dusty slickers triumphantly.

"Sorry," I mumbled, picking up the long, heavy tote.

"It's all right, sweetie. It's just the tent."

I patted the tote as I propped it back up. "Was this the one that replaced the yellow one from all those years ago? You know, right before that big storm?"

He shook the slickers out, distracted. "We never had a yellow tent," he uttered quickly.

What he said was like a paper cut, sharp at first but then dull as the pain settled in to stay. His hands gripped the jackets and remained still for a moment. I wasn't sure what it was about his words that stung me like that.

It lasted a few seconds. But it was there.

He shook the jackets even harder, making flapping noises that wrapped around us both until one fell out of his hands.

"We should go. Before the rain gets too heavy," he said, pushing one of the jackets into my hands and brushing past me.

I pulled a sleeve on and watched him march ahead of me, tearing his jacket on with his head ducked down. He was smaller, shrunken—nothing like the tall figure I had grown accustomed to as my father.

We remained that way, me a few yards behind him as he led the way to the falls.

They roared. Tumbling and louder than ever, snarling at us for our prolonged absence. A grand display of mist and wetness. We stood staring out at its vastness and never-ending depth, the water strands of long thread pulled down and yanked into whatever lurked below. I could see him looking at me out of the corner of his eye, not quite turning to face me. What was he looking for? Was I lost to him? Where had I gone that he needed to search?

I stepped forward, disturbing the dirt loosened from the rain, and a few small, gray stones tumbled down and into the falls below.

Fall and disappear forever.

What were the stories Dad used to tell me?

I felt the beats of the waterfall in the pit of my stomach, the beginnings of a recollection that contained nothing to look back on fondly. They were pieces floating around, crawling back together, creating what exactly—I was afraid to try to understand or even know.

He turned to venture back to the cabin. I stayed behind a few minutes longer, tipping my face down toward the bottom of the falls, light-headed from the thought of how far I would plunge.

I felt drained and wet as I strode back the way I came. I found Dad standing still at the back of the cabin. He was staring at something.

She stood in front of the windows. It dawned on me it was in almost the exact same spot where I first saw her. Her arms were crossed, and she spread her mouth open into something between a grimace and a grin.

"Hello, Isla."

CHAPTER 51

THE INTERVIEW

2021

[Studio]

JODI LEE: Are you going to be okay to finish the interview?

MARLOW FIN: Yes . . . I'm sorry. I'm ready now.

[Voice-over]

JODI LEE: After thirty minutes away from the set, Marlow did come back to our interview. This time alone, without any of her team. She insisted they stay out of the studio, much to their objections. She seemed calmer and more alert upon her return.

It was at this portion of our interview that things began to take a turn toward the unexpected—something neither myself nor my producers could have ever anticipated.

[Studio]

JODI LEE: Are you sure you're ready, Marlow? I'm going to be asking some really tough questions. You agreed to this. No holds barred.

MARLOW FIN: Let's finish this.

JODI LEE: September 7, 2020. Your sister, Isla Baek-Ford, goes missing. You are the last person to see her alive.

The last person.

How do you explain that?

MARLOW FIN: I can't.

JODI LEE: Her blood was found in the shed. On your dress. Why is it, then, that you can't explain your sister's whereabouts?

MARLOW FIN: You don't understand, Jodi. I simply can't explain it.

JODI LEE: Do you understand why it sounds like you are lying?

MARLOW FIN: Yes.

JODI LEE: Your father seems to think he can explain it. He seems to think you did it. That you murdered your sister in cold blood.

[*Roll package, recent footage of Patrick Baek*]

JODI LEE: Since the disappearance of his daughter, Patrick Baek has been very clear and vocal as to his belief that Marlow is responsible.

[*Patrick followed by reporters going into his house, turns and shouts at them*]

You want to know the truth? She killed her. She killed my daughter. Marlow Fin killed my daughter!

[Studio]

JODI LEE: Your father has not referred to you as his "daughter" since that September 2020 day. He refers to you only as Marlow Fin.

MARLOW FIN: Just like everyone else.

JODI LEE: Yes. Does this bother you?

MARLOW FIN: That he doesn't call me his daughter? Or that he thinks I'm a murderer?

JODI LEE: Marlow. [*Leans in*] You truly can't look me in the eye and tell me what happened the night of September 7, 2020? You can't finally give it some peace . . . let the truth come out?

MARLOW FIN: No. I can't.

JODI LEE: [*Pauses*] Why?

MARLOW FIN: Because . . .

JODI LEE: [*Nods*]

MARLOW FIN: [*Voice shaky*] I don't remember.

JODI LEE: You don't remember.

MARLOW FIN: [*Inaudible*]

JODI LEE: Marlow?

MARLOW FIN: Yes. [*Crying*]

JODI LEE: I'm here. Don't forget that. I'm here. Just you and me right now. Everything else is background noise. Okay?

MARLOW FIN: Okay.

JODI LEE: [*Moves down next to Marlow, places hands over hers*] Let's help you remember. We can do that together. All right?

MARLOW FIN: [*Nods slowly*]

JODI LEE: The beginning. Let's start from the beginning of that day. What is it that you do remember? Take us to that morning. Did you know you were going to drive to the cabin?

MARLOW FIN: I followed them.

That's why I ended up there. I wanted to talk to Isla so badly. I wanted to be able to tell her so much. I didn't have the nerve to go inside our house. I waited that morning parked outside. I thought I could try to talk to her from a distance. But then Patrick came out the front door with her. He carried two backpacks. And then she came out quickly and they got into his car and started driving. So, I followed them.

JODI LEE: When did you realize they were going to the cabin?

MARLOW FIN: Almost immediately, when they started going north.

JODI LEE: Did you ever think, maybe I should stop? Turn around?

MARLOW FIN: I was on autopilot. I didn't think. I just drove behind them. They pulled into a local pie shop that's a little over an hour before you get to the cabin. We used to always stop there as kids.

But I didn't stop with them. I kept driving and got to the cabin first. I parked my car on a side road and walked the rest of the way.

JODI LEE: When they got to the cabin, did you make your presence known right away?

MARLOW FIN: They didn't come inside. They went on a hike first. By the direction they were going, I knew it had to be Covet Falls.

JODI LEE: Covet Falls. That's the waterfall close to the cabin. Do you know why they were going there?

MARLOW FIN: [*Shakes head*] I decided to wait for them in the back. The lakeside of the cabin. Patrick came back first. And then Isla saw me.

JODI LEE: Did she seem happy to see you? Surprised?

MARLOW FIN: She was . . . nothing. She didn't react. She walked past me into the cabin. Patrick wasn't super pleased to see me either. There was no explosive confrontation. It was worse. It was like I didn't matter. Like I didn't exist to them.

JODI LEE: Did this frustrate you? Maybe even anger you?

MARLOW FIN: No . . . no. I felt sadness. I was overcome with sadness.

JODI LEE: When did you eventually speak?

MARLOW FIN: Patrick brought out the fishing poles from the shed onto the dock. She followed him, and I kind of waited back. I wasn't sure, really, if I should even stay. I considered giving up and leaving.

But I followed them once again. I sat down next to her on the dock, and she didn't get up or anything. She finally turned to me once, told me she didn't want to go there. I respected that and we just fished. Quietly. Next to each other. Our legs dangled deep in the lake. The water was so high.

JODI LEE: By this time, was it still light out?

MARLOW FIN: Yes. But the sun was setting. Patrick caught two walleyes. They were actually quite big . . . he cleaned and gutted them in front of us. Fried them. We ate pretty much in silence outside. Patrick had made a bonfire. That's when . . .

JODI LEE: That's when what happened?

MARLOW FIN: That's when Isla just lost it. She blames me for it, you know.

JODI LEE: For what?

MARLOW FIN: His death. Sawyer's death.

JODI LEE: How did she lose it?

MARLOW FIN: Screaming at me. Like she was finally saying everything she wanted to say. She looked like a different person, there was so much anger. It was . . . pure, unadulterated rage.

I may have said some things back . . . things I shouldn't have said. I regret them completely. I wish I would have just taken it. I should have taken it. It was . . . it was horrible.

JODI LEE: Did it ever get physical?

MARLOW FIN: No . . . no. This was worse than that.

JODI LEE: What was Patrick doing during all of this?

MARLOW FIN: He finally told us to stop. Stood between us and then took Isla inside. I don't know what was said between them once they went inside the cabin. I stayed by the bonfire.

I was already so warm from all the fighting . . . all the hostility with Isla. My face, the fire. I felt like I was on fire. I was so upset after our fight. I was shaking . . . I was not myself.

It all gets so foggy after this. It's like I'm in the woods and they're on fire. And I can't get out. I can't see past the smoke.

I can't see anything.

JODI LEE: So, this . . . this is when you start to lose your memory of that night?

MARLOW FIN: I've tried so hard. I'm so tired of not being able to remember. My past and how I was found. That night. I can't . . . I can't do it anymore. [*Head goes down and shoulders shake*]

JODI LEE: Marlow . . . it's okay. I can help you.

MARLOW FIN: How? How can anyone help me?

JODI LEE: Just concentrate. Focus. Your sister left with Patrick. Then what? What did you do next, Marlow?

MARLOW FIN: [*Closes eyes, tilts face up*] I . . . I walked down to the dock. There was water. I wanted to be near water.

JODI LEE: Why did you need to be near water?

MARLOW FIN: I was hot. I was just so hot.

JODI LEE: Did you get in the water?

MARLOW FIN: No . . . I don't think so. I think . . .

JODI LEE: What next? What did you feel? Hear?

MARLOW FIN: I heard the water lapping against the dock. I stood there for a while. Letting the night breeze cool me.

JODI LEE: Was anyone else there?

MARLOW FIN: I don't know . . . I . . .

JODI LEE: Who else is there, Marlow?

MARLOW FIN: [*Crying*] I wanted it to stop burning.

JODI LEE: What was burning?

MARLOW FIN: Me . . . I was.

JODI LEE: You can tell me, Marlow. You can. Was anyone else there?

MARLOW FIN: [*Gasps*] Yes.

JODI LEE: Who? Who was it?

MARLOW FIN: I did get in the water. I remember now. I was in the water.

Oh God . . . Oh God, help me. I remember now. I remember . . .

CHAPTER 52

ISLA

The Night before the Interview

Everybody knows Marlow Fin.

Everybody thinks she killed her sister.

Everybody thinks I'm dead.

I am perched. I am patient. *Just one more night.* I feel myself holding my breath already with the rest of the world, watching and waiting for that face to show up.

That face I saw in the window.

I see it again and I bend down and spread my hands wide over the television.

She is exiting a restaurant, her head bowed low as a bevy of paparazzi take her picture. Each flash makes me flinch.

"Marlow! Marlow!" they cry out, as though she's in peril.

She steps down from the curb. I can see her ache. Her pain. Her sorrow. She is my sister. I don't need to see it. I can feel it just by touching the screen, the glow of it giving me even more of a measurement.

"Are you going to tell the truth?"

"Did you do it, Marlow? Tell us what really happened!"

Yes, tell them. Tell them what happened.

You would think it would have been maddening to always see her face on the news. An endless montage of her red-carpet premieres, her modeling shots, her movies, her face flashing like a disorienting strobe light. But it was the opposite.

The more her face was shown, the less mine was ever brought up. I was missing but she was the focus. The hot intensity on her made me feel safe. I was the buried lead, disregarded, the part of the story most people forgot about.

Isla is missing. But she *is the one we care about, the one we love to obsess over.*

I was always the unseen sister, and it was a gift.

My apartment has become a cocoon of protection and illusion over the last nine months. I'm dizzy with no longer existing, cut off from anyone who ever knew me. Within the walls of this apartment, I'm shielded from the rest of the world.

But the ability to ignore time has now dwindled.

I close all the windows and draw all the shades. I check the dead bolt on the door twice, then once more. I sink back deeper into the cushions. I sit in darkness, and it calms me. The remote is slippery in my hands as I slide it down and grip the buttons. I focus my attention on the latest story.

There is a brief mention of my name on CNN, but no new developments or leads. It is a stagnant and dead part of the story, but they keep running it. Bringing it up like some mandatory prerequisite, the warm-up to mentioning Marlow Fin.

I switch to NBC to see lead-up promos for the interview. Older clips of Jodi Lee as an anchor followed by shots of Marlow being chased by a media mob. She ducks into a car, then they roll footage of her at the last movie premiere she attended. Posing regally on the red carpet, one ankle crossed over the other, her hand on her hip. She is a professional.

She is a professional liar.

You can't trap a tiger just by catching him. You have to make him think he has won.

Isn't that what modeling and acting are? Pretending to be anything but what you are in that moment? I don't see it as deceitful. I see it as a talent. An endowment of having all your faculties together, right there, ready to execute on cue.

I am ready to watch her.

Come on, Marlow. Let's see that beautiful face.

My knees bounce and I steady them, but there is nothing steady about the rest of me. I need the interview to begin, to hear the familiar intervals of her voice, her pauses and hesitations.

Marlow, the wild one. The unpredictable one. Always full of surprises.

Always one step ahead.

CHAPTER 53

ISLA

Labor Day: September 7, 2020

She looked like the ghost she could become and the ghost I wanted her to be.

I stood on the bottom of the steps below her, making her Amazonian in height, a warrior who blocked my path.

"What are you doing here, Marlow?" I heard Dad say.

The straps on my backpack were damp from the falls. They cut into my shoulders as I gripped them hard. I put my head down and brushed past him as I walked up the stone steps to the cabin.

"Isla. I'm here to talk to Isla," she replied, looking only at me.

I would not reciprocate. I would not breathe or make a sound. I would not acknowledge her presence.

"Please, Isla. I need to tell you something. You have to know—"

"Marlow," Dad cut in. "I don't think this is a good idea."

I shut the door behind me, drowning out any more of their noise. I looked up to my old bedroom and walked with purposeful, shuffled steps toward it. I stared down at the bed and fell in. I had never felt so exhausted, so drained of all energy. My arms and legs turned to solid tree limbs. Stiff, rooted. I slept into blackness.

There was no dreaming. No lingering memories of images in my head. I woke up to nothing. I saw the door to the lake was open downstairs as I leaned over the railing.

Murmurs, low and strong, came through between sounds of the water kissing the shoreline and distant boats turning in for the day.

The words were undecipherable, the tension of them palpable.

I appeared before the two of them and they stopped. There was an eerie pause in their exchange and everything around us halted.

Dad stood up from his chair and smiled as though we had been there for days, a course of uneventful, enjoyable ones at the lake filled with swimming and s'mores and what any other happy family would do. A family that we were not.

"You're up. Did you sleep okay?"

I nodded.

He acted like there was nothing abnormal about his charade of cheerfulness as he rubbed his hands together.

"You know what we haven't done in forever, girls? Dockside fishing. What do you say? You want to join Dad for a little sunset fishing?"

We deliberately looked at each other, as if a magnetic field drew us together, and followed him down the steps to the dock, briefly united against his unnerving, enthusiastic front. We had no control over our bodies, drones that submitted to commands, our autonomy briefly gone. For there was no other option. He retrieved the poles from the shed, the fishing knife nested in its brown leather sheath on his waistband.

We sat down next to each other on the dock. The wood felt surprisingly soft, as worn as we were. I felt her eyes rove over me and I shook my head, casting out a line.

"No. Just let it be. For now. Let it be."

I gazed out over the water to show her. It had become a mirror as the light left us, the rows and rows of liquid metallic ridges that shone for us. The hues of the sun bruised the top of it, dark blues and pinks that glistened together.

She nodded as if to say she understood.

We couldn't talk. Not now. Not in front of all this.

Dad yanked a walleye up out of the water. It flopped twice on the dock before he pulled the line and slid its mouth off the hook. We watched as he gutted it right there. The knife made ripping sounds as he cut through its flesh. Pinkish liquid dripped down his hands. He caught a second and did the same.

Night had fallen once we went back up to the cabin. He lit a bonfire and laid out a grate for the fish to cook on. The flames made my cheeks quickly grow hot, and the tiny hairs on my skin seemed to melt off. I rubbed my hands over my face and felt a sudden hunger. I eagerly ate the white flaky meat with a fork, drinking wine to ease it down. I had another glass and fell back into my chair. I could see Dad's eyes observing me above the fire, the sparks dancing around his face, glowing like a shaman, an invocation cast over us.

Marlow remained quiet. She didn't drink and ate very little. I envied her ease. I envied her ability to return again and again, a creature that could not be put down. Stronger each time, unstoppable in her growth. She was untouched and more beautiful than ever.

And I had been altered in every single way possible. Beaten by death before even dying. A woman who lost everything that meant anything to her.

"Look at you," I muttered, barely holding my glass up, the stem sliding down my hand.

"What?"

"I said, look at *you*."

She stared back at me with disappointment. "Isla, there is so much you don't know."

"I know enough," I said, pouring what was left down my throat.

"No . . . you don't understand. I need to tell you—" Her eyes went to Dad, who had stood up.

"I don't care. I don't care because there is nothing you can say that changes anything."

"Oh, Isla . . ."

She became even more serene. As if what I just said was a flowing compliment for her to bathe in. The heat in my face surged, and everything I had resented her for, everything I had blamed her for, flashed bright. I wanted to engulf her into ashen pieces right in front of me.

"Oh, Isla?" I mocked. "Oh, Isla, you poor thing. You poor thing who lost everything. Do you know what it's even like? To barely make it through the pain each morning? And when I finally have the strength to get up, when I walk down the street . . . the first thing people wonder is if I'm your sister."

"No. I can't."

Her eyes were so sad. Or were they amused?

My confusion rattled what was already so enraged.

"Stop!" I screamed.

I felt Dad's hand on my shoulder. I jerked away.

"Stop! I want you to stop!"

She shook her head. "Do you think this is what Moni would have wanted? Sawyer?"

A snarl rose up and out of me. "Don't you say their names! Don't you say *his* name!"

Broken glass shattered on the ground, and I looked down to find my hand empty and shaking. A sob shuddered in my throat, and I turned to get away from them. I stumbled up the stairs and into my room. I lay on the floor. My hands opened and closed against it with each cry. The emptiness put me to sleep.

When I came to, there was no light.

The lights in the cabin were out. The bonfire hissed from being extinguished.

I went down the stone steps and covered my arms from the cold air. The lake was unforgiving at night; no one would be comforted as she slept. I turned to go inside but heard a shout.

A shout cut off before it could ring out—scissors had snipped the thread.

I stared out at the dock to see someone at the end of it.

I walked slowly at first, my bare feet padding against the grain of the wood. But the figure at the end grew smaller. I walked faster and then began to run.

My arms reached out. They knew before I could see him. They knew what he was doing to her.

He knelt down, one knee tucked in as if in prayer before flattening his body out, crossing the dock like a railroad track. He shook from the resistance.

The water splashed playfully as her hands remained above the surface, striking left and right to come up.

CHAPTER 54

ISLA

The Day of the Interview

I dial the number on my phone and let it ring.

"Hello?" she answers.

There is skepticism in her voice. She doesn't recognize this number, after all. She's likely getting dinner ready and annoyed the phone rang.

"Hello?" she asks again.

"Mom," I say. I feel so cold saying it. *Mom.*

She is silent.

"Don't hang up."

I hear deep breathing and then a succession of small gasps.

"I knew . . ." she whispers.

"What?"

"I always knew you were still out there. A mother always knows."

A mother . . . a mother always knows.

Her voice is muffled and I realize she is crying.

"I can't talk long," I finally say.

She sniffs a few times. They sound wet through the phone. "Where are you?"

"I'm . . . away," I answer, looking around the apartment. "I'll be okay."

"But why—"

"I have to ask you something."

"Ask me? I don't understand." She grows frantic. "We need to get you help. We need to get you—"

"Please. Just let me ask you this," I cut back.

I can hear her trying to calm herself. "Okay. I'm listening."

I close my eyes. I can't ask with my eyes open. If I do, somehow, I will see her reaction even though we are nowhere near each other.

"Have you always known?"

I force the question out like it's hot, as if it burns my lips.

"What? I don't quite—"

"Listen to me, Mom. Have you always known?"

She goes silent again.

"Mom?"

"Known what?" She sounds fearful. She sounds resigned.

"About Marlow's mother?"

"Dear God," she says.

"About my—"

I stop there. I can't say it. I expect her to go quiet as well. I expect her to never be able to answer and, somehow, I wish for that.

"I knew," she answers.

I sit down at the table. My legs can no longer support me, each of her words a new weight clipped to my belly.

She heaves a huge sigh and sob all at once.

"I was the one who told him to take care of it. But I never in a million years thought—"

"Mom . . ."

"She wouldn't leave us alone, Isla. She was determined to hurt our family."

I shiver. I shake my head.

"She must have followed us. I don't know. But when I saw her . . ."

"Please. Mom . . ."

She can't end it there. She rattles on and the more she speaks, the words sliding out all too easily, the more I feel like I'm going to vomit.

"He was so angry. Furious. He went out to talk to her and then he came back. And he told me she wouldn't be coming back anymore. I didn't know what he meant by that. But then—"

"Stop. Please stop," I whisper.

She is crying again now. "We had to. We had to do it."

"Do what?" I tremble and put my head down.

It's suddenly quiet before she speaks again. "They haunted me every day, you know."

She breathes in, the sound raspy from crying. She can't speak. I am ready to let go. I am ready to hang up.

"Her eyes. She has her eyes."

CHAPTER 55

WREN

1980s

The bathroom floor was cold as Wren pushed her legs out and sat. She wished she was in any bathroom but the one in her basement apartment, with the dirty tiles that, no matter how much she scrubbed, never looked clean. The scratched mirror with a crack that split diagonally. She couldn't look in that mirror. She didn't want to see her face like that anymore.

She didn't want to live like that anymore.

This was her key to the exit door.

She clutched the plastic stick in her hands and rested her head on the vanity cabinet. If she closed her eyes, she could still see Stella's face. The shock and happiness that filled every crevice.

"You don't understand what this means to me . . . to us," she had whispered through tears. And then, realizing what was going to have to happen—what she had asked of the young woman in front of her—she sobered.

"We tried everything. *Everything*." Her eyes hooded over. "We aren't like most married couples—we don't *look* like most married couples. And with adoption"—she shook her head—"with adoption, if you aren't anyone's first choice, then you are no one's choice."

They decided to wait until after Christmas. As if it were inappropriate to proceed during the holidays. As if it really mattered when it happened.

Wren followed their precise instructions two days after New Year's. She knocked on the hotel room door at the requested time. It was a nice hotel, nicer than any she had ever stayed in before. Stella answered. She could barely look her in the face.

"Thank you for coming," she said.

She could see him in the corner, sitting in an armchair.

"Patrick? Did you want me to—"

"I think it's best." His voice suddenly shot out, curt. He turned his head and looked out the window. "I think it's best if you leave the room."

"Yes," Stella replied.

She stuck her hand out. A white envelope. "This is the first half. As we agreed." She brushed past Wren, their shoulders bouncing off each other.

She paused, not turning around. "When I saw you out the window of the coffee shop . . ." She began to close the door. "I saw what our child could look like." Her voice broke as it shut.

Wren kept her head turned, afraid to look forward.

He was waiting for her on the bed.

"You're one of my students," he said.

She said nothing.

"You aren't really a student . . . are you."

"I want to help you," she said, meeting his eyes.

He took his jacket off and laid it carefully next to him. "I love my wife very much. I'd do anything for my wife. But this—"

"This is what she wants."

She wasn't sure where her voice came from. Forceful. Insistent.

As she lay there and she felt him flood her insides, she imagined Stella outside the room, her hand placed on the door as if she could still be the one, still be the woman who could carry his child.

They repeated this once more that week. She assured them her cycle was never off.

And now here she was, holding the answer for all of them. She stood up and flipped the stick over. Two pink lines boasted their darkness at her.

CHAPTER 56

ISLA

The Night of the Interview

It's not what people forget. It's what they pretend to forget.

Of course, she remembers everything.

I told you she is good at it. She is good at convincing us all.

I watch as Jodi Lee looks as though she has caught the biggest story of her life. There's both pleasure and revulsion in her face. I can't look away.

I can't imagine anyone can look away from their screens.

She's Marlow Fin, after all.

Every pixel of color swarms to collect around her stunning features, like wasps fighting for their station in the nest. She's magnificent. Her hair cascades perfectly down one shoulder. There are a few streams of tears down her face. She looks up to Jodi and sits up straighter. She has an announcement to make after all.

"He tried to drown me."

"Who? Who tried to drown you?" Jodi asks.

She puts her arms out as if to demonstrate for the audience.

"I stood there alone on the dock. I thought I was alone. And I feel this big shove. I'm in the water before I can react. It's so cold, it feels like shockwaves throughout my whole body . . . and I see his face. He doesn't smile. He doesn't cry. He's just looking down at me."

"Who, Marlow? Who is looking down at you?"

"My father."

"Patrick? Patrick Baek tried to drown you that night . . . but why? Why would he do that?"

"Because . . ."

"You can tell us. You can tell us, Marlow."

Her mouth shakes as she continues.

"He had his hands on my shoulders and then my head. He's so strong I can't do anything but move my arms in the water. I can't see him anymore. And the whole time I can't breathe. I can't breathe . . ."

Jodi Lee looks like she's going to be sick. But she holds it together.

"Why, Marlow? Why would he drown you?"

"Because I remembered the truth about my mother."

CHAPTER 57

WREN

1980s

She made the phone call she promised them she would make.

"It's time," was all she had to say into the phone.

He picked her up at the corner by the deli and told her to lie down in the back seat. When they reached the house, he draped his coat over her and led her up the front steps. The contractions seized her as they crossed the foyer.

"Can you make it up the stairs?" he asked flatly.

She nodded.

Stella was waiting for them in their bedroom.

"I have everything prepared, Wren," she said, motioning toward a miniature threaded fortress of blankets and towels.

They both helped her onto her side. The sheets smelled like lavender. She smoothed her hand over a wrinkle.

That was the last complete memory she had before the pain fogged out the room. Their faces became blurred masks that spoke to her incoherently.

Her body felt like it was cracking in two halves when she pushed the baby out. She couldn't recall how long it had been since she first lay down on the bed. Her scream was muffled by the rolled-up washcloth that had been placed into her mouth.

But none of that mattered. She was here. She held her baby's tiny body in her arms and cried. How was it possible to feel such love for someone she didn't know? She cried even more and then laughed through the tears, delirious with euphoria. She looked up at them, expecting them to be just as she was.

They looked down at her with faded expressions.

Her joy had muted theirs.

"We've picked out a name," Stella announced.

Wren looked down at the baby girl, who rooted at her chest. The slight tug of her lips pressed and then peeled away like a snail.

Stella's fingers felt like spears as they dug against her skin, pulling the baby away. She handed her to Patrick, who stiffly held her and then stared down with amazement.

"Wait," she started to say as he left the room.

She tried to get up but then sat back quickly, light-headed.

"Shhh. Rest now," Stella cooed, smoothing her hair back.

"What did you name her?"

She didn't answer as she turned to leave.

"Please."

"Isla," she finally said with her back facing her.

They sent her home with another envelope, thicker this time. She held it against her chest in the basement apartment and cried for something she didn't know she wanted. There was a part of her missing—no, many parts missing—as if every one of her organs had been torn in half and taken from her.

She went back to their house a few months later. She knocked. They were home. She had watched them in the window at first, Patrick holding the baby so carefully as Stella cleared the dishes away after dinner. She had already grown so much.

"Let me see her," she said to the door.

She knocked urgently.

"Please. Let me see my baby," she said louder.

She reached up to knock again but the door opened, and he grabbed her wrist.

"Quiet," he said through gritted teeth.

Her baby cried somewhere in the house, and she heard Stella comforting her.

"I want to see her. Just once."

He held on tighter, and the thin skin around her wrist burned with his grip.

"Don't ever come back here."

His eyes were dark, and she could see that he wanted to do more than hold her wrist.

She felt like vomiting. Even the contents of those envelopes could not help her. She couldn't turn to anyone for help.

She was not someone in a position to ask for help.

Something had to replace her void, the space inside her growing to where she felt it twisting, thick and ferocious up through her throat. Something had to take its place.

She walked around in search of it. Julien smiled at her from the window of the restaurant as she passed. He held on to her tight later that night, telling her how much he liked her. How much he had wanted to be with her. She nodded, breathing hard and trying not to let him see her tears as he lay between her legs.

The next morning, the bus fumes gave her a headache as she sat in the back.

It was warmer where she had decided to go. She quickly wanted to rethink that decision, as the extreme summer heat made her already-swollen feet feel like the skin over her toes would split open from the pressure. Her belly was already round again.

It was another girl.

But this time . . . *this time* she felt no elation. The disappointment, the hope that this would cure what she saw as her ailment ate away at her like acid. This new, tiny body that squirmed in her arms felt like an intrusion. A reminder of how far away she was from what she was trying to reclaim.

This little girl had her eyes. She took her by the hand and led her from city to city until she couldn't take it anymore.

She went back to where it all started. Where she was forbidden from ever returning to.

She watched them again. This time the three of them. The trees of the forest near the lake were her guardians, shielding her from being exposed.

This time would be different. This time he would listen.

CHAPTER 58

ISLA

Labor Day: September 7, 2020

The force of my cheek hitting the ridge of his backbone speared pain up my jaw and throughout my skull. I wrapped my arms around his neck, yanking it upward. His arms seesawed up and he reached for me, clawing at my forearms. I tightened my grip and screamed out. His legs pulled up under him and tipped us both into the water.

Three seconds. Three seconds of abrupt peace took over me.

There was nothing to see but liquid darkness, inky and composed. My legs made a slow, thick dance, kicking to break through. When I came up, hair floated toward me, slithering out in waves.

She was face down in the water.

I grabbed at her, not knowing, not even sensing whatever piece of her my hands had gripped and dragged up. She sputtered and weakly grasped at the nearest plank. I pulled myself up first and then clutched her hands as she toppled sideways onto the dock.

I twisted forward, searching each side to find him climbing up a few yards away from us. I could hear the heavy sound of water pouring from his wet clothes, each hard step coming closer to us as we instinctively reached for each other.

Who was this man? Older than I had ever seen him, defeated, with shoulders that sloped so narrowly. This was not the father I knew.

"Why?" It was the only word I could utter.

He lumbered two more steps toward us and then sank down onto his knees. His hands were flat on the dock as he caught his breath.

"Because I remember," Marlow said.

"Remember?" I turned to her, and it was then I saw the cloudiness of a forgotten past churning in her eyes.

"I've known for some time now. But I never told you. I never told anyone. But I remember exactly what happened the day you found me. My life before this family."

"Enough, Marlow," Dad said, still breathing heavily as he stood up. "You're making up lies. You're using again. Everyone knows it."

His expression went flat, dejected at how weak his own words had become.

She glared at him with piercing venom. "*Me?* The liar?" She looked back at me slowly and my heart stopped.

I wasn't ready. Whatever she had to say next . . . I would never be ready.

"My mother came up here . . . our mother."

Her words scorched my ears and tingled up the back of my neck.

Our mother.

My hands pressed down on the dock, pushing me away from her as though I could escape it all. "What do you mean?"

"I remember exactly what she looked like," she said, leaning closer to sit next to me.

My whole body trembled. From the cold or the shock, it didn't matter.

"Looked like?" I whispered.

"You look just like her . . . our mother."

There it was again. *Our mother.*

"Stop it, Marlow! I'm warning you . . . stop with your stories," snapped Dad, his hands clenching into fists, flashing anger reemerging.

"Do you think she's really going to believe you, of all people? Does anyone?"

She remained steady, unflinching, and put her hand on my shoulder, claiming me—all the while staring at him.

"Or what? You'll try to drown me?" She half grinned.

I thought for one second he was going to push her. But his hands opened, releasing the last of whatever energy that remained. He sat down in a heap, overcome by it all.

Exhausted.

She slid her hand down my arm gently, her eyes glowing. "It took me a while to figure it out. But you could have been her twin. My memories of her face—sometimes I thought it was you I was remembering."

A face . . . my face that made her remember.

Dad clutched his head as if in pain. "Please don't do this. Not now."

"I'm right, aren't I?" she shot at him.

"Right?" He flung his hands down. "What's there to be right about?"

"And you think what you and Stella did was right?" She spoke with such force, her lips moved harshly.

He bowed his head, placing it down between his knees. "All we ever wanted was a family," he barely uttered.

"Dad?"

I said his name like it was a question. Full of all the disappointments and horror he would never be able to answer. His paternal status had been altered, his title forever stripped away with one word.

"Tell us. Tell us how," Marlow demanded.

How . . . how we became a family. How we had turned into this.

His wrists crossed over his lap, as if they were chained together.

"We couldn't have children," he said, staring out into the lake. "We tried and it never happened. That was difficult enough. But Stella? She took it further. She became obsessed with it—it consumed our lives."

He snapped back to us, making sure he had our attention.

"I wanted to do anything to make her happy again—*anything*. And then one day she came to me with this insane request. As if all our problems had been solved because she had figured it out once and for all. I wonder now if she knew what was real then, if—you see, nothing else mattered to her. Nothing."

We watched him go silent. As though it was impossible to go on. As though he couldn't say it.

Her request.

He looked away from us both.

"She said if our child couldn't come from her, at least part of it could come from me. That we could do it on our own . . . it was all in our hands, she kept telling me . . ."

His fingers curled and shook as he drew them next to his mouth.

"She had even picked out who it would be."

The air around me disappeared and I wondered if I would ever breathe again. Marlow took my hand.

His next words were transactional. "We paid her. She needed money. And we needed a child."

"Her," I muttered.

"Huh?" he met my eyes as if he forgot I was there.

"You said *her*. What was her name?"

"Wren," he answered quickly. "Her name was Wren."

He didn't stop there, like it was pain that had to be pushed through.

"All our friends knew we were having trouble getting pregnant. They only assumed we had used a surrogate when Stella never showed. People didn't really ask questions back then—you kept these kinds of things private. But we had Wren deliver the baby at home, and forged affidavits that it was Stella who had the home birth."

The way he smiled then made me sick. "We were so happy, Isla. We were so happy to finally have you. You don't know how it changed your mother. How it brought her back to life." His smile faded. "But that woman . . . Wren. She wouldn't leave us alone. She kept trying to take you, our baby. Can you imagine what you would do if someone tried to take your baby?"

He paused and looked at Marlow. "She came back with you. That week we were at the cabin. But we didn't know about you, I swear. We didn't know she had another child."

Marlow lifted her gaze up toward the cabin, as if she could see it all again. "She brought me with her. We camped out in the woods to be near all of you. She kept telling me I was going to meet my sister soon."

She held tighter to my hand, and I felt myself recoil.

"I'm not saying what she did was right or wrong. But she didn't deserve it."

"What didn't she deserve?" I asked forcefully.

Marlow turned her head back to him. "Why don't you tell her . . . *Dad?*"

"You don't get to call me that . . . not anymore," he said through gritted teeth.

I placed my hand out, to guide and steady myself. "You lived in the woods . . . before we found you. With our mother . . ."

Our mother. I had let that fall through my lips.

I pointed to her. My hand quivered and kept pointing, as if it were a gun in my hand, aimlessly looking for a target until it settled on Dad.

"The tent. The yellow tent I saw you with that day. You were throwing it away. I remember . . . I remember that tent."

He shook his head. "How would you even remember that?"

"It doesn't matter. The only thing that matters is that I do."

"Isla," he said pleadingly.

"No. Tell me I'm wrong." A cry caught in my throat.

"I want to . . ."

"No. Tell me it isn't true. That you couldn't have . . ."

"I can't," he said, hushed.

"Why not?" I demanded. *"Why not?"*

"It was the right thing to do!" he yelled. His shook his hands in front of him, the potency of his shout causing flickers of water to fly through the air.

I bent forward, my midsection contracted, and the back of my throat opened up. There was nothing left inside me to be sick. I would have given anything to be sick, to release the disgust that foamed inside me.

He got up slowly, on his knees, as if still trying to find a way into our good graces.

"She was coming to take you, Isla. She wasn't going to stop until she finally took you away from us. I tried to make it all go away. She wouldn't leave us alone. And then to follow us . . . our *family* . . . up here. To this place. I tried to talk some sense into her. I tried. I really did."

He stared at Marlow.

"She was beautiful."

I felt her shudder next to me.

He shook his head rapidly, trying to erase what happened.

"I still don't know how it got to that point. She wouldn't listen to me. She wouldn't let anything I was trying to explain to her make sense. I was screaming at her to leave us alone, but she wouldn't stop asking me to give back her baby . . . *her* baby. She was like this—this machine that you could never turn off. But she had agreed to it, remember—she knew exactly what she was getting into. Didn't that mean something? She knew how much we wanted a child."

"Jesus!" I shouted out, doubling over, hugging myself.

"She threatened me. She threatened our family. She was going to finally go to the police, a lawyer, whoever could help her, and tell them. She was never going to stop. I put my hands on her shoulders and I . . ."

The lake became hushed right then. Every wave of water still. Every possible sound sucked away.

"I pushed her away from me."

I had never seen him so scared, so out of control.

"I didn't mean for her to fall . . . I didn't!" he cried. "She must have slipped. I don't remember how but suddenly she was there. Under the water. She was so still. So beautiful. And I just . . . I let her go. She floated down the river. Down the falls . . ."

His eyes teared up as he wrenched his hands together. He sobbed once and then caught himself.

"You have to understand," he said, lunging closer to me. "It was the only way to protect our family. It was the right thing to do. We did the right thing by taking Marlow in, didn't we? Isn't that what we all strive for? To do the right thing? To sacrifice for those we love?"

"You're crazy," I whispered.

I stood up and stepped away from him. The man I had called my father.

I don't know you. I don't know who you are anymore.

"No," Marlow said firmly. "No. Don't give him that. Crazy would mean he's ill. Don't give him that."

"Why keep it a secret?" I turned to her abruptly. "When it all came back to you. You remembered it all. Why keep it a secret so long? All this time?"

Her face softened deeply. "You still don't get it, do you, Isla? I would do anything to protect you."

"Protect me?"

"It would have ruined you. Everything you had grown to trust, and love, would have crumbled. I couldn't do that to you."

"You kept it all in . . . for me . . ."

Why? Why would she do that for me?

"Yes . . . and it would have ruined this family. This family I had once loved so dearly. That once meant everything to me. I did everything to please every single one of you. To make you believe I was part of you all. But no matter what I did, I was still somehow an outsider. Stella, my so-called mother, looked at me every single day with such . . . *hatred*. Even my real mother didn't want me."

She looked so lost and angry, it made me shake my head at her.

"Marlow—"

"When I remembered the truth, when I remembered what he did to my mother, I realized something."

"What?"

"Nobody wanted Marlow. But everybody wanted you." There was both pride and ice on the edge of her voice.

"*You*. You and Moni were the only two people who would never betray me."

Moni.

I hated her name being brought up. Her sacred name mentioned among these unleashed secrets, a pure brass ring tarnished.

"What are we going to do now?" I asked wearily.

"Nothing," said Dad.

Marlow's eyes narrowed up at him with loathing.

He stood. "There is nothing you can do now. There is nothing *for* any of us to do now."

She rose up to meet him. "You murdered a woman in front of her child. No one gets away with that."

Indifference.

It was the indifference on my father's face that made the hairs on my body stand up. He was so beyond what he had done that he truly believed he deserved to move on. Deserved to get away with the unforgivable.

"There is no trace of her left," he responded flatly. "If there was, it would have shown up by now. It's been over twenty years and no one—*no one*—has ever given a shit about her. Why would they now?" His eyes went wide and distant. "I'm going home to your mother now."

He walked with heavy steps down the dock, a pathway toward the exit door of a theater he was escaping. The show he refused to acknowledge, refused to be a part of.

I turned my head. I heard her voice. Faint at first.

"Now, my babies . . . pay attention and remember this . . ."

It grew louder as he walked up the stairs. Each stride up the stone steps was a heavy stomp on my heart. A drum beat so deep, disturbing anything I had ever believed.

"You can't trap a tiger just by catching him . . ."

We watched as he disappeared up into the darkness. The drumming grew faster.

"You have to make him think he has won."

I looked at Marlow to see a little girl. A little girl from the woods staring back at me with hollow eyes.

"Only then have you truly trapped him."

CHAPTER 59

THE INTERVIEW

2021

[Studio]

JODI LEE: The truth about your mother?

MARLOW FIN: In the summer of 1995, a woman was drowned in front of her daughter near Covet Falls. That woman was my mother. That little girl . . .

That little girl was me.

JODI LEE: You're saying there is a body in Covet Falls?

MARLOW FIN: Patrick Baek murdered my mother. And then he murdered my sister when he found out she had learned the truth. *[Sobs]*

JODI LEE: Marlow . . . Marlow. Take a deep breath. What do you remember from that night? Do you remember . . . do you remember your father hurting Isla?

MARLOW FIN: Yes . . . yes.

He thought he had drowned me, but I was still alive. Somehow, I had survived. I woke up in the water down the shore. I had drifted before I came to. When I stood up, I could see him in the distance, stabbing her. She was crying. She kept asking, Why? Why, Dad?

JODI LEE: Dear God . . .

MARLOW FIN: I must have passed out because that's the last thing I remember. I think I went into shock. When I came to, I was dazed. I was so confused as to where I was and how I even got there. I looked around and went to the shed.

There was blood in the corner. I bent down and got some on my dress. I couldn't remember anything . . . I couldn't remember how I got there. I sat by the lake with blood on my dress.

JODI LEE: Marlow . . . I have to ask. Where do you think he put her body?

MARLOW FIN: Where do you think?

CHAPTER 60

ISLA

The Day after the Interview

The scar on my forearm feels satiny as I trace my finger over it. I twist it back and forth in the mirror, watching it shine and change colors, a chameleon that lives on my arm.

I look up and see the square reflection of the television.

I see them both.

She is hounded by a mob of reporters as she leaves her hotel; the flashes and shouting buzz around her like insects. This is nothing new for her. She disappears into the waiting car faster than she had appeared, a vision of dark sunglasses and a trench coat wrapped tightly around her.

He is being led by another man into the police station. His gait falters; he is unsteady and unsure of what to do in this new microscope he has been thrust under. He does not look up once, blinded by the sea of reporters begging for just one acknowledgment. One look for the shot that would grace every front page and every feature story online.

I walk to the television and shut it off. It won't be coming with me.

There is only one item left to pack.

I wrap it in a dish towel. If I focus hard enough, I can smell a hint of the lake, maybe even brine and flesh. But maybe I am imagining that.

The towel goes in a large, padded manila envelope, addressed carefully in black ink and stamped accordingly. Ready for the day it may get sent.

I am not sentimental today. I pick up the last bag and shut the apartment door quickly behind me. It is dark, but the sun has already begun to flush the edges of the sky. I slip into my car and the engine starting sends trills of exhilaration throughout my body. The road is nearly deserted at this hour, but I welcome the solace.

I always welcome it.

Where I am going, no one knows who I am. No one knows who Sawyer is. Who Marlow really is. We were never meant to be in the same world, she and I. Two beings setting each other on fire.

Maybe there I can be satisfied with only my thoughts.

My foot gets excited and pushes hard on the gas pedal. I ease up as I see a brown patrol car out of the corner of my eye. I hold my breath and keep driving. I must not be worth the time. I find myself zoning out, the lines in the road a hypnotic pulse to each empty thought.

I stop to eat. I reach for him in my pocket. I have not allowed myself to touch it or look at it in a while. He is worn but still there as I set him atop the dashboard. I think about the last time he held it. The last time he thought of me when he looked at it.

He didn't feel anything. He felt no pain.

My phone is slippery and bothersome as I dial her number. Each ring and I am closer to her voice. Somewhere she is waiting for mine.

I reach for my scar once more, remembering how it felt when it was open.

When she had sliced my skin so willingly.

The shed had been as dark and damp as we were. My back to the corner as she stood there, more lovely than I had ever seen her. Waves of hair stuck across her forehead, her lips silken from the lake.

I had held out my arm, staring down at her hand flexing with the fishing knife. Intent on each finger wrapped around the ivory handle, so tight and fixed.

Branding.

My eyes had met hers and, for a second, I thought she wouldn't do But I nodded, bracing myself for the pain of blade to flesh. A flash pleasure went off in those eyes of hers. The last time I ever wanted see those eyes. But nothing seared through me. Nothing hurt as the ood trickled down onto the floor.

I felt nothing. I felt no pain.

Her voice breaks through now as she answers.

"Isla." She speaks with certainty. A clarity I want to take away.

I stay silent.

"It's over . . . you can rest easy now," she says.

I nod as if she can see me.

"Where are you? Are you—"

"Tell me what happened, Marlow," I cut through, willing each word to embed deep into her like a parasite. "*Tell me* how my husband died."

She says nothing. I am willing to wait. I am willing to wait forever.

"I told you. I told you what happened. I can't remember," she finally speaks, flat and emotionless.

"No," I growl, low and tumbling, a warning of disruption—of what I have kept so long inside me. "The truth."

She is shaky. "Okay, Isla."

I suck in all the air around me, holding my breath.

"Is this what you want from me?"

Her voice sounds wet, but I don't believe the tears. I don't believe anything anymore.

"Then I will give it to you," she sputters. "The truth? The truth is I remember. I remember *everything*. I remember every detail of the moment Sawyer died."

"Marlow," I start to say, but nothing comes out. Nothing is left inside me to expel. I am an empty vessel of misery.

"Yes," she answers. "The answer to your question is *yes* . . ."

Yes. Yes. Yes.

A shrill tone pierces my ears, its high note deafening me until her voice breaks through.

"I pushed him," she says.

I close my eyes and pain spreads out over my face, stinging every cell it touches. I see him. I see Sawyer, his beautiful body flying in front of the truck. I see her crouched low where she belongs, watching with a mixture of terror and allure at what her hands have just done. I feel a sickening relief . . . relief that she is the reason.

Relief that I can tear her apart.

"Do you believe me?" she finally asks, with such an unearthly innocence and purity to her voice that I nearly hurl the phone. "Do you believe that I could do something like that to you?"

But it doesn't matter, Marlow. It doesn't matter anymore.

"Oh, Isla . . ."

It's my turn now.

"You never asked me what I did with it," I say with precision. I am purposeful, sharp.

"What?"

"The knife."

She goes quiet.

"I know," she finally breathes out. In that breath I hear a resignation, one that sweeps in thoughts of us as children. Our laughter echoes as we splash in the lake, floating in and eating away at what I hold on to dearly. The bitterness of what I have become.

"You want to hurt me so badly . . . don't you?" she asks, all too sane and sound.

No. I don't want to hurt you, Marlow.

"What do you think I did with the knife, Marlow?"

She doesn't answer my question. She only plays one kind of game. Marlow's game.

Yet her tone begins to tremble.

"I needed to see what you would do. I *needed* to see if you would protect me. Like I protected you, Isla." Her voice breaks off with my name.

I do not yield. I press on.

"Do you think I got rid of it? Down the falls. Wiped clean and gone forever?"

She doesn't respond. I wait patiently. I have all the time in the world now. Vacant, space-consuming time.

I want you to suffer. I want you to suffer from doubt until it eats away all reason.

"Or maybe . . . maybe I kept it. I kept it to show the whole world what you really mean to me, Marlow."

"What is it then? What do I mean to you, Isla?"

She asks this with feigned strength, and I relish it.

I touch the knight with one finger and smile brightly, the last of any light left inside me. I am extinguished.

I am Marlow Fin's dead sister.

The phone slips down my cheek as I prepare to hang up. "Oh, Marlow," I sing.

She is desperate on the other side. I can feel her need for an answer with every muffled sound in my ear.

"Uncertainty is such a terrible thing."

All is fair now, sister. All that is left is a knife for a knight.

ACKNOWLEDGMENTS

This book would not be possible without all the *Moni*s or *Halmoni*s in the world. Yes—that special Korean maternal figure, grandmother, mother, or whatever you may call her in your own life. The one with the quiet strength, sacrifice, and unmatched love for offspring. A generation of fearless immigrants whose enduring spirit we only hope to carry on. We only hope to honor you.

To my parents, Jung and Kyung Won, who embody every bit of this and more. Admiration doesn't even begin to describe how much I am in awe of your bravery.

To my sister, Jennifer Grilli, thank goodness our sister relationship is nothing like that of the one in this book! You have been there for me in countless ways this year, and I am forever grateful.

To everyone at Liza Dawson Associates for their support and especially my amazing literary agent, Rachel Beck. Over four years later and I still pinch myself that I get to work with you. Your constant guidance is infallible, friendship cherished, and I hope you know just how spectacular you are.

To the entire wonderful team at Lake Union, this book would not be possible without all of you, and of course my editor, Alicia Clancy. Your talent, wicked insight, and encouragement have made my first forays as a published author so fulfilling and delightful.

To every author, writer, blogger, and individual I have encountered in the writing community who gave me that boost of confidence when

I needed it. Thank you. You are all amazing lights in this crazy journey of publishing.

To my beautiful sons, Preston and Archer. I love you more than you will ever know. You two are my beacon in life.

To my A. J. You are and always will be my number one fan. You are my hero.

ABOUT THE AUTHOR

Photo © 2022 Caitlin Bielefeldt

Ellen Won Steil grew up in Iowa in a Korean American family and earned her BA in journalism from Drake University and law degree from William Mitchell College of Law. She lives in Minnesota with her husband and two young sons. The author of *Fortune*, Ellen believes most good stories have at least a hint of darkness in them. For more information, visit ewsteil.com.